GRACE ACROSS THE MILES

BOOK 6

CHRISTINE DILLON

LINKS IN THE CHAIN PRESS

www.storytellerchristine.com

Grace Across the Miles

Copyright © 2021 by Christine Dillon.

All rights reserved. This book or any portion thereof may not be reproduced or used in any manner whatsoever without the express written permission of the author except for brief quotations in a book review.

Scripture taken from the HOLY BIBLE, NEW INTERNATIONAL VERSION®. NIV®. Copyright © 1973, 1978, 1984 by International Bible Society. Used by permission of Zondervan. All rights reserved worldwide.

This book is a work of fiction. Names, characters, any resemblance to persons, living or dead, or events is purely coincidental. The characters and incidents are the product of the author's imagination and used fictitiously. Locales and public names are sometimes used for atmospheric purposes.

Cover Design: Lankshear Design

ISBN: 978-0-6453547-3-7

For my friends.
You are such a gift to me. For laughter and memories and much prayer.
You encourage me to follow Jesus and you're there when I need someone to listen. I am blessed.

*And especially for **Joy Lankshear**.*
This journey would not have happened without your beautiful designs. You have generously shared yourself and expertise along the way. I thank God for your friendship.

NOTES TO READERS

* This book is unashamedly Christian. All books are written from a worldview, be it secular, communist or New Age. If you're not a Christian the views expressed by the characters might appear strange BUT it's a great opportunity. Why? Because this story allows you, if you're not yet a follower of Jesus, to see things from a perspective totally different to your own. Are the character's views consistent and does their worldview make sense of the challenges in their lives?

* Should this book contain spelling, grammar, punctuation and word usage that are unfamiliar it is most likely because it is an Australian story. It seemed wrong to write an Australian story according to the Chicago Manual of Style.

PROLOGUE

October 1988
Nepean River, Sydney

"*T*hat's impossible!" Gina's voice rose as she stared at her father. "Totally impossible."

Her dad moved over on the grassy hillock, where they were watching the Head of the River rowing championships, and put his arm around her.

Gina shook off his embrace. "How can I be adopted? All those photos in my album!" Including photos of herself as a newborn clearly labelled with the date she'd always celebrated as her birthday.

"We took you home three days after you were born," he said.

So was the date on the photos her real birth date or the date she went home from hospital? Had she been celebrating the wrong birthday all these years? She shivered and pulled her knees up towards her chest.

Was it only this morning that she had been bubbling with excitement to go and watch her brother Bruce compete in the championships? Rowing was a family sport. Dad had missed out on the Commonwealth Games due to illness, but he had always dreamed that one of his sons might make it. To give the boys the greatest possible chance they'd been sent to board at a top private school. It cost a fortune, but Bruce's First VIIIs and IVs were the favourites for this year.

She jerked her chin towards the boats. "What about Bruce? And Grant?"

"No, they're not adopted."

Her father touched her shoulder and she willed herself not to push him away again. He was the one family member she was closest to.

"We love you just as much as your brothers."

Her eyes teared up. He might love her as much, but she couldn't say the same about her mother. Not that her mother was exactly a model of motherliness to Grant and Bruce either. They'd all been tiptoeing around her for years, anxious not to tip her over some unseen edge.

Gina took a deep breath and deliberately relaxed her tense shoulders. "I had no idea ..." Her voice shook. "We all seem to fit together. I even look like you."

"I love it when people say you look like me," her father said. "You've made me proud every day of your life. We didn't think we'd ever have children, and then you came along."

Up until that moment, she'd never suspected she didn't belong. Her chest ached as though the wind had been knocked out of her. "Why didn't you tell me earlier?"

"It was tricky," he said. "I wanted to tell you when you were eighteen, but your mother objected."

So he'd backed down. Protecting mother had become the family's preoccupation. None of them wanted to ever again experience years like those when Gina was in junior high school. Back then, she'd had to help her father do all the housework because her mother had retreated into her own world. Gina had buckled down and carried far more of a load than any teenager should have had to. Her cheeks flushed with past embarrassment. She had never mentioned her mother in case people asked questions. Sometimes her mother had been almost normal, just kind of spaced out. Yet other times, she'd been downright peculiar. The problem was that Gina had never known at breakfast whether the day was going to be good or bad, and things often deteriorated rapidly. It had become easier to avoid inviting friends around altogether.

And if Gina hadn't made that casual comment today about her disappointment with her own rowing form compared to her brothers, perhaps her father wouldn't have said anything. When had he intended telling her she was adopted? When she was about to get married? When she'd had a baby? When Mum died?

In the rational part of her brain, she understood there were problems with revealing the news at any time. But right now, she wasn't feeling logical. Right now, she was angry he'd left telling her until now. And she was disappointed that he had put her mother's needs ahead of hers. As usual.

The rowers were now approaching the finish line. Gina couldn't see who was in front, but it looked like a tight race. She got to her feet. Other groups scrambled up too, and tension crackled through the air. Would the favourites win, or would something unforeseen happen? Gina's father joined her, and they watched in growing anticipation as Bruce's team came level with where they were standing. It was a close contest between three crews. Less than a minute later, Bruce's team crossed the line first and the elation of his win overlaid the churning in her gut.

"I know this discussion isn't over," her father said, setting off towards the finish line, "but let's go and congratulate Bruce."

Gina scurried after him.

She still had so many questions, but whether he'd answer them was the big unknown.

CHAPTER 1

Post-Easter, 1998
Sydney, Australia

The worst thing about parties was the dishes. Gina stood with her hands in a sink full of sudsy water, greasy plates stacked all over the counters around her. The dishwasher was running through the first load, but it bothered her to see so much clutter. She'd started washing the rest by hand.

The soothing sound of classical guitar music wafted through the open window, not quite loud enough to cover the chatter of the partygoers.

Footsteps came down the hall and Pete, her housemate's fiancé, popped his head through the kitchen door. "Gina, there you are, I wasn't expecting to find you in here. Rachel is wondering if you could come and dish out your fabulous pavlovas."

Gina had made three huge desserts the day before for Pete and Rachel's engagement party. She took off her gloves and apron and smoothed down her hair. Then she wound her way in between the small clusters of people in the living room and onto the broad back veranda where they'd laid out the dessert table. Rachel had scattered bright coloured lanterns among the bare branches of the garden trees, but only a few intrepid guests still huddled outside in the late-autumn chill. The smell of barbecued meat and onions lingered in the air from where the barbecue was cooling in the carport. Most of the guests had moved onto the veranda or into the lounge areas.

Rachel's grandmother, Naomi, had died six months ago, and Gina had moved in to keep Rachel company. It wouldn't be long before Pete and Rachel were married and Gina would have to move back to her own one-bedroom apartment. Gina tightened her lips and turned her back to the guests while she set portions of pavlova on plates. There was no use pretending it wouldn't be tough to go back to living on her own. She was happy Pete and Rachel were getting married—of course she was—but why was it always someone else? She'd lost count of the number of weddings she'd attended in the past ten years. Next weekend it would be her brother's wedding—a brother six years younger than herself. Even her youngest brother looked like he'd found a potential life partner, yet Gina had never even been on a date. Not one.

The piece of pavlova on her cake server wobbled and fell off. She pushed it to the side to save it for herself after everyone else was served. The messy blob of meringue seemed to sum up everything she felt about her love life.

Gina concentrated on the next piece, carefully sliding the cake server underneath and making sure it looked perfect. The next guest in line took the small plate without even looking at her. Gina watched them go, a tiny spark of irritation stirring inside.

Half her life seemed to have been serving food. Maybe that was the problem. She was just part of the furniture. "Gina, you're a treasure for helping us out." "Gina, how could we do without your help in the kitchen?" She'd heard words like these so often they no longer surprised her. Yet they still managed to give her a deep-down feeling of warmth.

"I'll help, Gina," said a loud voice.

Gina looked up with a grateful smile. "Thanks, Josh."

The stocky man lumbered over and insisted on her tying him into the apron he'd brought from the kitchen. Then he took a tray of desserts and offered them to the people closest to him.

Bless the guy. He might be in his mid-twenties, but his childlike joy had endeared him to her ever since they'd met on a kayak trip last year. She might only have been invited because Rachel had been a bit worried about supervising Josh while learning to kayak herself, but Josh had quickly found a place in Gina's heart. Rachel and Pete loved Josh like a younger brother, and he'd been going around telling everyone that he was going to be a groomsman at the wedding. Gina wanted to think she'd been invited to be a bridesmaid because of her friendship with Rachel, but maybe it was to make sure Josh stayed on task.

Josh came back for more servings of pavlova, and then twice more. Once Gina had filled all the plates, she leaned back to stretch her back. It would have been better not to have worn heels tonight, but she liked the extra height they gave her. If only being artificially taller also made her slimmer. Next to Rachel's sylphlike figure, she always felt dumpy.

"Everyone has some," Josh said, his voice a slightly overloud monotone. "And some people are almost ready for seconds."

Gina handed a big serving to Josh. "Then we'd better eat ours."

"Thanks, Gina. You make the best pavlova. Even better than my Mum's."

Josh's parents were around the place somewhere. Most of the guests were linked to the nursery that Pete and his family owned, or were from Rachel and Gina's church. Pete had only moved over to Sydney after his father had had a heart attack, and the only guest from Western Australia was Pete's ex-father-in-law. Or was he still a father-in-law? 'Ex' usually indicated divorce, and Pete wasn't divorced. His wife and kids had died. It was complicated, and Gina didn't know the whole story.

She'd enjoyed talking to Binh earlier, hearing how he'd migrated to Australia during the Vietnam War and become a Christian soon after. He and Pete were obviously close, and he was going to be Pete's best man. Gina had hoped to be Rachel's chief bridesmaid. Sure she'd originally been Rachel's sister's close friend, but after Esther had died and Gina had moved in with Rachel, they'd grown close. It stung that someone called Alice would get that privilege. She'd apparently been Rachel's friend in her old job at David Jones and had had some sort of role in Rachel coming to know Jesus.

Gina hated these little drips of bitterness that seemed to be poisoning her lately. Maybe it had something to do with her age. It hadn't been so hard to be single in her twenties, but now she'd entered her thirties, it was increasingly difficult to believe her chance would ever come. Last year, on her thirtieth birthday, she'd spent the whole day in tears. If she didn't watch out, she'd become a man-hater who people avoided and labelled 'spinster'. Spinster. Such an ugly word. So much less pleasant than the word 'bachelor'. Spinster sounded like someone as thin as a stick, with grey hair pulled back in a tight bun and a pinched mouth hiding a sharp tongue. Someone she had no desire to be. The possibility yawned like a gaping sinkhole at her feet.

Being a Christian was supposed to make a difference, but it was hard to be enthusiastic every time Rachel burst into the house gushing about her wonderful Pete. Rachel, who'd had her chance at motherhood but who'd thrown the child away.

Gina had longed for her own children from the day when the first of her two brothers had been placed in her arms. She'd taught the tiny-tots Sunday School class during high school, and it had surprised no one when she'd become a Kindergarten teacher. What bitter irony, that the person surrounded by small children most of the week might never hold her own. And sometimes it was the church folk who made it the hardest. She had often begged God for a husband and family, but so far her pleas had landed on seemingly deaf ears.

Pete stood with his arm loosely draped around Rachel's shoulders, and Rachel alternated between looking up at him and laughing with her mother and his parents. A diamond flashed on her finger. Gina went back to the kitchen. At least there she belonged and could look useful and fulfilled.

God do you hear me? Do you care?

CHAPTER 2

"*H*aven't I seen you somewhere before?" a male voice said.

Gina glanced up from the shoe she was considering buying and resisted rolling her eyes. Of all the overused pick-up lines. Not that any guys had ever tried the line on Gina, but she'd heard others joking about the kind of guys who used it.

She looked into the dark eyes of a man a bit older than herself. He did look familiar.

She took a step away from him. "Do you normally use that line with people you've just met?"

"I wasn't trying to pick you up—" The man flushed. "Not that I mean …" He gave a crooked grin. "I'm not doing a very good job of this, but I've been puzzling for a few minutes about where I've seen you before." He frowned. "Not school, nor university." He shook his head. "No, somewhere much more recent than that."

He was right. She'd seen him somewhere in the last year. She ran through a list of possible places. Work? No. Victory Church? No. But … a church. "Esther's—"

"—funeral," he finished. "You were Esther's good friend."

"And you're Tony. You spoke about how Esther introduced your wife …" Gina's neck warmed. Maybe she shouldn't have mentioned his wife.

"It's fine to mention Anna. We miss her every day, but she's been gone two years now." He swallowed. "We make it a practice at home to talk about her. Otherwise it seems a sort of denial of how important she was to us. You know—"

Gina nodded. "That's how we feel about Esther. I share a house with her sister, Rachel, and we talk about Esther all the time. It was hard at first, but it gets easier."

"Yeah, it does." Tony glanced at his watch.

"Don't let me keep you," Gina said gesturing towards his shopping bag.

"Oh, I've finished shopping." He held up the bag. "My eldest is growing like a weed and needs new school shirts." He grinned and a playful dimple flashed in his left cheek. "I was checking to see if there was time for a cup of coffee before I collect the girls from my parents. Have you got time to join me?"

She did have time, but did she want to? A cup of coffee seemed innocent, but what strings were attached? Was he asking her because he was being polite, or because he saw her as Esther's friend, or something else?

"It's okay if you don't have time." He looked like he was about to leave her standing there with her mouth open.

"I'd be happy to," Gina said with a rush, putting down the shoe she'd been examining more closely than was really necessary.

He glanced towards the shoe. "Did you want to buy that pair? I'll wait."

Gina shrugged. "I was just looking. I always check out the sales, but I don't need any shoes at the moment."

He laughed. "You're not one of those people who has to buy everything you like?"

She shook her head. "Not on my salary. I'm more of an a-few-good-things-that-will-last-a-long-time buyer."

"Wise woman."

She bent her head so he couldn't see her flush of pleasure.

"Do you prefer coffee or tea?" Tony asked as they went out the door.

"Either is fine," Gina said, walking beside him.

The café was only a short walk away, and he led the way inside.

"Ciao, Antonio," the man behind the main counter said as they passed.

Gina blinked. It had never occurred to her that Tony was Italian, he sounded completely local.

They took a seat and ordered, and the coffee was on the table almost before they'd settled themselves.

"You obviously come here often," Gina said.

"It's my daughters' favourite café, and the boss and I have known each other since the start of primary school."

So Tony's family must have migrated when he was fairly young. "That explains why you speak English with an Aussie accent. Do you also speak Italian?"

He laughed. "It depends who you ask. My parents tell me my Italian is terrible, but I can get by. What about you? What's your background?"

She shrugged. "Nothing special. My parents live at Lake Macquarie. Dad has just retired from PE teaching." She wasn't going to expand on any more details with someone she didn't expect to see again. "I have two younger brothers. The youngest is just starting work, and the oldest is getting married next weekend."

"That should be a good family time."

"I hope so. Our parents aren't Christians, so that causes a few tensions."

Tony rubbed his eyebrow. "Yeah, I know how difficult that can be. How did you become a Christian then?"

"It wasn't part of my parents' plan." Gina relaxed back in her seat. "They wanted child-free time on the weekend, and it didn't cost them anything to send us to Sunday school." Gina laughed. "They hoped we'd learn to be good and not get too fanatical about the whole thing, but they got more than they bargained for, because we all became Christians."

"How old were you?" Tony asked.

"About fourteen. After I got too old for Sunday school, I asked Mum and Dad if I could help teach the younger kids. That meant I could keep an eye on the boys, so they agreed. Each week as I prepared the lesson, the meanings of the stories became clearer." She blew on her coffee and took a sip. Was she boring him? It didn't look like it, as he leaned forward to listen.

"One holiday, I went with friends to a Scripture Union camp, and the speaker talked about why Jesus had to die. Suddenly I understood I was a sinner who needed a Saviour."

Tony nodded. "I can't believe how many years I sat in church and never grasped that simple fact even though I could recite the catechism and Hail Marys with the best of them."

Gina drank some more of her coffee. "You said something at the funeral about coming to understand who Jesus was after your wife died."

Tony nodded. "That was because of Esther. She got to know Anna in the chemo clinic and Anna noticed Esther wasn't afraid of dying." He sighed. "Both of us were struggling. Anna's cancer wasn't caught until late and there was always a high probability she wouldn't make it. She dreaded leaving the girls while they were so young, and I was terrified of managing on my own."

The weight of his words hung in the air. Gina felt an urge to comfort him, but she held back. She didn't know him well enough to pry.

Tony finished his coffee and checked his watch again. "I'm sorry, I have to go. I've enjoyed talking, but I have to be at my parents' place before they go out." He picked up the coat he'd draped over the back of the chair and hesitated.

Would he say anything more? Oh, she hoped so.

He paused, hands on his coat. "I'd like to get in touch again. Would you mind giving me your phone number?"

Her heart rate sped up and she tightened her lips to prevent herself grinning like a lunatic. The more they'd talked, the more she'd felt at ease, but she hadn't dared to hope that he might want to see her again. Things like that didn't happen to her.

Gina bobbed her head, unable to say a word and scared to look up at him in case her eagerness frightened him off. She dug into her purse and pulled out a pen and scrap of paper. Perching on the edge of her chair, she wrote her name and phone number as clearly as possible. She didn't want there to be any possibility of a mistake.

Tony read the number out, smiled, and headed out the door. Gina followed but found a bench and sank down on it, hugging the past forty minutes to herself. She took a deep breath. *Calm down.* Asking for a number was easy, but would he follow up? Would she ever see him again?

CHAPTER 3

*G*ina's brother, Bruce, and her almost sister-in-law stood under the flowery arch Gina had designed. Behind them, Lake Macquarie glinted in the pale sunshine and the guests teetered on chairs that kept sinking into the lawn. Oh, well. Bruce and Sue had chosen an outside wedding so the mainly non-Christian relatives felt more comfortable. Gina would still have gone with a church, but this wasn't her wedding—a fact she was more than aware of. She'd already had four people say, "Your turn next." She'd smiled in what she hoped wasn't a grimace and muttered some polite banalities.

"… In sickness and in health, for richer, for poorer …" Vaughn, Bruce's pastor, said.

Much as Gina longed to be married, there were no guarantees things would work out well. Wedding vows were like signing a blank cheque with life. Had her father had any idea that he'd spend most of his marriage protecting his wife's mental health? Did Rachel and Pete have any real idea how the traumas of their pasts would impact their marriage day to day?

Oh Lord, maybe it's a good thing Tony hasn't rung back. Having a wife die in her thirties has to have a major impact on a family. Only you know whether there are major cracks in their foundations.

Gina's mind wandered as the wedding vows continued. On Sunday, the day after meeting Tony, Gina had hurried home from church and hung around the phone the entire day. Nothing. She'd rationalised that Tony was busy with the children and didn't want to look too eager. Surely he'd ring on Monday. The phone remained silent on Monday evening. On Tuesday, it rang three times for Rachel, but there were no calls for her. Maybe Tony had rung while the phone was occupied. Wednesday … silence. Thursday, Rachel talked to Pete for an hour and Gina had returned to her room so that Rachel wouldn't see her impatience. There were still two hours after Rachel finished talking, but the phone remained stubbornly silent. Gina had even checked that the phone hadn't been accidentally left off the hook. Twice.

She'd gone to bed depressed and shed some quiet tears into her pillowcase. Her pillowcases had seen lots of tears over the years, like the three times during university and her early work years when she'd thought someone was interested in her, but it turned out they wanted help with their studies or contact details to ask out one of her friends.

"You may now kiss the bride," Vaughn said.

Concentrate, Gina. She'd missed half of the vows. Behind her, the guests erupted into clapping or hoots. Bruce reached towards Sue and kissed her tenderly.

I'm happy, happy, happy, Gina rehearsed in her mind. But around the edges, envy curdled in her throat. Gina swallowed. She was not going to ruin this day with her own issues. *God, help! Bitterness is a choice, but I don't know how to get this out of my system. Why are there such longings in me, and how do I deal with them?*

The guests settled down, and Bruce and Sue walked across to seat themselves off to the side to listen to the pastor.

Lord, help me to stop thinking about myself. There are so many here who don't know you. Let them hear something today that leads them closer to you.

"I've been meeting with Bruce and Sue to do marriage preparation for the last six weeks," Vaughn said. "Did you know that churches did this?"

A few in the audience shook their heads.

Did the average Aussie even do marriage preparation, or was it only a church thing? Maybe not, when so many couples used weddings to legitimise an existing relationship.

"We do these sessions because God, who created marriage, has a high view of it and he created us for certain purposes," Vaughn continued. "I don't know if you're the kind of person who gets a new piece of flat-pack furniture and tries to put it together by instinct, or if you follow the instructions. I'm usually overconfident and waste a lot of time before admitting the instructions aren't such a bad idea."

There was a ripple of laughter, and Vaughn waited for it to die down.

"My wife shakes her head at me every time. Similarly, we can avoid a lot of mistakes when we follow the maker's instructions for marriage, and following the instructions brings a lot of joy—they're a package deal. I thought I'd let you in on some of the secrets of what God tells us about marriage." He grinned at his listeners. "But sorry, I'm not going to tell you Bruce and Sue's answers."

Most of the guests laughed, and Gina relaxed. Even non-Christians would listen to this sort of talk, whether to gain a tip or two, or to listen and criticise.

Vaughn started with mutual respect and kindness, points most people could agree with. He sprinkled Bible verses into each point and told several real life stories to illustrate. Gina glanced around. People were listening. Really listening.

Except Bruce and Sue, who were holding hands and gazing at each other. The all-too-familiar longing for someone to have and to hold surged through her. *Lord, help me to get through today, and help Vaughn. Everyone is waiting for him to say something controversial.*

Vaughn made a few more points and then said, "... and I know you've all been waiting for me to say something about God's view of sex." People shifted in their seats. "It's an issue everyone seems to have an opinion on, but today I'm asking you to listen in to the Maker's instructions. I'm hoping you'll be surprised."

Give Vaughn courage, Lord.

"First of all, I want to say that sex was God's idea. Does that surprise you? God designed sex as a wedding gift. It was to be the icing on the cake in a marriage."

For five minutes there was silence apart from the birds and the wind in the trees. Vaughn did an excellent job of explaining the positives in God's design and giving hope for those who'd gone their own way. He finished by painting a picture of marriage done God's way by sharing about his parents, a marriage which had lasted sixty-five years.

After the signing of the marriage certificate and a final prayer of blessing on the marriage, Vaughn raised his voice and said, "And now let me introduce, Mr and Mrs Reid."

Everyone stood to clap as Bruce and Sue walked forward to greet their guests.

***

*G*ina joined the line to choose food from the buffet. The caterers were set up inside the lower floor of her parents' home. The full-width French doors were open so guests could choose a spot on the deck or sit in groups on the grassy verge next to the lake.

"Yes, Gina would love to be married." Her mother's shrill voice carried in from the deck. "She's so good with cooking and children."

Mother! Gina's ears burned. It sounded as though her virtues were being paraded to be sold to the highest bidder.

"Your mother obviously appreciates you," said the older woman in the line behind Gina.

Gina half turned and made a face. "Mothers are often our greatest fans. But they can also be embarrassing."

"She means well, dear," the woman said, patting Gina's shoulder.

"Maybe." Gina wished her mother would learn some lessons in tact and keeping her voice down. Their relationship was rocky nowadays. As a young child, she'd often felt smothered by her mother. She'd struggle in her mother's arms, trying to break free and her mother would say, "You're my baby, my precious baby. Don't you love me?" A question Gina had always answered in the affirmative but she'd resented having to reassure the supposed adult in her life.

After selecting her food, Gina went over to join some of the people she knew from the church she'd attended as a child.

"Good to see you, Gina. When are you going to move back out of the big smoke?" Maude, an older woman, asked.

Gina had moved to Sydney because that's where she'd found a job. But it had also given her a little distance from her mother. "I like the school I'm working at and they've treated me well."

"But you haven't found a husband," Jacqui said.

Gina drew in a breath. When would she ever be free from such comments? She lowered her voice so their conversation wouldn't carry to anyone else. "There are worse things than being single."

"Perhaps your problem is that you're too clever," Bernice said. "Or too fussy."

Pardon? Did she just hear that correctly? "I wouldn't claim to be clever," Gina said. "And I'd like a husband who loves me for who I am." If that was too fussy, then so be it.

"What are you looking for in a husband?" Bernice persisted.

Tension spread along Gina's spine. The women seemed to have

decided it was open-season-on-Gina-day. What would they do if she got up and moved elsewhere? Except where could she go? Locking herself in the bathroom might be the only option. They'd probably call her a flirt or desperate if she talked to any male under seventy.

"I'd love to marry a man who puts Jesus first and who loves me, a man who is kind, forgiving, and patient," Gina said. "And willing to admit he's wrong and say sorry."

"Wouldn't we all?" Jacqui said.

"Maybe you need to pray more about it," a lady who hadn't said anything yet, chimed in. She was the same age as the other women but Gina didn't recognise her.

So now Gina was being blamed for her lack of husband.

"God has promised to give us the desires of our heart," the now not-so-timid lady continued. "The Bible says so in Psalm 37."

This had gone on long enough.

"I have never figured out how Psalm 37 has become applied to finding a spouse," Gina said, throat tight. "It's actually about trusting that God will vindicate us in an evil world and that he'll give us everything we need. If you'll excuse me, I need to talk to other people." Gina stood up, inclined her head to acknowledge everyone, and made a beeline for her father. He had to rescue her. That was part of his role, wasn't it?

In her painful experience, it wasn't her non-Christian colleagues and friends who pestered her about whether she had a boyfriend. It was Christians. Somehow, the one group that should have been her greatest refuge made her feel like a misfit.

Once Rachel was married, Gina would be the sole single in her thirties at church. There'd been one other woman her age, but she'd gone overseas as a missionary last year. She said it was easier to be a single woman on the mission field.

If Tony didn't ring back, maybe Gina should start considering that option.

CHAPTER 4

*E*arly the next week, Gina opened the front door of their home and beamed a welcome at the middle-aged Asian woman outside.

"Come in Joy," Gina said. "We're so glad you could come while Blanche is still here."

Blanche, Rachel's mother, had flown over from Lord Howe Island where she and her husband were pastoring a church. She'd arrived two days before the engagement party and was staying a full two weeks to help Rachel with the wedding planning.

"It has been a long time." Joy handed Gina a beautiful basket of fruit.

"You didn't need to bring anything," Gina said. "We just wanted to get the quilting group together while we had a chance and hear what God has been doing in everyone's lives."

"Most Chinese bring fruit or tea when we visit," Joy said.

"More practical than flowers." Gina closed the front door behind Joy and ushered her through into the room at the back where the others were.

Blanche took orders for tea and coffee with the familiarity of a resident. She'd stayed here with Rachel and Naomi after she'd separated from William, at around the time Esther went into palliative care. The quilting group had supported each other through the grief of Esther's death and the months it took for God to work a miracle in William's life.

Gina served the carrot cake she'd baked.

"It feels strange not to be working on a quilt while we're together," Joy said.

"I've been quilting a lot recently, using all my fabric scraps from past projects," Blanche said. "The island is a great place for beauty and swimming but limited with craft materials. It's also not the place to forget an item on your grocery list since everything has to be flown in."

"I can't imagine you living in such a place, Mum," Rachel said.

Blanche laughed. "Not easy for a city girl like me, but I've come to appreciate the slow pace of life and amazing neighbours who spend so much time encouraging us in our Christian life." She smiled broadly. "It's been like a second honeymoon. God has changed William so much. I never thought he'd ever become a man who valued prayer and quiet reflection, but amazingly he does." She turned to Rachel. "And he looks forward to your letters every week."

Only Gina had seen how much it cost Rachel to write to her father. The first few letters had been a real battle, but Rachel had persevered, urged on by Pete. She was determined to give her father every chance to redeem his past. William wrote long screeds in return and sent photos of the island. He'd also sent occasional bunches of flowers or tickets to concerts. Gina had twice enjoyed those benefits.

"How's your job going out there?" Gina asked.

"It's certainly different from being at Victory. Our congregation of forty is mostly retirees or tourists coming once or twice while they're on holiday."

A huge contrast with Victory Church with its thousands of young adults.

"William has been excited to see a second church member's husband come to know Jesus, and there are another two doing Bible study with him."

"And what do you do, Blanche?" Joy asked.

"I'm leading the women's ministry and visitation teams," Blanche said. "I love it all, but I especially love meeting one-on-one with various ladies."

Gina needed to get back to meeting one-on-one with someone. She'd studied with Rachel for a while and they'd completed Ephesians and Hebrews, but recently Rachel had been too distracted by wedding plans. Maybe looking out for the needs of others would make Gina feel less depressed about not hearing from Tony. She hadn't picked him as the sort of person to let others down. Then again, it might be her fault for having such high expectations. One coffee, and she was dreaming about a future together.

Rachel shared a little about wedding plans and then it was Gina's turn. She talked about her brother's wedding and work but didn't say anything about her struggles or disappointments. It didn't seem like the right time or place.

"And what about you, Joy?" Gina said before anyone probed too deeply.

"Nothing unusual. I continue cleaning at the hospital and praying for the patients and staff, and I've just finished translating two more Christian books into Chinese." Joy leaned forward and beamed at them. "And we might be seeing an answer to some of Esther's prayers."

"What do you mean?" Blanche asked.

"I'm sure you remember Paul Webster."

Gina nodded. "Esther's medical specialist? I was surprised to see him at her funeral."

"Esther and I prayed a lot for him," Joy said.

"Didn't Esther also send him a letter to read after she died?" Rachel asked.

"Yes, but somehow that letter got lost and arrived much later than all the others. Whatever Esther said pushed him to spend some time investigating Christianity with another of Esther's friends from the clinic," Joy said.

"Could that be the science teacher?" Blanche asked. "Esther used to talk about him a lot."

"I don't know who the person is, but they're reading Luke together once a week."

Gina leaned forward. "Joy, how did you find out what's been happening?"

"Dr Webster wanted to talk to me because he'd had some weird things happening to him, and Esther's letter suggested he ask me if he had any questions."

"Wow," Rachel said. "I'm surprised he actually dared to talk to you."

"It's not easy for someone to approach a stranger to ask questions. Especially the kinds of questions he had." Joy looked around. "I'm not going to tell you the details and you mustn't say anything outside this group, but those men need our prayers. It's obvious that God's at work. Esther warned Dr Webster in the letter that if he ever started to take Jesus seriously there might be some sort of counter-attack."

"You mean from Satan?" Gina asked.

"Yes. He's had some terrifying nightmares that made him want to give up on studying Luke. So I want us all to pray for these two men. That they'll not only read the Bible but meet Jesus."

"And I can ask William and our neighbours to join me when I get back to Lord Howe," Blanche said.

They bowed their heads and first spent time praying for each other. Then Blanche prayed for Paul. "Dear Lord, you know how often Esther prayed for Paul and Rob and others at the clinic. We know of at least one who believed."

Anna, and through her Tony.

"Please protect Paul from distractions. Help him and his friend to keep studying the Bible. Not doing it casually to tick a box or to search for excuses not to believe in you. Help them to see that you are not only true but worthy of following."

Everyone else prayed for Paul as well.

Lord, help me to be faithful in praying for this man and to be like Esther in looking for opportunities to share about you with others. Please deal with this bitterness in my heart. I want to be like Esther, who ran her race well.

CHAPTER 5

*G*ina tried to walk for an hour every day after school. It helped her relax after six hours keeping twenty-five Kindergarteners moving in the same direction. Teaching Kindergarten was like trying to herd a group of cats, but by the end of second term they had adjusted to each other and she'd worked out each child's strengths and weaknesses. Some children arrived already reading and others couldn't sound out a single letter. The Year One and Two teachers thanked her every year for breaking in their future students.

That morning, while Gina had washed the breakfast dishes, she'd asked Blanche if she'd be willing to join her on her afternoon walk. Now Blanche walked along beside Gina. "I hope Rachel hasn't been giving you a hard time."

"I wouldn't ask you to work out any problems between me and Rachel. Actually, living with Rachel has been great," Gina said.

Blanche laughed. "She loves it that you do most of the cooking."

"And she does nearly all the gardening. A good number of our vegetables are from the garden."

"I'm sorry you have to move out after the wedding."

"It makes sense for Pete to move in here. Rachel has come to love the place, and Pete's place wouldn't work for the two of them."

They kept walking. Gina wanted to ask a question but didn't know how to start. She cleared her throat. "I was tossing up whether to ask you or Joy for some advice."

"I would feel privileged if you asked me," Blanche said, turning slightly towards Gina.

Gina took a deep breath. "Ever since I turned thirty, I've been struggling with being single. Everywhere I go seems to remind me of what I haven't got."

This year alone, she'd attended four weddings and three of her colleagues had had babies.

"I guess your brother getting married last weekend didn't help," Blanche said.

"I was doing okay until I had to fight my way through marriage mongers and their probing questions," Gina said with a wry smile.

"What were they saying?"

Gina repeated the comments. She'd been able to laugh them off when she was twenty-five, but now too many pierced her defences and stung like a multitude of bee stings.

"How insensitive people can be, and misquoted scriptures make it even more annoying," Blanche said as they turned the corner and started down another street.

"I was worried I'd start bawling and wreck Bruce and Sue's big day."

They kept walking. Was Blanche silent because she didn't know what to say?

"I'm praying," Blanche said, answering Gina's unspoken question. "Asking God to show me what questions might be helpful. When all the problems erupted between me and William, I just wanted to run. But if I had, I'd have missed out on a great chance to grow spiritually."

"And your marriage might not have survived."

Blanche dabbed at her eyes. "God used Naomi to give me the help I needed."

"You must really miss her," Gina said.

Blanche was quiet for a long moment. "Wanting to be married is not wrong. It's wired into us, but maybe it would be helpful to ask why you want to be married." She sighed. "I married for the wrong reasons. William's attention made me feel good about myself, and he offered an escape from my family situation."

It was a good question. Gina hadn't really pondered the why. Was it so she'd feel special to someone? Her family should have been enough, but there'd been a hole in her core ever since she'd discovered she was adopted. If she ever had a child, she could never give it away, yet her parents had done just that. Why? That question gnawed away at her.

Her adopted father was a blessing. He'd never shown any preferential treatment towards the two boys, but her mother had been different. Gina had felt smothered for the first six years of her life, yet, her mother had barely noticed her after Bruce was born. Her father had worked hard to make sure Gina never felt neglected.

"Is that question helpful?" Blanche asked.

Gina nodded. "But it will take me a while to think through it."

"I have another question or two, if you're willing." Blanche crouched down to tie her shoelace.

"Ask away. I'm too close to the situation. I've been going around in circles, getting upset then beating myself up. I'm afraid of becoming bitter."

"The next question digs deeper." Blanche stood up. "When we get bitter about something, what are we saying about God?"

Gina frowned. "I'm not sure I get what you're asking."

"Sorry, I don't have William's way with words." Blanche paused, wrinkling her brow. "When we get bitter, it says something about our relationship with God—"

"You mean, it reveals that we don't trust God?"

"Mmm, and that we don't think he cares."

And Gina's adoption was sure to exacerbate those issues.

They started walking again. Gina stared at the footpath in front of her. Finally she said, "Your questions have given me plenty to think about."

"And you don't need to fear the process. Emotions are an outward sign of what is happening inside. If God is letting these things come to the surface, it's because he wants to lead you to a higher level of freedom and maturity."

"I know that here." Gina touched her head. "But I need to know it in my heart too, so it impacts my thinking."

"As we learn to trust that God always knows what he is doing, then our emotions will get in line."

"That will be a relief. I hate all the turmoil."

"Yes, but be careful not to stuff it down and ignore it. William and I both did that, and it wrought havoc."

"I think all these things are coming to the surface because I met someone nice, but he hasn't called me."

"There might be a good reason for his lack of contact," Blanche said.

"It doesn't take much time to pick up the phone," Gina said, weariness in her voice.

"Keep trusting God. He does know exactly what he is doing even if we often doubt him."

CHAPTER 6

*T*he phone rang the next day, but Gina ignored it. There was no point in wishing for the moon.

"Gina." Rachel knocked on Gina's bedroom door. "There's a phone call for you."

It was probably just someone from church, but Gina's heart rate sped up all the same. She put the bookmark into her book and headed for the phone. "Gina speaking."

"It's Tony."

Tony. She'd reconciled herself to never hearing from him again.

His warm, deep voice sounded sheepish. "You probably thought I'd died or something."

She definitely hadn't thought he'd died.

"I felt like I was dying for a few days. My eldest got a gastro bug the day after we had coffee, and it spread to the other two. I've never changed so many sets of sheets in my life. I thought I'd avoided getting sick but no, I got the bug worse than the whole lot of them."

She didn't want to rejoice at others' struggles but she was glad to hear there was a legitimate reason he hadn't called. "It sounds horrible."

"It certainly was, and it's taken longer than I expected to recover. I hoped you hadn't given up on me."

"I had rather."

"I'm sorry but I'm still hoping you might be willing to come to dinner with me. Do you like Italian?"

She'd have eaten plain rice with him if that was all he'd offered.

"I have a favourite place in Leichhardt," Tony said.

They finalised the details for Saturday night and he asked her about the wedding. She'd only talked for a few minutes before a wail came down the phone line. "Dad, it's not fair. Grandma gave that book to me and I haven't even read it yet."

"Sorry," Tony said. "I'll have to go and sort this out. I'll see you Saturday."

Gina hurriedly said goodbye to the accompaniment of another wail.

She stared at the phone in her hand. Dinner. On Saturday night. That sounded like a date. Was she excited? Yes. Nervous? Yes, definitely.

"What are you doing, sitting here in the dark?" Rachel came into the room and switched on the main light. "That guy didn't sound like any of your family." She raised an enquiring eyebrow.

"Do you remember Tony from Esther's funeral?"

"Not sure I do." Rachel sat down and pulled up a stool. She put her foot on the edge and started to paint her toenails.

"Esther helped his wife, Anna, become a Christian," Gina said.

"Oh, yes, I do remember him. How do you know him?"

Gina's face warmed. "I met him at the shopping centre the weekend before last."

"And?" Rachel looked up from her toes.

"And we had coffee that day and he asked for my phone number." Gina avoided looking directly at Rachel.

"And he's only just ringing you back now?"

"He and his daughters have been sick." Gina shrugged. "I'd decided he was never going to call."

"How many daughters does he have?"

"Three, I think."

"Um," Rachel said, looking directly at Gina as though to read beneath the surface.

"Yes, it might be complicated, but I'm going to take one thing at a time, and enjoy a nice Italian meal and what I hope will be good company."

"Good on you. We all have issues of some sort, and three daughters is a lot less tangled than Pete and my situations."

And Rachel and Pete had made progress on their issues with lots of prayer, counselling, and taking things slowly.

Rachel looked at her toes critically, gave them a little wriggle, and closed the top of the bottle. "I'll be praying for you."

"You might need to do more than that. I need a fashion consultant. I've never been on a date."

Rachel clicked her tongue. "The men you know need their heads read. You're a serious catch. Poor Pete is going to have to be the cook of our family, and I'm not much better at housework," Rachel said with a chuckle.

Yes, but Rachel was beautiful, sporty, and fun to be around. Things like that counted. So few people went beyond that first look. Gina would love to say Christians were different. She knew some who'd made wise choices based solely on character, but too few. If she was such a 'nice girl', why did no man want to marry her?

---

*G*ina had never been to Leichhardt, but it was immediately clear that it was a hub for the local Italian community. Restaurant after restaurant lined the main street and many signs were in Italian. Brightly coloured Italian flags fluttered from the awnings, and occasional notes of accordion music wafted on the evening breeze.

Tony had picked her up right on time in her Rachel-approved casual wear: jeans, blouse, tailored jacket, and mid-calf boots.

"Here we are. It doesn't look like much, but it's the real thing," Tony said as he led her into a particularly small Italian eatery.

Tables were crammed into the long, narrow space. The smells of garlic, onion, and bread swirled around them, along with the clatter of plates and cutlery. They only waited a minute in the line near the door before being led towards the back.

"A bit quieter here," Tony said.

Once again, he was greeted by name.

"Another friend?" Gina asked.

"Cousin." Tony shrugged. "My parents were both from families of nine and most of the younger generation migrated to Australia."

"What part of Italy are you from?" Gina asked as Tony pulled out her chair.

"A small village in the north, where everybody knew each other and their business."

"Have you ever been back?"

"A few times. Once when I was about twelve, and three times since. Anna and I had our honeymoon there so I could introduce her to the country and my relatives."

He handed her a laminated menu offering a lengthy list of salads, pizza, pasta, and main meals.

"This looks overwhelming," Gina said. "What do you recommend?"

"Almost everything," Tony said with a chuckle. "The main thing to remember is to leave room for gelato or sorbet. I know it's a cool evening, but a good portion of the clientele comes just for dessert."

"It's never too cold for icy desserts in my book," Gina said.

"My family would agree." Tony looked at the menu. "Is there anything you don't eat?"

Gina made a face. "I'm afraid I don't like olives or anchovies."

"Ah, that's something I hope to help you get over. My girls prefer olives to lollies."

"So do you give them a jar for Christmas?"

He laughed. "We sure do. One jar each."

Maybe she'd learn to like them if she bought a jar and ate one a day.

"Why don't we share a pizza, a pasta, and a salad?" Tony said.

"Sounds good."

Tony gestured to the waiter and ordered in Italian. The waiter took down the order on his notebook and winked at Tony.

"Trying to impress the pretty lady?" the waiter asked in English.

Gina's face heated.

Tony grinned. "None of your business."

"Your mama will be happy," the waiter said with another wink and headed back to the main counter.

"Sorry about that," Tony said. "I told you everyone knows everyone's business, but they don't mean to be offensive."

"I'm not offended." The waiter's words underlined that this was a real date. She looked over at Tony. "What did your parents do when they came to Australia?"

"Dad came first, under the Snowy Mountains Scheme."

They'd learned about the scheme in school history. The huge hydroelectric project supplied electricity to three states.

"Dad was one of thousands of European migrant workers. He said the dorms were spartan and it was back-breaking work. It did force them to learn English quickly, as the bosses used English."

"And what about the rest of the family?"

"Towards the end of the second year, Dad sent the money for boat tickets and I came out with Mum and my older sisters."

"Do you remember it?"

"A little. It was such a momentous thing for an almost four year old. The ship seemed like a giant playground designed just for me. I was always trying to escape and visit the other passengers."

"It must have been a nightmare for your mother."

"Being so young, I was blissfully unaware of how stressful it was for her." He shook his head. "Moving across the world with three children and not speaking any English except 'Please' and 'Thank you' and 'Can you speak Italian?'."

"What did they end up doing?"

"Dad had been a grocer in Italy. They moved into this area and supplied all the new migrants pouring into Sydney."

"So your family would have been well-known here."

"Yes, very," Tony said dryly.

A waiter wended his way from the kitchen carrying three dishes. He put the pizza down. "One pizza capricciosa, one house salad without olives, and one carbonara."

"The pizza has olives on it, but you can always give them to me," Tony said. "It's hard to avoid olives entirely."

"I'm willing to give them a try."

Tony waited for the waiter to leave and then said, "Let's pray and thank God for the meal."

It thrilled her that Tony took the lead on such a thing and didn't seem embarrassed to be seen praying in his old neighbourhood.

After eating a portion of each, Tony asked, "What do you think?"

"It's fabulous. I've never had pizza this thin before."

Tony snorted. "Real Italian pizza is like this with a few excellent ingredients and cooked in a super-heated clay oven."

"I'll never be able to eat the other stuff again," Gina said, wiping her mouth with her napkin and looking across at Tony. "I'd love to hear more details about how you became a Christian."

"Is this some ploy to make sure I can't eat?"

"Not at all. I'm almost full, so most of the rest is yours."

"Then I'm willing to talk." He finished his piece of pizza and reached for another. "My family are your typical small-town Roman Catholics. The church is our community centre. Every child is baptised, and we make a big deal of the first communion ceremony with special clothes, gifts, and photos. Now Mum has more time, she goes to Mass every day."

"And was Anna a Roman Catholic too?"

"I wouldn't have dared to marry a non-Roman Catholic. The thought of disappointing my parents would have been too much."

"So they're not too thrilled with your current beliefs?"

"No." He grimaced. "It's been really difficult. They didn't know Anna had changed because she was already too sick to go to church by the time she became a Christian."

"And how did you feel when Anna told you what had happened?"

Tony ate some more pasta and offered the last of the salad to Gina. "It was tough. From my point of view, she'd joined the enemy."

"The enemy?" Gina said.

"In our home, you didn't make friends with Protestants. You couldn't even go to a Protestant wedding without special permission from our priest. Becoming a Protestant was the equivalent of exiling yourself."

"So were you angry?"

"Not angry. I loved her too much for that. More puzzled and sad. I was worried she was headed for hell." He swallowed. "But as Anna told me the stories Esther shared, I had to admit something dramatic had happened. All her fear of death was gone, and she was looking forward to heaven. I'd always been taught that being confident about going to heaven was arrogant."

"So you were never sure you were going to heaven?"

"Our family was relying on good deeds and religious behaviours to get there. The problem was, I never knew when I'd done enough." He finished the last piece of pizza. "Anna said one thing in her last week that really hit me. That she had known about Jesus before, but now she knew God personally, as both her heavenly Father and friend."

"It's a big difference, isn't it?"

"It certainly is. Esther visited just before Anna died and she urged us to each spend time with her saying goodbye." Tony rubbed his eye. "I told Anna I'd investigate everything she said, and I meant it. I didn't want to be separated from her for eternity. Being separated here is hard enough."

Gina had worried that hearing about Anna would bother her, but it didn't. A man who loved his wife was the best kind of man. The more important question was whether he was the kind of man who only ever loved one woman.

"That last night Esther read Psalm 23. I loved the intimate image of God leading his sheep through life and protecting them every step of the way. She finished by saying to Anna, 'I'll see you in the morning.' I knew the morning she was referring to wasn't the next day. It was Esther's absolute confidence about the future that got to me, but I didn't have the time to think about it then."

"That's understandable." Tony had not only his own grief to bear but his daughters' as well.

"I asked our priest if we could have people sharing memories about Anna at the funeral, and Esther shared how she'd gotten to know Anna and how Anna had come to know Jesus." He chuckled. "She'd prepared well and avoided offending anyone by suggesting that Anna hadn't been a Christian before. But as she told Anna's experience of coming to a deeper knowledge of Jesus, it really hit me. She used the story of the thief on the cross like Joy used at Esther's own funeral."

"How long did it take for you to understand what Anna had been trying to say?"

"Not long. About a month after the funeral, I approached one of my accountancy colleagues who was a Christian and asked if we could meet up. I told him what had happened, and he offered to read the Bible with me. We read all of John, then Romans. I asked a million questions and finally understood about a month before Esther's funeral."

Tony handed Gina the menu again. "Are you ready for dessert? I suggest getting two or three different flavours."

Gina took the menu. After some deliberating, she chose passionfruit and lemon sorbets with pistachio gelato.

While they waited Gina asked, "And how did your parents take it?"

"I didn't immediately leave our church, so they didn't notice for a while. My colleague introduced me to his Bible study group and that was where I really started to grow. Those guys have broad life experience and are super keen about following Jesus."

"And now?"

"I've recently started attending the same church as all the men from the Bible study group. My parents have chosen to ignore my decision and hope it's just a fad. They'll really object when I move the girls into Sunday school. Up to this point I've been reading the Bible with them at home."

"Tell me about your girls."

Tony reached into his jacket pocket, extracted his wallet, and pulled out a photo. "Here are my three treasures."

Gina took the photo and Tony pointed to the eldest. "That's Sophia. She's twelve and in Year Seven. Isabella is eleven and in Year Six, and Elissa is nine and in Year Four."

"Sophia looks like you."

Tony pulled out another photo. "And the youngest two look like their mother."

Gina took the photo and her heart sank. Anna's light bulb smile made her beauty even more luminous. How could anyone compete with a woman like that? Blanche would remind Gina it wasn't a competition, but the theory was so different to what actually happened in the human heart.

"She looks like such a warm person," Gina managed to say, concentrating hard so there was no wobble in her voice.

Tony looked up. "She was, and I'm thankful we had thirteen years together. The last two years have been tough, but I've been grateful for the terrific bunch of men who've walked with me through it."

"Tell me about them," Gina said. Where, oh where, was that dessert? As though in answer to her inner plea, the waiter materialised at her elbow and laid their dessert bowls on the table.

"Let me eat a few mouthfuls first," Tony said.

A few turned into a few more but eventually he said, "They're a real mix. Mostly married, plus a single guy, and myself. A plumber, a doctor, an engineer, and an author." He ate a few more mouthfuls, slowly and with obvious enjoyment. "But what we have in common is a desire to follow Jesus and support each other."

They continued chatting as they finished their dessert.

"I really enjoyed tonight," Tony said once the bowls were cleared away. "Would you be willing to meet again? I can only do Saturdays because the girls need me around on school days, but either set of grandparents is happy to have them on the weekend."

Gina nodded. "I'd like that."

"I chose this time. Why don't you choose the next time?"

They hadn't even discussed hobbies yet but if he wanted to get to know her, she had just the thing. "What about coming kayaking with me on the Parramatta River? I'll bring everything we need."

They discussed the details, and then Tony drove her home.

She did like him, but she wasn't going to fool herself that she was only dating Tony. In the background were three hurting children. Sure, she was good with kids, but at school she could send them home. Tony on his own, so far, a definite yes. Tony plus three daughters? That required a lot more thought and prayer.

CHAPTER 7

*G*ina stood next to her kayak at the Meadowbank launching spot. A car tooted behind her and she turned to wave at Tony.

As he got out of his car, she walked over to join him, dragging the wheeled trolley that she used to manoeuvre the kayak.

"I don't see your car, so how did the kayak get here?" he asked.

She pointed across the park. "It lives in my friend's shed, so I can get it down here on my own without needing help."

"Lucky you to have a friend nearby. Do you kayak often?" Tony asked.

"Every Saturday unless it is pouring with rain or too windy." Gina clicked the backrests into place and checked the scupper plugs were tight. "I brought an extra pair of waterproof shoes which should be big enough to fit you. Your wind jacket is perfect." She'd told him what to bring during their last phone call.

"Do you have anything you'd like me to put in the car?"

Gina laid a few things next to the trolley, including her shoes and socks. Tony took off his tennis shoes and socks and replaced them with the shoes she'd brought.

"I'm thinking we'd better just take snacks to eat on the way and come back for our picnic. If we stop midway, we'll get too cold."

"You're the boss." Tony grinned. "I haven't been kayaking since I was in university."

While Tony went back to the car, Gina stored the snacks, her camera, and her binoculars in a dry bag and attached them to the kayak.

The car door closed, and the central locking clicked. Gina looked up. "Ready to go?"

Tony put on a broad-brimmed hat. "I am indeed."

"You get the front." Gina picked up the back of the kayak, and Tony grabbed the front. They walked into the shallow water and set the kayak down. Tony settled himself awkwardly in the front. Once he was in, she slipped into her place, gave a thrust with her paddle, and they shot forward.

"We'll go across the river before any of the passenger catamarans come by and work our way along the other shore," Gina said.

"Sounds good to me."

Tony soon remembered the basics. Within minutes, they were working as a team.

"When did you start kayaking?" Tony called over his shoulder.

"I don't know. It was one of the first things I did with my Dad. He nearly went to the Commonwealth Games as a rower but got pneumonia and missed out. Rowing wasn't so easy to do with kids, so he switched to kayaking. Both my brothers competed at state level in rowing."

"And you didn't?"

She'd been considering when to tell Tony more about her background and how much it would matter to him.

"No matter how hard I worked at it, I couldn't reach the standard and I didn't know why."

"Sometimes it's just because that wasn't how God made you,"

Tony said, stroking smoothly forward, water dripping off the end of his paddle.

A band of tension tightened around her chest. Would it bother Tony that she was adopted? Even if it did, she had to tell him. "That's what I thought, I expressed my frustration about my abilities compared with my brothers and Dad told me I was adopted." The memory of the emotions of the day swirled through her.

"Was that hard for you?"

"It was."

"Hmm," Tony said.

Was his response because he understood or because he didn't know what to say? Was her being adopted a problem for him?

"The whole situation is made harder because my brothers don't know, and my mother doesn't know that I know." Gina sighed, tension gripping her neck. "Mum can't cope with much stress, and Dad protects her. Perhaps he overprotects her, but he's the one who's seen the worst of her episodes."

"It must have been a difficult childhood."

"Not really. Dad was amazing at stepping up."

"And worked full-time?" Tony asked. "I'm doing that now, and I wouldn't have coped without my parents and in-laws."

That was the problem with going out with someone like Tony. Was he interested in her for herself, or did he merely want someone to share his load? She pushed down the thought. *Enjoy the moment, Gina.*

"I was about fourteen when I worked out how much Dad was doing, and I took on as much of the housework as I could. Things like the cooking, which he hated, and laundry."

She'd liked to feel useful and to see the gratitude on her Dad's face when she cooked a particularly good meal.

"That's quite a burden for a teenager."

"It didn't feel like a burden because cooking became something I loved."

They were now working their way downstream towards the city. Big houses in both Federation and modern style lined the riverbank, rising up away from the water in terraces that maximised the view.

"Look at the size of that house with the pool." Tony pointed.

They continued to move forward. If they spotted any floating rubbish, Gina would scoop it up and place it in a bag dragging along behind them. "The rubbish levels are much better than they used to be. Better guards on the stormwater drains and higher fines for littering."

"Do many of you collect the rubbish?"

"It started with one or two of us. Now lots do it. There are places to dump it near where you parked."

They kept paddling.

"I'm surprised your brothers didn't spot that you looked different to them," Tony said.

"I don't. Some people even comment on how much I'm like various members of the family."

It was one of the reasons she'd been so shocked to discover she was adopted. It had never occurred to her because she seemed to fit so well.

"Have you ever looked for your birth parents?"

"No, but I have thought about whether I should," Gina said.

"I have a friend who recently found his birth parents."

The tension in Gina began to relax. Tony seemed to be taking her news well. "Was he pleased he'd done it?"

"Yes and no," Tony said, changing his position in the kayak. "His birth mother didn't want anything to do with him, but he's in regular contact with his father."

Gina sighed. "It's a big risk, and it isn't easy to find out the information. Dad showed me my birth certificate, and it only has his and Mum's names on it. It's as if my birth parents don't exist. I don't even know if Gina is my original name."

"That would be unsettling."

"Some months I think about searching, but something else always seems to take priority."

"If only we didn't have to earn a living."

Gina laughed. "Exactly. I'd be happy to kayak three times a week instead of having to make do with walking, and there are plenty of other things I'd like to do if I had more time."

"Like what?" Tony stopped paddling and stretched his shoulders.

"Sewing, painting, anything crafty. What about you?"

"I'd like to have more time for friends and family. I still feel like we're surviving rather than thriving."

And now she was taking up his one half-day of spare time. Did his daughters resent her before they'd even met her?

"Do your daughters know about me?"

"I think Sophia suspects something because she's heard me talking on the phone and caught me whistling *Funiculì Funiculà* down the stairs the other day."

A warmth filled her chest. It was amazing that she, Gina Reid, could make a man happy enough to whistle.

"And my mama and sisters are certain to guess something is going on soon. This is the second Saturday in a row that I've asked for babysitting. I'm trying to ask a different family member each week so they take longer to notice, but it's only a matter of time. I never could keep secrets from them." He chuckled. "They always worked out Anna was pregnant before we told them."

Was Tony the kind of guy who would be willing to have more children? It wasn't the kind of question she could ask. Not yet. There were lots of questions she couldn't ask yet. Right now, she'd still be holding her breath at the end of this date to see if he'd suggest another. If the day came when he asked her to meet his family, she'd feel they'd moved up to another stage. At the moment things were so tentative. She breathed a sigh of relief every time he rang. He hadn't seemed bothered by the fact she was adopted, but maybe he was good at covering up his thoughts.

"Why don't we go around to that next point and have a drink and snack," Gina said.

"Sounds good to me. I'll work hard for one of those biscuits I saw." He dug his paddle in and she kept her eyes focused beyond him, trying to ignore the breadth of the shoulders in front of her.

They settled into a rhythm, heading arrow-straight for the little beach ahead.

Once they arrived they remained in their kayak and Gina handed out Anzac biscuits, still one of her favourite standbys. Just the right mixture of crunch and chewiness.

They ate and chatted until Gina looked upriver. "Here comes the RiverCat. We'll turn the kayak towards it so that we ride the waves."

They adjusted the kayak and rode the resulting swell. Several people waved and they waved back.

"Ready to head back?" Gina asked.

"How far have we come?"

"About four kilometres. Far enough for two people with indoor jobs."

"Now, now," Tony said. "Enough of that. I went for an eight kilometre run yesterday. This is a nice change for me."

"And the weather was kind."

She'd anxiously checked the weather report a few times during the week. If she was ever going to convince him to come again, it would be easier if the first experience hadn't been a cold and wet misery.

"Any more of those biscuits once we get back to the car?"

Gina chuckled. "There might be after lunch."

"What are we going to do next week?"

"I'm not sure I'll be available next weekend. I usually go home once a month and spend Friday night and Saturday at Lake Macquarie then come back early on Sunday for church."

"I might have to call you twice this week to make up for it."

The corner of Gina's mouth rose in a grin. She certainly wouldn't be objecting.

CHAPTER 8

Gina arrived at her parents' place on Friday for a late evening meal, a stone of dread heavy in her stomach. Her mother asked the same question every month. "Do you have a boyfriend yet?" Dad had asked her mother to stop pestering Gina, but it hadn't stopped the interrogation. Month after month, her mother probed into a wound that barely healed between one visit and the next.

Her relationship with Tony was like a tiny, tender plant and Gina wanted to hug her secret to herself a little longer. To suck every drop of joy from it without having to analyse such a fragile thing. Analysing it might kill it.

Sure enough, the question came. Gina dropped the cutlery into the sink with a clatter, hoping to distract her interrogator. Her mother wasn't fooled. "You didn't shake your head as usual."

Why, oh why, couldn't her mother leave this alone?

"No." Gina swallowed. "I have had a few dates this month."

"With different fellows or just one?"

"One is more than enough for me," Gina said, concentrating on stacking each dish carefully in the drainer.

"Well, tell me more."

There was little chance Gina would get away with the bare details, but she'd try. Maybe something would happen to rescue her before she'd be drained dry.

"His name is Tony and he's an accountant."

"And?"

"And we met because of a funeral," Gina said.

"That doesn't sound very romantic," her mother said.

"Perhaps not, but real life isn't a romance novel."

"How old is he?"

"I haven't asked directly but I think he's thirty-eight or thereabouts. He's healthy, kind, easy to talk to, and loves Jesus. The last is what matters most to me." Gina pulled out the plug and watched the water drain away.

Her mother ignored the last comment and rushed in with another question. "Why is someone his age not married? There's not something wrong with him, is there?"

Tension gripped Gina's neck. "His wife died of cancer two years ago."

Her mother fixed her gaze on Gina. "Don't tell me he has children."

Gina sighed. "He has three beautiful daughters."

"I can't believe it." Her mother stretched out the words. "That you'd be willing to take on some other woman's children. That will be a whole heap of trouble, mark my words."

Tears welled in Gina's eyes. "Can you not believe someone might like me just for me?"

Her mother ignored her.

Gina turned her back towards her mother. "I'm going to bed." Without waiting for her mother to respond, she fled, throat tight, holding the tears until she reached her room.

---

*G*ina slipped out of her parents' house at six-thirty the next morning. She'd arranged to go kayaking with her father and youngest brother. Going this early in winter allowed them to set off in the semi-dark and see the sun rise over the water.

She shivered. A warm bed was so much more desirable at this moment, but she unlocked the chain connecting the three kayaks to a tree on the water's edge. Behind her, a door clicked closed and she turned her head to see her father coming down. He carried his paddle, a life jacket, and the backrest for his kayak.

"Good morning, sweetheart." He kissed her cheek. "I'm not sure if your brother will make it. We were in bed before he came home last night."

Well after eleven, then. "Let's set up and if he doesn't come, I'll lock his kayak back onto the tree."

It only took five minutes for them to get ready to go. Just as they were about to get in their kayaks, her brother came stumbling down the lawn, dropping his gear as he came.

"Don't wait for me," he said. "I'll catch up."

And he would. He was the best kayaker of the family and still trained hard for rowing. He'd been disappointed that rowing was no longer a part of the Commonwealth Games, but dreamed of competing at the 2000 Sydney Olympics.

The glimmer of a golden sunrise was in the east, and they headed towards it. Gina had put on gloves to prevent her hands turning into ice blocks, but vigorous paddling would soon get her blood pumping.

It had taken Gina ages to get to sleep last night. All the doubts she'd ignored had been let loose by her mother's comments. Did Tony really like her, or was he just looking for a mother for his children? Their last conversations had been great—easy flowing and talking about things that mattered. They'd talked about their own churches and what they liked about them. Then they'd switched to favourite memories from their childhood, and he'd finally asked why she limped. She hadn't felt embarrassed as she told him about the juvenile arthritis diagnosis at age eight following years of lower joint pain and mysterious rashes that appeared and disappeared.

Tony had asked some intelligent questions about how it was controlled: medication and exercise. About whether it still caused problems: no, she'd been in remission since she was sixteen. In contrast to her mother, Tony hadn't made her feel like she was being interrogated and failing in some way. Instead, he'd told her about the TB scare he'd had as a child and rejoiced that her condition hadn't been too traumatising.

Grant had overtaken them, and Dad paddled closer. It was better she tell him what was going on rather than let Mum relay her version of events.

"Dad, did Mum tell you I'm seeing someone?"

His smile warmed her down to her frozen toes. "That's wonderful, honey. I hope he realises the treasure he's found."

Gina blinked back tears. "It's still early on. We met not long after my last visit here. He only has time to see me on Saturdays, but we talk at least once a week on the phone."

"Why is he so busy?"

One of their neighbours greeted them as he kayaked past.

"His wife died two years ago, and he has three daughters to look after."

"That explains the busyness. How old are they?"

"Nine, eleven, and twelve."

"Have you met them yet?"

She stopped paddling and allowed the kayak to glide forward. Her father stopped to match her.

"Not yet. It's tricky to work out when it would be the right time to meet."

"If anyone can win them over, you can," her father said.

His support warmed her. "Tony is going to talk to a counsellor friend for some advice."

"I'm sure you'll be praying about it," Dad said with a gentle teasing tone.

She glanced sideways at him. He seldom mentioned anything to do with her faith. "I have been since day one, and several of my friends are too."

"Sometimes I envy you having praying friends."

Before she could say anything further, he'd dug his paddle in and shot forward.

Lord, you know why Mum and Dad have never been open to spiritual things. Please help me to be faithful in praying for them.

---

*O*n Sunday evening, Gina found Rachel in the kitchen nursing a cup of tea.

"The kettle just boiled," Rachel said. "Good weekend?"

"Yes and no." Gina got out a mug and some camomile tea.

"Let me guess. Your father and kayaking were the yes, and your mother was the no?"

Rachel knew about her difficulties with her mother, as Gina knew about Rachel's difficulties with her father. At least Rachel's parents followed Jesus and things were moving in a positive direction.

Gina sat down with her tea and told Rachel about her mother's questions and how they'd stirred up all her own fears.

"You remind me of myself last year," Rachel said. "I was afraid of so many things that I almost didn't give Pete a chance." She paused. "As Gran once told me, we fear fear itself and don't deal with it. But so often what we fear never even happens."

"But how do I stop it?" Gina asked. "My mind starts churning with all sorts of scenarios the minute I get into bed—most of them worst-case scenarios."

Rachel laughed. "Good thing you couldn't read my thoughts last year. I was terrified to share my past—which was much more of a mess than yours—in case Pete rejected me and went after someone else."

"I can understand that," Gina said. "Fear of rejection is a big issue, and the problem is we don't know what people will react against. Our culture, our family, or the fact that our health isn't one hundred percent."

"And the stumbling blocks can be hidden and unpredictable. Pete felt he'd disqualified himself from a second chance because he was driving the car his family died in."

Everyone had a distorted view of grace. "We too often think everything has to be earned." Gina took several sips of tea. "Grace seems illogical."

Rachel nodded as she put down her empty mug. "It's taken me a long time to begin to trust that God acts with grace, but I still don't expect grace from people." She shook her head. "Yet I've received so much grace from Gran, from Esther, from Pete and his family. And from what you've told me, Tony seems to be the same kind of person."

Yes. There hadn't been any warning lights in their relationship so far. No pressure or manipulation in any way. Last time they'd talked, he'd asked if they might pray together at the end of each phone call and she'd been delighted to do so. He prayed as if he meant it, without any flowery language or special talking-to-God voice.

"And I'm slowly learning to show grace to others," Rachel said. "Pete and I have been discussing the wedding list. I'm struggling with the tradition that Dad is supposed to walk me down the aisle, but there's still time to decide."

Gina hadn't even thought ahead to that issue. "I don't think you have to follow tradition for the sake of tradition."

"Maybe, but I haven't been able to get the parable of the unforgiving servant out of my head. God's forgiven me a heap, and I have to pass on that forgiveness to others."

From all Rachel had told Gina about her father, it wasn't a surprise to hear Rachel was struggling. "I have to practise forgiving with my mother too. She has hurt me so much over the years. I'm going to double my prayers for her and Dad's salvation."

"Pete and I are already praying for you and Tony."

Gina swallowed around the lump in her throat and reached across the table to squeeze Rachel's hand. "Thanks."

"Why don't I pray for you right now," Rachel said.

They held hands across the table and Rachel said, "Dear loving and gracious heavenly Father, thank you for knowing us, truly knowing us, and still loving us. Thank you for always treating us better than we deserve. For lavishing us with gifts, including the gift of knowing you better. Lord, you know our hearts are often full of fear. Help us to take those fears to you and pray through each one. Help us to not look at the storms but to look at you. You put all our fears into perspective. Help Gina to trust that if you mean for her and Tony to be together, that you will deal with every obstacle in their path. And Lord, if you don't mean for them to be together, help that to become clear quickly for the benefit of everyone. Please protect Tony's girls from extra hurt."

Yes, Gina was most concerned about the girls. She would adjust to whatever happened, but children didn't have the same maturity and life experience.

CHAPTER 9

*G*ina reached Meadowbank Wharf thirty minutes early. She'd woken at 5 a.m. with a tension headache, the kind that only settled with getting out for a walk and prayer time. After two months of dating Tony, today was the day to meet his daughters.

She paced along the water's edge muttering to herself. "Patience, perseverance, prayer, and love 'em," the mantra Tony's friend, Greg, had shared. Not only was Greg a friend from Tony's Bible study group but he was also a professional counsellor with a specialty in children.

At the end of the path, Gina turned to walk back the other way. At this rate she'd create a furrow in the cement. *Calm down. The children won't eat you.*

She and Tony had had several conversations about this first meeting. Her teaching experience had been useful in choosing the place and kind of activity—something that didn't demand the children be stuck next to her the whole time.

They'd both agreed that a boat ride from Meadowbank down the river and under the Sydney Harbour Bridge was the best option. Then they'd walk from Circular Quay into the Botanic Gardens for a picnic.

Tony assured her everything would be fine, but it was hard not to imagine all the things that could go wrong. He'd told her about each child's personality, but she'd have to wait and see if they blurted out what they thought or shut up like clams. *Thank you, Lord, that you're with us. Please help today to go okay.*

She continued walking but slowed down and took some steadying deep breaths. Tony had taken some photos of her to show the children when he told them about Gina. He said he'd been proud of how they'd responded, but Elissa had been more clingy since and Sophia shut herself in her room more often. He'd taken them on a few walks and made time to talk with each one separately.

Gina looked up as Tony's car swung into the carpark. He waved, she responded, and three blonde heads swivelled in her direction. She walked back to her car and got out the large picnic basket. Tony was bringing the drinks.

She locked the car and went to stand on the footpath. Today was not a day for running towards them. They needed to come at their own pace.

The two older girls took their time getting out of the car, faces averted from Gina. Elissa skipped forward then stopped, hanging back to wait for the others.

Gina smiled, stomach cramping, as the silent group walked towards her. It would have been easier if the children were younger, but the girls were at the age of developing their own minds and opinions. Wary like wild deer. Waiting to respond rather than embrace.

Tony smiled broadly. "Girls, this is my friend, Gina. Gina, this is Sophia."

Sophia nodded.

"Isabella."

"Good morning," Isabella said.

"And Elissa."

Elissa gave a tentative smile, as though unsure if she was allowed to do such a thing.

"Let's go get our tickets. That looks heavy." Tony reached down to pick up the picnic basket. "Let me take it."

The RiverCat arrived on time. Tony pointed out its twin hulls and explained how catamarans were different to other boats.

"Can we go right up the front?" Isabella asked as they boarded.

"It'll be cold," Tony said. "You'll probably need your wind jacket."

It was cold, but they were prepared and the views were better from the front. The boat was surprisingly quiet as it glided over the water from one pick-up point to another.

"Look, Dad." Elissa tugged her father's hand. "We can see the cars crossing the bridge above us."

"There's my favourite place." Gina pointed to a building like a gatehouse on the edge of the water. "It would make an amazing small house. Does anyone else have a favourite?"

"I like that white one." Elissa pointed to a modern design.

"I prefer the older ones," Isabella said.

Sophia stood to one side, saying nothing, and looking in a different direction to the rest of them.

Two out of three talking was a good start but Sophia, as the oldest, looked like being more of a challenge. A tight knot settled in her stomach.

Tony looked across at her and winked.

"What about boats?" Tony asked. "Which one is your favourite?'

The river was broadening out, and boats of all shapes and sizes were moored along the edges. Elissa chose based on colour, while Isabella went for yachts rather than motorboats. Sophia moved further away from them, as though to disassociate herself from the rest of the family.

"Look, there's an island." Isabella ran to the starboard side. "A big one."

Industrial buildings and chimneys reared up, and a great chunk of sandstone rose in the centre with an old house on top.

"I think it's Cockatoo Island. They used to build big boats there," Tony said.

"Aren't there rumours it's going to open up to the public?" Gina said.

"I didn't know that," Tony said.

As they passed the island, the city centre came into view with more pointing and exclamations from the girls and in a mixture of languages from behind them— Chinese of some sort, Greek, and several European-sounding languages. Centrepoint Tower gleamed gold in the sunshine.

"Look, Dad," Elissa said with a little hop, "There's the Harbour Bridge. Do we go near it? Do we?"

Tony grinned down at her. "We're going right underneath it."

A warmth coiled in Gina's abdomen. Tony was a good dad. Not that it surprised Gina. He kept the children together, checking on each one but letting them have their freedom as long as they didn't bother anyone else.

The boat glided within the shadow of the bridge before turning between the brilliant white sails of the Sydney Opera House and the nineteenth century buildings of the Rocks area.

As they waited their turn to cross the gangplank, Tony said, "We're going to walk along towards the Opera House and into the Botanic Gardens. Everyone needs to carry something."

"Do we have to?" Sophia muttered.

Tony gave her a look with the hint of a frown and handed her a bottle of drink to put in her backpack. She packed it in and headed off in front of them.

"She'll be fine," Tony said quietly to Gina. "Coming in on the RiverCat was a great idea. I think they'll want to do it again."

Elissa walked, holding Tony's hand and claiming his attention to look at various street performers scattered along the harbour front: a juggler, a quick-sketch artist, and a cellist. They stopped to look at a statue—or was it a man covered in silver paint? He stood so still it was hard to tell at first. Various tourists took photos with him and even Sophia watched him until she said to her dad. "He blinked. Did you see it?"

They meandered their way into the Botanic Gardens. Elissa stuck close to Tony, Sophia either trailed behind or strode way out in front, and Isabella seemed uncertain where to be. Dragged each way by different loyalties. Gina walked beside Tony, torn between understanding where the kids were coming from yet wishing it had been different. It was hard for kids to understand that loving your mother didn't mean you couldn't let anyone else in. She reminded herself that they weren't rejecting her, but the hurt still swirled inside. She'd always prided herself on how quickly she connected with children, and she'd thought it might be easier for her to win them over.

They walked through the gardens, looking at various sections, before setting up a picnic blanket on a lawn near enormous trees. The youngest two scampered over to join other children climbing the trees but Sophia hesitated.

"It's fine to go with the others. Gina and I can manage here," Tony said, and she wandered over to the others.

"I'd normally get them to help but think it's better to give them some space today," Tony said.

"Good idea," Gina said, getting various things out of the basket. Once everything was set up, Tony called the children and had them run over to the nearest water fountain and wash their hands.

During lunch Gina thought hard for a question to break the ice. "Sophia, I hear you're in Year Seven. Is that right?"

Sophia shrugged. "Yeah."

"Do you have a favourite subject?" Gina asked.

Sophia stared off into the distance, looking as if she was trying to read a street sign across the other side of the harbour. She didn't answer.

Elissa looked from her sister to Gina and back again. "Sophia always helps me with maths. She says that's her best subject. I'm no good at maths, but I love reading. We have to do twenty minutes of reading room at the beginning of the day, and Mrs Arnold always lets me sit on the beanbag because I read so well. After reading groups—"

"Thanks, Liss." Sophia folded her arms. "She doesn't need to know every single minute of your schedule."

Isabella was willing to answer questions, but only enough to be polite. She looked anxiously between her father and Sophia.

Tony kept things moving and asked Gina questions about her job and interests. She answered as best she could and even generated a few laughs when she told them funny stories about things her students had said and done.

It was a relief when lunch was done. All the girls helped tidy up afterwards. They'd been well brought up.

"Daddy." Elissa pointed towards a big fig tree. "Can I go and climb that?"

"As long as one of your sisters goes with you."

"I like climbing trees," Gina said.

"Really?" Elissa said. "I didn't know that adults climbed trees."

"Well, this one does." Gina stood and brushed some leaves off the seat of her jeans. She'd chosen tennis shoes rather than boots because she'd wanted to be prepared for any games they might want to play.

"This I have to see." Tony packed up their picnic things.

They each picked something up and placed it in a pile near the tree. Tony gave Elissa a hand up to the lowest branch and Gina followed. Isabella scrambled up too, but Sophia plonked herself on the ground near their things. Tony bent down to talk to her, but Gina couldn't hear what was said.

"Come on, Daddy," Elissa called. "I want to see you climb."

"Do you think I can't?" He came to the bottom of the tree and reached up to grasp the bottom branch.

Tony spent the next ten minutes helping Elissa move around the tree while Isabella and Gina went higher.

"Hey, Soph," he called. "Take a photo, please."

Sophia moved sluggishly to obey and after some instructions, finally found the camera and took some photos of them all.

After Sophia had finished taking the photos, Gina climbed down and went over to her. "If you go up the tree, I'll take some photos for you."

"I'm good, thanks," Sophia mumbled.

There was no point in pushing her. When the others came down, they went for a walk around the gardens before heading home on the train. The girls read their books and she and Tony were able to talk.

It hadn't been super easy, but she'd survived. Gina would pray it would get easier each time. And if it didn't? Then they'd deal with that as they needed to. She wasn't worried about Elissa and figured Isabella could be won over in time, but Sophia? Only time would tell if Sophia would come to accept her.

CHAPTER 10

Several weeks later, after staring at her wardrobe for what seemed like an eternity, Gina rang Tony. She was due to meet his parents for the first time today.

"Tony, I've been standing here for twenty minutes trying to decide what to wear. I want to make a good first impression."

"Gina, take a deep breath. It will be okay."

She'd known he'd say that. It was okay for him. He'd done this before. How conservative were his parents? Were they the kind to frown if women wore trousers? Would they think she was trying too hard if she wore a dress? Tension pulsed in her jaw. Tony had already told them she wasn't Roman Catholic. Would they hold that against her?

"Why don't you wear what you wore last week? That orange-coloured skirt."

She didn't wear orange. She cast her mind back. Oh, he meant the peach-coloured one. That was easy enough.

"Just be yourself," Tony said.

Maybe that was the problem. She wasn't sure who she was. Gina Reid or someone else entirely.

"Why don't we pray, and I'll be there to collect you in two hours."

"*G*ina, what do you do for work?" Mr Agosto asked as she and Tony sat with him in the formal sitting room. Mrs Agosto was busy in the kitchen and had insisted that Gina was the guest and should sit and talk. She would have been much more relaxed with something to do.

"I'm a Kindergarten teacher, and I've worked at the same school since I finished university."

"And where did you study?"

"Newcastle."

"Newcastle?" he said. "So you're not from Sydney?"

"No, I grew up in the Lake Macquarie area, and my parents still live there."

"I haven't been there. Have you, Tony?"

"Not that I can remember."

The heap of questions weren't a surprise. It was human to be curious and normal for a family to be protective of their son. Tony was the youngest of three and the only son in a traditional Italian family. They wanted to make sure anyone who might join the family was suitable. The problem was she wasn't certain about their criteria for 'suitable'.

"Do you and your parents go to church?" Mr Agosto asked.

She should have known that her family might be as important as who she was as an individual. A prickle of sweat moistened her hairline.

"I do, but my parents don't."

"And why is that?"

She wasn't sure which part of the question she was answering— why her parents didn't go to church or why she did, but she and

Tony had prayed she might have a chance to share about her faith. He'd warned her what to expect from his parents.

"My parents don't have any sort of religious background, but they sent us three children to Sunday school."

"That seems unusual if they did not believe," Mr Agosto said.

"Not in Australia. Up until recently lots of people sent their children to church on Sunday so they could have some peace and quiet."

"Families should be together," Mr Agosto muttered.

Gina smiled. "I agree. I'd have loved my parents to have been at church with us, and I'm still praying they might come to know Jesus."

"Know Jesus? That's a strange thing to say."

How could she explain it? "I guess it is, but when I first went to church when I was about ten, I began to learn about Jesus. I heard stories about the things he did and said, but it was all a little distant. Like learning about King Henry the Eighth or—" *Quick! What was an Italian example?* "Julius Caesar or the Emperor Constantine."

Mr Agosto sat up straighter in his seat.

"It wasn't until I was in my mid-teens that I understood Jesus wasn't just someone who lived long ago and died, but that he rose again from the dead and so he's still around. Still around for me to know personally and not just know about."

"Humph," Mr Agosto said.

Gina glanced at Tony, who gave her a flicker of a smile. As she'd started to talk, Tony had briefly clasped his hands together out of his father's line of sight to let her know he was praying.

"So you're not Catholic then?"

Gina shook her head. "The church my parents sent me to as a child was a Baptist church and I've stuck with that. Our congregation isn't big, but they love Jesus and the pastor faithfully teaches God's word so we can understand and apply it."

She had spent last night trying to guess what questions they might ask, and thought about possible answers. Tony had previously told her a little about the faith he'd grown up with and she'd wanted to use words they'd understand and which might raise a few questions.

Mrs Agosto bustled into the room, carrying things from the kitchen towards the dining room.

"Mama, I can help you with that," Tony said, bounding to his feet.

His mother patted his cheek. "You're a good boy."

"And what do your parents do?" Mr Agosto asked.

Gina answered this question and other questions about her brothers and their professions—high school teacher and engineer—and whether her family were close and what they liked to do with their spare time.

Gina was relieved when Mrs Agosto came into the room and asked them to come and eat.

Tony was seated on the other side of the table, but he touched her foot with his and she tapped back as Mrs Agosto served large bowls of pasta in a creamy sauce.

Once they were finished Mrs Agosto asked, "Would you like more?"

"It's delicious, but more than enough for now," Gina said. Tony had warned her that pasta was only the entree. Mrs Agosto served the main dish, pork cooked with lemon.

"Papa, why don't you tell us a little about your family background," Tony said as they ate.

"Ah, young people today aren't interested in such things," he said.

"Actually, I'd love to hear about your family," Gina said.

Mr Agosto nodded with a tight smile. "Tony comes from a good background. Hardworking people. People proud of their large families."

"I can see that." Gina gestured towards the walls and sideboard, which were covered in photos.

"One day I'll introduce them all to you, but not today. Today we enjoy the meal my Faustina has cooked. She's a good cook, no?"

Gina nodded. "She's an excellent cook." If she ever got the chance, she'd love to learn from Tony's mother.

"My mother taught me. Did your mother teach you to cook?" Mrs Agosto asked.

"Not really. I learned because I liked cooking," Gina said. Tension tightened around her neck, but Mrs Agosto went on to talk about her mother and aunts and all she'd learned from them. No more questions that might probe into Gina's background.

They finished the main course, and the dessert was brought in.

Gina turned to Mr Agosto. "What was it like working on the Snowy Mountains Scheme?"

"Cold, cold, cold, and hard work. Work, eat, sleep. Work, eat, sleep, and never enough rest."

"But you did make some good friends, Papa," Tony said.

"Si. Many of those friends are still around."

"Dad plays bocce—Italian lawn bowls—twice a week," Tony said.

"And eats too much." Mr Agosto laughed as he tucked into his cannoli with vanilla custard.

When they'd finished, Tony cleared the plates and Mrs Agosto brought in coffee to finish their meal. Gina was uncomfortably full.

"I am sorry to see that you limp. Is your foot painful?" Mr Agosto asked.

Gina shook her head. "Not any more. I had arthritis as a child."

Mrs Agosto looked across at her husband, and he said something in Italian. She nodded in response. "I thought that was something only old people got."

"There are some kinds that happen in children, but mine is in remission."

Mr Agosto translated again.

"So is it something that can be inherited?" he asked.

"The doctors don't think so."

"So it might be?" Mr Agosto looked across at his wife, and a look passed between them.

A flicker of anxiety sprinted through Gina's stomach. What did that look mean?

"Have any members of your family had it? Brothers or sisters, parents or grandparents?" Mrs Agosto asked.

Gina's gut churned. She'd hoped to avoid any talk about this topic. Tony might be relaxed about her being adopted but his parents might not be.

"I don't know," Gina said.

"Have you never asked them?" Mrs Agosto persisted.

Tony touched Gina's foot under the table. She glanced across at him, grateful for his support, even if this was her battle.

"I don't know who my parents were. I was adopted at birth."

Again that look between Tony's parents. Was she being tested? If so, it wasn't clear what things would gain or lose her points. If the looks meant what she thought they meant, she was rapidly losing points. She swallowed. It looked like only one of four parents was happy about her relationship with Tony. It wasn't fair. All these years, she'd never had anyone interested in her. Now Tony had come into her life, and everyone had an opinion on the matter … and wasn't afraid to share them.

To her relief, the questions stopped. Mrs Agosto directed her back to the lounge and asked Tony to come and help her do the dishes. Was it about helping with the dishes, or having a little chat like Gina's mother did so often? Gina took a shaky breath. She hoped she hadn't let Tony down.

After all the questions before dinner Mr Agosto seemed to have run out of words. Gina's shoulders relaxed and she looked around the room. It was overfull to her taste and many of the pictures were religious in nature. Several statues of Mary took pride of place. She'd have to ask Tony about how his family viewed Mary and what his views were now.

Perhaps she could use the bathroom. When she asked, Mr Agosto pointed down the hall and told her it was at the very end of the passage. As Gina headed past the kitchen, she heard Mrs Agosto say in a loud whisper, "She's adopted. Doesn't that bother you?"

Gina paused, frozen, bile rising in her throat.

"No, it doesn't. I judge Gina on her character and her's is the finest."

"But you have no idea who she is. That disease could be from her family and you don't know if any of them are ..." Mrs Agosto went off into Italian, her voice rising and falling, each word emphatic.

Gina crept down the hallway and back to the living room. Tony had seemed fine with her being adopted, but his mother definitely wasn't. Not one little bit. Tension surged back into Gina's body. How much longer did she need to be here?

CHAPTER 11

*G*ina thanked Tony as he opened her car door. Then she clicked in her seatbelt and leaned her head back, forcing herself to relax, while they set off.

"I'm sorry they gave you a bit of a hard time," Tony said. "I don't remember it being so bad for Anna."

Anna had been beautiful and from a Roman Catholic family. Gina was more foreign to them. "They love you and the girls, and they want the best possible outcome for you all."

"Yes, but I want them to trust me. Mum and I had some words in the kitchen about it."

Gina didn't say anything but his defence of her warmed her heart.

"She was overly concerned about your being adopted." Tony changed gears and glanced across at her.

"She might be right. I don't even know if there is anything I should be concerned about. Genetics is about a lot more than disease. There might be aspects of my personality and the way I do things that are inherited, but I'll never know unless I find my parents."

Tony geared down as he approached a red light.

"Ever since I've known I was adopted there has been a will-I-won't-I tug of war in my heart."

The traffic moved forward. "What are the pros and cons?" Tony asked.

He talked like an accountant, with everything in lists. It wasn't that easy for her. "I guess it would be good to know." Gina gnawed her lip. "Not knowing is hard. I find myself wondering what things are inherited and what are due to being raised where I was."

"How much is nature and how much nurture?"

"Exactly. And there is a sort of hole." She tapped her chest. "Like I have a beginning but it's blank before that. I don't know if I have grandparents or aunts and uncles—"

"—or half siblings?" He changed lanes to move around a slow-moving car. "Does it make you feel like you've been abandoned?"

Gina worried her lip again. "A bit. I've tried to work that one through and remind myself that God loves and knows me, but it doesn't feel enough. Not when other people know where they come from." She'd been unable to avoid all the family photos in Tony's home. "Look at your family. They're a big family, and they're proud of it. When your parents talked about all their siblings and your cousins, they exuded a sort of ..."

"A sort of what?"

"Groundedness. Like their feet were solidly in the soil of both Italy and here. I don't even know my racial background or where my name came from."

"You might even be Italian," Tony said. "That would please my parents."

"I'm not sure anything else pleased them." She wished she'd bitten back the words the second she said them. They sounded self-pitying.

"They'll come around. It's me they're disappointed in, not you.

My leaving their church has been hard for them. They hoped that any girlfriend I had would lead me back into the fold."

So whoever she'd been, they'd be predisposed to find fault with her. Gina took a deep breath. She'd get through this. And poor Tony might get the same kind of third-degree treatment from her mother. Why couldn't people accept others without finding fault?

"What about the cons of looking for your birth parents?"

"There are lots of cons. If I was given away as a baby, presumably my parents didn't want me. That's not something I want to confirm."

"You'd prefer to live in uncertainty?"

"Not knowing means I can imagine a happy ending. If I met them, I might have all my hopes dashed."

"But isn't reality better?" Tony asked, turning the corner.

"I don't know. I fear knowing the truth in case it's a truth I don't want to hear." Gina hugged her arms across her body. "That my mother didn't want me, and my father doesn't know I exist."

She didn't want to be the result of a casual encounter or worse. At least now, she knew her adoptive parents had wanted her. Her father had always said that natural parents had to put up with the baby they birthed, but she had been chosen. They'd taken one look at her and wanted to take her home. His words had often warmed her heart when the cold winds of doubt blew.

"But it isn't necessarily the truth. When you were born, few young unmarried women got to keep their babies. Maybe she did want you, but everyone else pressured her to give you up for adoption."

"Then why hasn't she looked for me?" The words shot out of Gina's mouth.

"Perhaps she tried. It's not that easy. Or perhaps she loved you enough to not want to unsettle you. I don't think giving up a baby for adoption is ever easy. I can't imagine ever being desperate enough to give up one of the girls. I have such a fierce desire to protect them."

She envied those girls. Even with their mother dying so young, they had wonderful memories of her, and they had an amazing father who adored them. What if she had stayed with her mother? Would things have been better or worse than now? That was just it. She didn't know.

Tony turned the last corner before her place. Rachel might still be out, and Tony would have to rush off to pick up the girls.

"Gina, why don't you pray about this. I'm willing to help you look for your birth parents if you want."

"It won't be easy. I don't know their names or anything, and I'm sure my mother won't tell me anything."

"But your father might?"

"Maybe. It depends whether he is willing to risk Mum finding out what he's done and getting upset about it." He'd been so careful for so many years, it had become an ingrained habit.

"Let's pray about it over the next few days and talk again during our next phone call," Tony said as he parked.

*G*ina picked up the phone on Wednesday evening.

"It's me," Tony said. They first talked about their week and then he said, "I've been praying for you all week. Have you had any further thoughts about looking for your birth parents?"

She'd been thinking of nothing else for the past four days. She'd talked and prayed it over with Rachel and written to Blanche requesting prayer.

"I think it's time."

Even as she said the words, her shoulders relaxed and the tension headache she'd had for several days eased. Any decision was better than none, and it was time to stop procrastinating out of fear. "I'm not looking forward to speaking with my parents about it and there is no guarantee of a good result, but I need to try."

"I came to the same conclusion. It's unfinished business and the sooner we get going, the better," Tony said.

"We? I thought you were only being polite the other night," Gina said.

"You don't think I'm going to let you do this on your own, do you?"

She blinked, hot tears welling up.

"Where do we start?" Tony asked. "I'm not going to have the time to travel vast distances but if there is research that can be done in Sydney, I'll help. I'm also happy to be your shoulder to cry on."

Gina swallowed the lump in her throat. This search was likely to make her more emotional than anything she'd tackled before, yet he didn't seem afraid of her emotions.

"I'll need to speak with Dad first. Then I guess we go and see if there is an original birth certificate."

"You're not planning to speak to your mother at this stage?" Tony asked.

"I'll ask Dad what he thinks. I've phoned him and asked him to meet me at Gosford on Saturday morning, so I'll have some news for you when we go out for dinner."

"And how are you feeling about it?"

"Pretty scared but sort of excited as well."

"What are you scared of?"

Fears scurried around like meerkats, popping up and disappearing before she could focus on them. She paused to gather her thoughts. Tony would wait until she was ready. "At the moment, I'm most concerned about my mother. I think Dad will take it in his stride, but my mother is highly sensitive and will take it as a rejection."

"And?"

"And we may not succeed. I suspect that different eras handled adoptions differently and the information might not be easy to find."

"Would not succeeding be a problem?"

"It would be hard because I'd always be wondering." She gnawed her lip. "And it certainly wouldn't please your mother."

"Don't worry about my mother. She'll accept you once she gets to know you."

Gina wished she had his confidence.

"I'm scared my birth mother might hate me or want nothing to do with me."

"She'd have to be a pretty messed up person not to love you."

Maybe, but Gina's imagination could easily come up with terrible what-ifs. What if her mother had been in prison or a drug addict or a prostitute? There were no guarantees of a good ending to this story.

"Would you like me to make some calls and find out if there are government procedures for searching?" Tony asked.

"That would be great."

They talked for another hour, then prayed together.

CHAPTER 12

*G*ina waved to her father as he came along the waterfront to their prearranged meeting point. Reaching her, he kissed her cheek and they found a seat on a stretch of grass looking over the water.

"What's this all about, honey? I gathered you didn't want your mother to know. She thinks I'm meeting one of my former work-mates for lunch."

She told him about her visit to the Agostos and the comments Tony's mother had made.

"And now you're wanting to look for your birth parents?" Gina's father said. "I can't say I'm surprised. Every adoptive parent thinks about this day."

Gina reached over and rested her hand on his shoulder. "Are you okay with it?"

"I'm fine. I know you love us and we won't lose you, but I don't think your mother will see it the same way I do."

"Why is that, Dad?"

He sighed and stared at the grass at his feet.

"Only tell me what you're comfortable with," Gina said. Her mother had always been a private person.

"When we got married, I didn't know the full extent of her abandonment issues. Her father, whom she adored, died when she was still in primary school and her mother married again very quickly." He sighed. "Her stepfather wasn't thrilled to find two children came with the deal and he packed them off to boarding school as soon as possible. Your mother never got over it, and she never learned to talk to anyone about whatever was bothering her."

"Doesn't she talk to you?"

He shook his head. "Not really. It would make a world of difference if she had some close friends."

"Perhaps she finds it difficult to trust others."

"I think you're right." He stared out over the water. "I've often wondered if I was the wrong match for her."

Gina put her hand on his shoulder. "No one could have been more patient with her."

"Yes, but is patience what she needs?"

Gina didn't know. Perhaps the whole family had spared her mother too much. Perhaps they'd all been part of the problem.

"What do you remember of your early years in the family?" her father asked.

"I remember Bruce's birth, of course."

"Before that?"

"I remember I could never go out to play with other kids and Mum used to grab me with no warning and hug me too tight. I fought to make her let me go." Then her mother would cry. She'd learned to put up with the hugs to prevent those tears.

"Do you know why she was like that?"

"I have no idea."

"Your mother isn't going to be happy with me telling you this, but you need to know. We tried to have children for several years.

First there were two miscarriages. Then we had a little boy who died when he was six weeks old ..."

Her father's face was pale and his voice flat. Gina touched his shoulder. "Dad, I had no idea."

He wiped his eyes. "It was terrible. She blamed herself, and nothing I said could get her to change her mind."

Gina had never seen a hint of this earlier brother. In fact, there wasn't a single photo of any of them as babies displayed around the home. Maybe her mother hadn't dared to take any until the children were past the dangerous first year of life. Gina had an album of photos of herself as a baby, which her father gave her when she turned eighteen.

"How did I come into your lives?"

"Honey, would you be willing to go and get us both a coffee? I need a few minutes to decide how much I can tell you."

Gina's heart sank. Was she going to be foiled at the first hurdle? If her father wouldn't talk, what chance did she have? She got to her feet and scanned the foreshore. "Do you want your usual?"

Her father nodded and she headed for the nearest café.

Please, God. Please help him to be willing to talk.

She gave him twenty minutes. He was pacing back and forth when she got back to the bench. She put down the coffees and went over to link her arm through his. "I'm sorry to put you in this situation."

"There's no need to be sorry. You're not the problem."

Mum was. Her father was the total opposite to her mother. He'd bend over to help her if it was just him. But how much would he say today?

They sat down and sipped the coffees. Gina had finished hers before he spoke.

"Your mother would never forgive me if I said too much. She'd feel I betrayed her."

One hint, Lord. Just something to get me started.

He took a deep breath. "Your mother was pregnant again, and we grabbed the chance to go on holiday up in the Tamworth area. We weren't doing anything strenuous when she went into labour." He clenched his fists. "And the baby, a little girl, was stillborn."

"Oh, Dad, I'm so sorry." A tear ran down Gina's cheek.

"It was a terrible three days. The doctors sedated your mother because she just stared at the wall and refused to say a word. I cried but she didn't shed a tear although it was obvious she was in a bad way."

Somewhere in this story might be the clues Gina needed.

"Your mother was in a private room. While I made the discharge arrangements, I heard whispering at the nurses' desk. That afternoon, the Sister approached us and asked if we would consider adopting a girl who'd been born the night before to a teenage mother."

Gina swallowed and repeated the two clues in her mind. *Tamworth. Teenage mother.* She kept as still as possible, as though breaking the silence might seal her father's lips forever.

"And that's how you came into our lives." He looked around at her. "And what a gift you were."

"I thought parents had to apply through an adoption agency."

"If you'd been born a couple of months later, that would have been true. The new Adoption Act stopped private adoptions but it didn't come into full effect until 1967, and things were a bit slower in country areas. It's unlikely we would simply have been handed a baby in Sydney or Newcastle."

"And how did Mum respond?"

"She was too out of it that afternoon to have any part in the proceedings. They took me to the nursery so I could look at you through the glass." He touched Gina's cheek. "It was love at first sight. Right then and there, I was determined to take you if we possibly could."

"But did Mum agree?"

"Well, I talked to her as best as I could and eventually the Sister just came and put you in her arms." He laughed. "And that was it. She wouldn't let go."

"It sounds awfully casual," Gina said.

"As I said, it was the country and things were more relaxed. A solicitor came to the hospital and I signed a heap of papers."

"And my birth mother?" Gina croaked.

"I never saw her. There was an older woman signing papers, but I only saw her back. I presume she was a relative, but I don't know."

"And the papers?"

"They might still be lodged with the solicitor."

Who might not even be alive. It wasn't much to go on.

"Did you choose my name?" Gina asked, voice raspy.

"Not really. As we were checking out of the hospital there was screaming from one of the rooms."

Gina swivelled on the bench to face her father, heart speeding up.

"Amidst the screaming the woman said something like 'Never forget, it's—Gina'. There was another word or sound in between but I couldn't understand it."

Gina hugged her body, suddenly cold. "Maybe my name is really Georgina."

"Perhaps, or Virginia, or even Regina. We didn't know, so we stuck with Gina."

A tight band squeezed Gina's chest. Gina. Her name—or at least part of it—might be a legacy from her mother. One tiny bit of connection. And perhaps, just perhaps, her mother hadn't wanted to give her up.

"Do you think there's an original birth certificate?"

"I really don't know. As I said, adoption laws were changing as you were born and there might have been some glitches."

"Glitches?" Gina raised her eyebrows.

"In the paperwork." He touched her arm. "But not in how much we loved being matched with you."

"A match in what sense?"

"I don't know, but that was the word the Sister used."

"You don't happen to remember her name, do you?"

"In those days, no one called nurses by name. They were all Sister. It shouldn't be too hard to find out because Tamworth is a fairly small place and many staff work all their lives in the same hospital."

Gina stared out across the water. A lone seagull flew in a low, straight line, parallel to the top of the gentle waves. "Thanks, Dad."

He squeezed her hand and they sat together, watching the sun glisten off the water. Tony was somewhere south of here. She'd talk to Tony first and then head to Tamworth as soon as possible.

CHAPTER 13

*T*hat evening, Gina had barely got into the car before Tony spoke. "I can tell you've got news."

"I've got a starting place for my search."

"I'll drive and you can tell me what you've found out," Tony said, putting the car into gear.

Gina poured out the story, her voice shaking with excitement. She finished just as they arrived at the restaurant. Indian this time.

"I knew we'd have a lot to talk about, so I asked for a quiet table in the corner." Tony reached around between the seats and picked up a small expandable file. He had been busy.

They got themselves settled at their table and ordered, but Gina paid little attention. What did Tony have in his file?

"I think you're more interested in the file than me." He winked.

"Sorry. That's really rude of me," Gina said.

He laughed. "I'm not blaming you. Now I've heard what you've found out, I'm ready to jump in the car and drive to Tamworth immediately."

"That's what I feel like."

He opened the folder. "You'll have to go a little more slowly. The government doesn't want you to rush off and do things your way."

Her heart sank but it made sense. "What are the steps?"

He pulled out a piece of paper and some photocopied sheets. "The article is a copy of the 1984 Adoption Act. It contains the long version of the process. The main point is that you're required to first have an interview with a counsellor who specialises in adoption issues." He looked at his own notes, a series of neat asterisked points. "The counsellor will gather whatever information they have and prepare you for seeing the file."

"It would be wonderful if they had my original file."

"Don't get too excited. When I told the woman on the phone that you were born in 1967, she told me that things were a little chaotic that year."

"Presumably because of the new legislation banning private adoptions."

"Oh, you know about that? She said that prior to 1965, more than half of adoptions were privately arranged but the government was concerned about the dangers of selling babies as had happened in the US. After 1967, private adoptions could only happen if the adoptive parents were relatives of the mother. Otherwise it had to be through a registered adoption agency."

"Dad mentioned that they probably shouldn't have been allowed a private adoption."

"I think he's right. The woman at the agency said there was a gap between passing the law and actually enforcing it."

"And I might have fallen in the gap?"

He nodded.

"The counsellor will give you guidelines for your search and let you ask all your questions."

The waiter came and placed a basket of naan and several different curry dishes on the table. "Chicken masala, beef vindaloo, dahl," he murmured, perhaps sensing that their attention was focused on the papers on the table. "Please enjoy."

Gina waited until he was gone. "It's going to be hard to eat with all this excitement."

"Let's pray. That might calm us down," Tony said.

She loved that he had made such an effort already on her behalf.

They ate most of the first course, the bread soaking up the pungent spices. "I wish I knew how to make Indian food," Gina said.

"I've made a homemade version of naan. It's not too hard."

She was going to see if she could find the spices for at least one simple curry and dahl.

"Gina, the lady on the phone did warn me that sometimes a mother has placed a 'do not contact' tag in the records. You need to be prepared in case that happens."

Gina looked up at him, eyes wide. "Why would she do such a thing?"

He shrugged. "Perhaps if the circumstances of the conception were too traumatic."

Gina gulped. What if her mother had been raped?

"Or if she's married to someone else and doesn't want her spouse or family to know about her past."

"Surely nowadays such backgrounds are quite common?"

"Maybe, but how we feel about our pasts can be messy."

Look at what she'd found out this morning about her mother. Gina's childhood had improved so much after her youngest brother was born. Maybe her mother no longer feared any more losses. Gina had a clear memory of her mother actually laughing after Grant was born, a sound she couldn't recall from before that time.

The phone number to make an appointment with the counsellor was on Tony's summary page. She'd be phoning to make an appointment first thing on Monday morning.

"Good morning, Ms Reid." The adoption counsellor, Ms Jones, rose from her place behind her desk. A pile of files sat on the desk and a small bookshelf of reference books were within easy reach.

Gina moved forward into the room, with Tony following. She introduced Tony. "We both wanted to come as Tony will be helping me on my search and he's the one who found you."

"Well done. A lot of people just start charging around on their own, then get upset when no one will reveal any information without a signed letter from us."

"I can see the danger that would pose," Gina said.

They took the offered seats and Ms Jones said, "You told us your birth date, name, and hospital of birth on the phone. I've had a look for any birth or adoption records and sadly, I've come up with virtually nothing. The only birth certificate at the Births, Deaths, and Marriages registry was the adjusted one with your adoptive parents' names." She clicked her tongue. "Most irregular."

"What do you think has happened?" Gina asked.

"I begin to wonder if there wasn't a little ..." she hesitated. "Going around the rules."

"If there was, does that mean anyone involved might not want to talk to us?" Tony asked.

"It's possible. You mentioned there may have been a relative acting for your birth mother. Country relationships are often ..." She paused, as if searching for the right word. "A little enmeshed. If the Sister of the hospital knew any of the parties involved, things might not have been done the way they ought to have been."

"Do you think the original birth certificate might have been destroyed?" Gina asked.

"There might not be an original birth certificate but there might be something in the original hospital records, if they still exist and if someone was following protocol."

Gina's heart sank. If she did get to Tamworth, would there still be records? And would anyone be willing to talk with them?

Ms Jones handed them a photocopied list of questions. "These are all designed to help you think through what you're trying to do and why. I gather you've only known you were adopted for ..." She checked her notes. "Less than ten years."

Gina nodded as she scanned the questions:

---

* WHAT ARE YOUR EXPECTATIONS AND HOPES?

   * HOW MIGHT THIS ALTER YOUR CURRENT FAMILY RELA-TIONSHIPS?

   * WHAT HAVE YOU ALREADY DONE TO PREPARE YOURSELF FOR THIS POTENTIALLY LIFE-CHANGING PROCESS?

"As you can see, there are pages of help for every stage of the journey. We suggest you take your time going through these. Rushing the process can result in a whole lot of unnecessary pain."

Gina had no plans to do that. She'd take her time, even if she didn't feel like going slow, to read all the relevant material and talk it through with Tony.

"People's stories are complex," Ms Jones continued.

Gina nodded and kept agreeing but her mind shouted at her to hurry, to get out of here so she could read the material and plan a strategy. Somewhere out there, her parents were waiting. Or so she liked to think. She pushed down any thought that they might not want to meet her. Or that they might not be around anymore.

CHAPTER 14

Gina stood outside the entrance of the Tamworth library at eight fifty-five on Saturday morning. She'd driven north directly after the school bell rang yesterday and stayed in a bed and breakfast Tony had booked for her.

Last night, she'd been buzzing with tension and finding it impossible to settle to sleep she'd pulled out a notebook and listed her options.

---

* Library
   * Hospital
   * Phone books
   * Local gossip
   * Newspaper office

The problem was that at least two of these places were probably closed early on Saturday and would definitely be closed on Sunday. She had to find any information in a relatively short time. Wednesday's phone call with Tony had mostly consisted of brainstorming how she'd use the precious time.

There was a sign on the heavy library doors. The library was open from nine until four. Good. She had time. If she was lucky, the information she needed to get started would be here and she wouldn't need to go to the hospital. The hospital was likely to be much more reluctant to give out information.

At nine on the dot, the lights came on inside the building and the heavy doors were pushed open from within and propped in place. She and a few others stepped into the carpeted space. Gina walked towards the front desk. This was not the day to waste time being overly independent.

"How can I help?" the silver-haired woman on the front desk asked with a warm smile.

Gina's heart did a little internal skip of joy. Just the right kind of person to answer her questions. Someone who looked like a long-term resident and who would know the history of the place.

"Would you have any kind of local hospital records which list significant people from its history?"

"You're in luck," the librarian said. "There was a book put out for the 150th anniversary." She looked up the Dewey classification number and wrote it on a scrap of paper to hand to Gina. She then pointed towards the correct row of shelves.

Clutching the paper, Gina went along the row. Once she found 994 for Australian history, she checked the more precise numbers after the decimal point and scanned the shelf. *There.* She pulled out the book and flipped to the table of contents. An appendix listed all the main staff linked with the hospital. Hands shaking she hurried to the nearest empty table, pulled out the seat, and sat down.

She found the correct decade and she was in luck. The head of the maternity department in 1967 was listed. Even better, she'd only left the post in 1988. If she'd left because of retirement, then she was probably in her seventies, so might still be around.

It was a pity about the surname—Smith—but her first name was more unusual. Noelene. Gina pulled out her notebook and wrote down the name. Then she checked the index and found out a little more information. Noelene was indeed a local girl. She'd worked in Tamworth her entire working life. A good photo was included. Gina got a photocopy just in case. Then she went back to the front desk, waiting until she and the librarian were alone.

"Was the book any help?" the woman asked.

"Yes, exactly what I needed," Gina said. "Do you happen to know if the former maternity Sister, Noelene Smith, is still alive?"

The librarian looked at her for a long moment before speaking. "She is, but I can't give you her address or phone number."

Gina had expected that answer. There was probably a set of phone books in the library, but she'd also spotted a phone box outside. If the phone book hadn't been defaced or stolen, she might be in luck. She thanked the librarian with a smile and headed outside.

The local area book was intact, and Gina flipped through to the S surnames. Even in this smallish area, there were still nearly one hundred Smiths in the book and five with the initial 'N'.

She wrote down the five numbers and addresses. Should she ring them all? But what if Noelene had used a different name for her work than for her personal life? Or if she'd gotten married and was listed under her husband's surname?

"Don't borrow trouble from tomorrow," she muttered to herself. She still had plenty of time to visit the newspaper office and see if they kept back copies of the newspapers.

She walked to the newspaper office. The reception area was fairly tidy but through the open door she glimpsed desks, computers, and a chaos of papers spilling out of boxes. A man with his glasses on the top of his head came through the door. "Sorry, no receptionist on the weekend. What are you needing?"

"Do you have some way to look at back copies of your papers?"

"They're all on microfiche at the library." He looked at her for a long moment as though weighing her up. "I've been here a long time. What do you want to know?"

Would he shut her down if she asked a direct question? "I'm trying to find Noelene Smith, who used to be the Sister in maternity up at the hospital. I found five possible numbers and addresses for N Smiths in the area, but realised she might not be listed as Smith in the telephone directory. Do you know if she's married?"

He scratched his head. "Why can't you city folk ask a direct question?"

"Because city folk are worried about privacy nowadays."

He chuckled. "Not in a newspaper office. Let's see the list." He held out his hand and scanned her notes. "Well, it's not those three addresses." He looked at the other two and tapped the paper. "I'm fairly sure it's that one and no, Noelene has never been married."

"So did your paper print births, deaths, and marriages in the 1960s?"

"It certainly did. Still does."

"Okay, what if an unmarried mother gave birth in the hospital back in the sixties. Would that be in the paper?" She'd kick herself later if she didn't at least ask.

He shook his head. "Very unlikely. Especially if there was no father in the picture, and the child was adopted out. Those kinds of situations were kept out of the public eye. Lots of people were ashamed of illegitimacy in those days. Still are, in some cases."

He perched against the edge of the desk. "You've hit me on a slow morning. If you have a date for me, I can do a quick check of the personal notices."

Gina grinned. "That's a deal I can't turn down. Will it take long?"

"Just long enough for you to go and get me a coffee. I'd appreciate that."

"That's fair enough. I'll go and get two." She took out her pen, wrote '10 April 1967' in her notebook, and tore out the page for him. "What kind of coffee?"

"Black with two sugars. How sure are you of the date?"

"Very." Her father had confirmed that he'd checked the exact birth date when they'd taken her away from the hospital.

"I'll check a week either side, just in case. The paper only comes out once a week."

He was already finished by the time she returned with the coffee.

"Sorry to be the bearer of bad news, but there is no mention of any baby born in April that fits. The only baby that we have a notice for was a boy." He took the offered coffee. "Thanks for the coffee. Since I'm usually on my own on Saturdays, I often forget to drink at all." He took a sip and sighed his pleasure, then looked at her. "Are you the baby?"

She nodded.

He pursed his lips. "It is possible that your mother was from here, but it's more likely she wasn't. In those days, unmarried girls were often sent to stay with a relative. Parents didn't want the news getting out to their friends and family."

"That's what I'm guessing, but the only clues I have are my birth date and the hospital."

"Noelene does have a fabulous memory, but she can be a bit cranky." He grinned. "But she has a thing for flowers and loves visitors."

"Thank you so much. I won't forget your help," Gina said.

"And if it turns into a story, remember me, won't you? People love a good mystery, and you look like you might be able to write something worthwhile."

Gina laughed and headed back to her car. On the way, she bought a bunch of daffodils. Anything was worth a try.

Lord, thank you for guiding my steps. Please help Noelene to remember my adoption and to be willing to tell me something.

*G*ina didn't phone ahead. She preferred to walk in unannounced rather than give Sister Smith time to flee. After checking the two addresses on her map, she drove to the closest. It was a Nicholas, not a Noelene.

The second address was on the outskirts of town, looking out over fields. The garden was weeded and pruned to perfection.

Lord, let this be the one. Give me wisdom to know what to say.

She rang the doorbell and waited. Nothing. No sound in the house at all. Her shoulders slumped. She'd been hanging her hope on this conversation. Of course, it wasn't likely that Sister Smith would remember an individual birth, but Gina had hoped the Sister could at least push her in the right direction. She had the official letter of approval for the search in her handbag to pull out if needed.

She turned from the door, went down the steps, and started back up the drive.

"Hello, can I help you?"

Gina turned. An older woman wearing gardening gloves, a tweed jacket, and a broad-brimmed hat was standing near the back of the house.

"Sister Smith?" Gina said, walking towards her.

"Who's asking?" the woman said.

"My name is Gina, and I've driven up from Sydney to find you."

The woman's head came up and she swept a searching gaze over Gina's face. Her eyes flicked and came back to settle on the right side of Gina's cheek, near her eye. Gina took a step back.

"So you've come," Sister Smith said under her breath. She pulled off her gloves. "I guess you'd better come in."

Heart pounding and clutching the bunch of daffodils, Gina followed her up the back steps and into a bright back room.

Now Gina had met Sister Smith, she wasn't going to call her

Noelene. The Sister did not look like a woman who used her first name.

"Are you wanting a vase for the flowers?"

Gina's face warmed. "Oh, yes. These are for you."

"Buttering me up," the Sister muttered. "I'll put them in water and get us a cup of tea." She headed further into the house, leaving Gina standing awkwardly in the middle of the room. Would it be okay to take a seat? She carefully perched on the edge of the one that looked the least used and listened to the sounds from the kitchen.

What had the Sister meant by her words? She seemed to know who Gina was, but how was that possible?

Sister Smith came back into the room with two floral cups and saucers, and a matching teapot, milk jug, and sugar bowl. She asked Gina her preferences and then handed her a cup. "You'd better tell me why you're here, although I'm fairly sure I know."

"I was born in the hospital here on the 10th of April 1967, and in my twenties I discovered I was adopted."

"Who adopted you?"

"Neil and Flora Reid."

Sister Smith nodded. "And you've come searching for answers?" She looked at Gina again with that searching gaze.

"I'm puzzled by how you knew who I was."

Sister Smith touched the skin near her own right eye. "You look like your mother, but that little birthmark near your eye confirms it."

A tightness gripped Gina's chest and she took a shaky breath. She looked like her mother. What an incredible thought. Somewhere out there, she had a mother. *Please God, let her be alive.* Somewhere out there was a woman she belonged to in a special way. Someone who had borne her so long ago. Someone who might not want her, but was still linked by a mother-daughter likeness.

Gina took a gulp of her tea, the cup clattering against her teeth. Was she finally going to learn her mother's name?

"I know you want to know more, but I can't tell you anything at the moment," Sister Smith said.

"Why not?" The words burst out. She was so close to the most important piece of information of all.

"I need to talk to someone first."

"And then you might be able to tell me more?"

"Yes, I think so. I don't think she'll object."

She. Was this 'she' Gina's mother? Or the other mysterious woman, the possible relative? Or someone else? Either way, she was still alive. *Please God, let her be willing to talk.*

CHAPTER 15

"*T*ony, I'm so glad to hear your voice," Gina said. "I've just had lunch and I'm back outside the library."

"Have you found anything?" His voice vibrated with excitement.

"I've found the Sister and she knows my mother's name and more details."

"But is she willing to say anything?"

"Sister Smith said she had to speak to someone. I don't know if she meant another nurse or a solicitor or even a relative."

"But she'll get back to you?"

"She asked me to go back to her place tomorrow morning." Gina swallowed. "I don't think I'm going to get much sleep tonight. It's pretty nerve-racking."

"Well, it's still early. You might have time to go out for a walk."

"Good idea. Before that, I'm going to see if there are any old directories listing solicitors who were practising back in 1967. I want to have the information in case a door slams with Sister Smith."

The phone flashed up the warning that it was about to run out of money, and Gina fed some more coins into the greedy slot. "How are the girls?"

"Sophia is out at a birthday party, and Isabella is at her piano lesson. It's been much better since you met them, because I can talk about you now and that's helping all of us."

Maybe they'd get used to the idea that their father was dating, and their next meeting would be easier.

"It would be great if you could come over for a meal when you return."

"I could bring dessert."

Tony chuckled. "That should win them over."

Someone tapped on the phone box.

"Tony, someone else wants to use the phone. I'll have to go."

"Stay safe and talk soon."

Gina hung up. Even talking to Tony for a few minutes had helped her process the disappointment that she still didn't have any more concrete information. She went back into the library.

An hour later, she walked out with a list of six local solicitors who had practised in the late sixties. She'd cross-check them with a phone book once she got back to her room. Now it was time to follow Tony's advice.

She was going to walk up the hill to the hospital to get a feel for the place where she came into the world. She went back to the car to collect her hat and sunglasses, then set off along Marius Street. Dawdling along the way it took her thirty-five minutes to reach the main entrance of the hospital. It had obviously been on the site for a long time. The maternity ward was probably the same place it had been thirty years ago, but she wouldn't go in. It was enough to be here. All those years ago, a mother had lost her child.

Had she regretted it? Or had it been a relief?

*N*oelene Smith rang at nine o'clock the next morning. "I didn't want you to waste your time coming over."

Gina sat down abruptly on the nearest chair, disappointment washing over her.

"My friend isn't always clear on what is happening, and is going through a bad patch. She didn't seem to understand what I was saying last night, and the nursing staff say she isn't any better this morning. They're going to call the doctor and see if she has a urinary tract infection."

"I have to go back to Sydney today as I'm teaching all week."

"If it's an infection, then a few days of antibiotics should settle it. Why don't I give you my phone number and you can call me on Thursday evening?"

Gina got out her notebook for recording her research, turned to the back, and wrote down the number. Was there anything immovable in her diary which would prevent her leaving Sydney next weekend? "I do appreciate you going to all this trouble."

"My friend would never forgive me if she didn't have the chance to talk to you. She has deeply regretted the way she treated your mother."

Gina clenched her free hand and dug the nails into her palm. *Please Lord, don't let bitterness have curdled any chance for a future.*

"And if she doesn't want to talk to me?" Gina asked.

"We'll cross that bridge if we come to it."

It was easy for Sister Smith to say that. This wasn't her life. But as her father had often told her, "You catch more flies with honey than vinegar." Gina thanked Sister Smith for all her trouble and hoped she'd be willing to talk, even if her friend wouldn't or couldn't.

And still she didn't have a clue to the identity of this mysterious 'friend'. Sister Smith was one careful woman. All Gina knew was the friend wasn't her mother, that she was elderly and lived in a nursing home. If only the Sister had let slip a first name, Gina might have been able to find out the surname. How many nursing homes could there be in Tamworth, population 32,000? It was going to be hard to wait a week for more clues, and she'd be puzzling over whether this friend was a fellow nurse, a neighbour, or a relative of Gina's. It seemed from what she'd heard so far that her mother had been alone and that Gina's father hadn't been in the picture. Why not?

CHAPTER 16

*G*ina going to Tony's place for the first time should have been a big event, but she'd been preoccupied with her family mystery since the weekend. Tomorrow night, she'd ring Noelene Smith and learn whether she had to head to Tamworth again.

Gina had been so distracted that she'd burned her cake. Instead, she'd whipped up an apple crumble. A tub of vanilla ice cream should also be acceptable.

She found the house, only three suburbs away from her own, and had a few moments to enjoy its neatness and cute dormer windows before Tony opened the front door, a border collie at his side. Tony came and opened the car door, and the dog thrust its nose in to greet her.

"This is Pirate." He reached down to pat the collie's head.

"Pirate because of the black eye patch?"

"Uh huh. The girls named him."

Gina bent to let Pirate sniff her hand.

"Welcome to our home. So glad I can finally invite you here. The girls said it was okay."

Sophia had probably given her grudging consent, but Gina wasn't going to worry about it. She and Rachel had been praying regularly for her relationships with Tony's family, and that her family would accept Tony too.

Tony took the bag containing her contribution to the meal, and led her inside. A broad hallway opened up to a big living room and open plan kitchen-dining room. Modern but homey. The air smelled of meat and herbs.

They went through to the kitchen. Tony opened the bag, put the ice cream into the freezer and then he asked her what she'd like to drink.

"Orange juice, please."

He poured a glass and gave it to her. "I'll ask Sophia to set the table."

"I could do that," Gina said.

"No, you're our guest and it's important for the girls to do their chores. I don't usually have to remind Sophia, but she might be a bit shy tonight."

Or a bit embarrassed at how she'd ignored Gina last time and now had to have her here in their home.

While Tony was gone, Gina looked at the chart on the fridge. Someone was obviously keen to have the girls doing household chores.

"Anna set that system up," Tony said as he came back into the kitchen. "I've continued it. They take turns at setting and clearing the table, and washing the dishes. They also make their beds and school lunches."

"And what do you do?" Gina asked, gently teasing.

"I ensure everything else gets done. After Anna died, I tried to do everything she'd done and it nearly killed me. Now, a cleaner comes every second week and I focus on the cooking and general organising."

And worked full-time, plus all the chauffeuring to music and church activities. He'd managed incredibly well, but it would have taken considerable strain and sacrifice to make sure the girls' routine was disrupted as little as possible.

Sophia came thumping down the stairs, said hello in a subdued voice, and went to lay the table.

"Sophia, if you'll call the others down, I'll serve dinner."

Gina went and stood on the dining room side of the counter. Tony dished the pasta and spooned on plenty of the meat and vegetable sauce. "It's pasta for the main course tonight. I haven't been home long enough to do a full multi-course meal."

"And I prefer not to eat too much," Gina said with a smile. "If you tell me where to put each plate, I'll put them on the table."

He directed her but stopped her when she headed to place his plate at the head of the table. "I'll put you at the head this time." His face warmed. "It will be easier for the girls if I sit in their mother's place."

Gina blinked back tears.

The children obviously weren't sure how to respond to her being here. They avoided looking at her, and went to their accustomed seats with little more than polite greetings. Once they were seated, they held hands to pray. Tony took her hand. After a momentary hesitation, Elissa put out her hand as well. Gina took the small hand in hers and tried not to think about Tony's hand enveloping hers on the other side. It felt so right.

Tony prayed. "Jesus, we thank you for bringing Gina to visit tonight. Thank you for her prayers for us all. Thank you for the work you provide, so that we can have this delicious food. Be with the girls as they finish their homework and help us all to have a good rest. In your name, amen."

He handed around the grated parmesan to sprinkle on the meal. "A little less, Elissa. Remember you're not the only one."

Elissa flashed him an apologetic look and he gave her a quick smile in return. They ate for a little while.

"It's Wednesday," Tony said. "What's our question for tonight?"

Elissa answered immediately. "What's one thing we're thankful for today?"

"Do you have a different question every day?" Gina asked.

"Yes," Isabella said. "Like what makes us happy, and what do we want to pray about."

"On Sunday, it's what we learned at Sunday school," Elissa said.

Tony looked round the table, a twinkle in his eye. "Who's going first?"

To Gina's surprise, Sophia spoke first. "I will. I'm thankful I'm in Year Seven and can study Geography and Indonesian."

"And I'm thankful we have kid's camp at church this weekend," Elissa said, bouncing in her seat.

"Is that just for primary school or high school as well?" Gina asked.

"Just for primary school, but Sophia is coming to help with the younger kids," Elissa said.

"What do you do at camp?" Gina asked.

"Us bigger kids get to go horse riding," Isabella said. "But there's also crafts and games and Bible stories."

"And I'm helping to organise a scavenger hunt," Sophia said.

Did Sophia realise she was talking at last? *Gina, play it cool. Don't make a song and dance about it.*

"And what about you, Isabella?" Tony asked.

"I'm glad my piano concert is finished, and I did okay," she said, beaming.

"You did more than okay. You were brilliant," Tony said. "Would you be willing to play your favourite piece for us after dinner?"

Isabella flushed. "Maybe."

"And Gina?"

She didn't want to say anything about what she'd done on the weekend. "I'm thankful that my students make me laugh."

"How did they make you laugh today?" Elissa dropped some of the meat off her fork onto her plate.

"We were talking about different sorts of nuts and one little girl insisted her favourite nut was a door-nut." Gina looked up. "Can anyone guess what she meant?"

Sophia frowned. "Did she mean a walnut?"

"Yes. She'd got the parts of the house mixed up!"

Elissa gave a giggle. "That's funny. I'm going to tell my friend tomorrow."

"And what about you, Dad?" Sophia asked.

"Apart from Gina coming for dinner and bringing dessert?"

"Yes, apart from that," Sophia said with a tiny blush.

"Mine sounds a bit boring, but I was thankful to finish some major tax returns for clients."

"Does that mean you have time to play a game with us after dinner?" Isabella asked.

"Only if you've all finished your homework."

"Yes Daddy," Elissa said.

"I only have two more maths problems to finish, which I can do while you're setting up the game," Sophia said.

"What say we work together to clear the table and do the dishes and then have dessert and a game?"

The girls nodded and each did their share of the tasks. Gina got Elissa to show her where the bowls and spoons were, and served the apple crumble. She'd add the ice cream when the dishes were done.

"Isabella, what about giving us some music while I finish the dishes," Tony said.

Isabella went out the door with a grin and got her music out of the piano seat. She sat down and played with confidence and a lilting joy. To Gina's untrained ear, it sounded like she was well on the way to being a competent pianist.

"Can we play Rummikub, Dad?" Elissa tugged on Tony's arm.

"Only four people can play that," he said.

"You could play with me," she said.

"Good idea, munchkin. Why don't you set it up on the dining table."

Elissa skipped off. Once she was nearly set up, Gina served the ice cream and brought the bowls over to the table.

"Dessert first, and then we'll play."

They played until seven forty-five and Sophia won. "Okay, bowls in the kitchen, and then teeth and Bible time." Tony looked across at Gina. "Can you entertain yourself until I come down?"

"Of course."

Once Tony went upstairs, Gina went into the kitchen, washed the last few dishes, dried them, and laid them in neat piles on the clean countertop. Tony was still upstairs, so she went into the lounge and pulled out some crochet, something she always carried with her. There was a single mother at church expecting her first baby, and making little blankets was easy. Something she could do while talking.

Tony came down the stairs. "The youngest two are lights out, and Sophia can read for an hour. She needs that slow-down time."

"How did you learn to be this good a father?"

He took a seat and put up his feet on a footstool.

"I wasn't nearly this good while Anna was around. Parenting is hard work, and it was all too easy to leave it to her." He leaned back. "The first few months after Anna's death were miserable. I wasn't sleeping. I kept snapping at the children, and they kept crying and telling me I didn't love them." He shook his head gently. "I got desperate and went and asked the guys in the Bible study group for their top advice. To my surprise, every one of them gave me words of wisdom from the Bible that they'd applied in their own lives. I hadn't known the Bible was so practical."

"I loved being here tonight."

"I'm glad. I'm hoping you might come every week from now on. What do you think?"

A smile began deep in her chest and bloomed out her lips.

"You are beautiful when you smile. Like one of those classic paintings."

Gina's face heated. She'd never considered herself beautiful. Pleasant-looking maybe, but in a world of models and movie stars, what hope did ordinary people have?

"It bothers me that you seem down on yourself."

"I used to go to a church that idolised perfection." Her voice cracked. "It was soul-destroying."

"It doesn't sound anything like what a church ought to be. It seems to me that modern women are under impossible pressures to work full-time, run a home and family, and look like they've never done anything but swan around, visit the beauty parlour, and have lunch with friends."

"Don't forget running the church fête," Gina said.

"Yes, well, Christian women seem to add another level of work." He leaned sideways, propping on his left elbow. "Please don't think I expect all that."

She wished she could believe he wanted just her, but no matter how much she'd tried to reject the idea, her mother's words had lodged in her head. The three reasons upstairs kept intruding. Three reasons that made her doubt this was anything other than finding someone to share the load. Someone willing to take on three children, not their own.

How could she work out if Tony was pursuing her for herself and not her usefulness?

"I noticed you finished the dishes," Tony said. "Thank you, but you were our guest, and I was happy to do them."

"It's my way of saying thank you," Gina said.

"I know, but I haven't invited you here to be a servant. I'm hoping you'll want to come every week for Wednesday dessert and games. We normally just have fruit for dessert, so it will make it special."

Gina blinked back tears. It wasn't dessert and games that made it special. His invitation moved things to a whole new level. He was risking the girls' hearts by asking her here regularly. Were they ready for it? Was she? This whole search for her birth family was a distraction, one with the potential to raise all kinds of emotions. After all the emotion of the last few years, Tony would quite reasonably be tired of emotion. What if he just wanted peace? What if her issues were just too much work?

CHAPTER 17

ina received a letter on Thursday afternoon and settled down to read what was now becoming a weekly exchange of letters with Blanche.

DEAR GINA

When Gina had first met Blanche, she wouldn't have guessed she might become a valued confidant. Perhaps Blanche hadn't known herself. William had confined her to traditional roles that hadn't included any kind of Bible teaching or pastoral care of others.

THANKS FOR YOUR RECENT LETTER. I AM DELIGHTED THAT TONY IS CONTINUING TO BRING YOU JOY. DON'T BE AFRAID OF JOY. I THINK YOU AND I MIGHT BE MARTHAS, ALWAYS IN A SERVING ROLE, BUT SOMETIMES TRAPPED BY IT AND A BIT RESENTFUL. LIKE

Martha, we need to learn to sit and delight in Jesus and his gifts.

Was she resentful? Gina put her head to one side. Yeah, maybe. She'd concluded that she couldn't shine in areas others regarded as important, so she'd carved herself a niche in the 'useful female' category. Better than sitting and weeping or going off the rails. There were days when she didn't serve others with joy. Days when she was tired of being useful, and would have loved to simply sit and talk.

Tony sounds like a special man. Don't let the accuser convince you that you somehow have to deserve him. Rejoice in the gift God has given. I know you're a little stressed by the fact he has three children. Of all women, you should not be stressed by the thought of a ready-made family, but I know these things defy logic. As a woman who has let fear control too much of my life, let me urge you not to do the same.

As you know (in your head), every marriage has challenges, but God is more than able to help you deal with anything that comes. He will provide the wisdom, courage, and strength needed. Look to him.

Blanche wasn't saying anything new but why did Gina and every other follower of Jesus she'd known have to learn the same lessons over and over again? Jesus' use of the sheep analogy was apt. Like sheep, Christians were constantly scattering then needing to be gathered up and moved in the right direction again.

I HAVE FINISHED MAKING YOUR DRESS. I'VE HAD MORE TIME BECAUSE RACHEL DECIDED TO WEAR THE DRESS I MADE FOR ESTHER.

Gina had been a little surprised at Rachel's decision, but then Rachel hadn't expected Esther's dress would be to her taste.

I AM DOING SOMETHING SPECIAL (I DID CHECK WITH RACHEL FIRST) AND EMBROIDERING WILDFLOWERS ON HER DRESS. IF I GET TIME, I'LL DO A FEW FOR YOU AND ALICE TOO. DON'T WORRY, THEY WILL BE SUBTLE.

Having seen Blanche's embroidery skills, Gina wasn't the slightest bit concerned.

I'VE BEEN TEACHING EMBROIDERY AND QUILTING HERE, AS IT GIVES ME A CHANCE TO BE WITH WOMEN OUTSIDE THE CHURCH. AS YOU KNOW, TALKING TO STRANGERS HAS NEVER BEEN MY STRENGTH, BUT TWO WEEKS AGO ONE OF THE LADIES STARTED ASKING ME ABOUT THE BIBLE. I EVEN MANAGED TO SHARE A BIBLE STORY WITH HER LIKE JOY TAUGHT US, AND SHE LISTENED!!! I'M PRAYING FOR MORE OPPORTUNITIES. I STUTTERED BECAUSE I WAS SO SCARED, BUT THE WOMAN DIDN'T SEEM TO MIND.

Lord, thank you for the reminder that I've stopped praying for opportunities to tell others about you. Please help me to do so more regularly.
See, yet another thing that dropped off the agenda too easily.

Sorry, Lord. I really am a wandering sheep. How did Tony share his faith? They'd already talked about their Bible reading and prayer habits and swapped ideas.

I'VE DISCOVERED I LOVE DOING VISITATION. WILLIAM NEVER LIKED THAT ASPECT OF MINISTRY IN THE PAST, BUT REG HAS SHOWN HIM HOW TO DO IT. THAT MAN HAS BEEN SUCH A BLESSING TO WILLIAM. HOW DIFFERENT WILLIAM'S LIFE MIGHT HAVE BEEN IF HE'D HAD SUCH A MENTOR IN HIS YOUTH. BUT THEN AGAIN, WILLIAM WASN'T WILLING TO LISTEN TO ANYONE FOR TOO MANY YEARS.

Even Rachel was coming to the conclusion that God had truly worked a miracle in her father. She regretted her early scepticism, and was loving being the daughter of four fathers. One heavenly, one earthly, and two potential fathers-in-law, since Pete's father-in-law had happily adopted her as well. Might that one day happen for Gina? She'd been more than happy with her father all these years, but was there a birth father out there? Did he even know she existed? Perhaps she'd know the answers to some of these questions by the end of the weekend.

WILLIAM VISITS THE MEN SEVERAL TIMES A WEEK, AND I VISIT ALL THE WOMEN. I DON'T KNOW WHAT I LIKE MORE. LISTENING TO THEM, PRAYING WITH THEM, OR SHARING FROM GOD'S WORD. I LEARN SO MUCH FROM EACH PERSON. LESSON AFTER LESSON ABOUT FORGIVING OTHERS, TRUSTING GOD, AND THE IMPACT OF PRAYER. IT WOULD BE EASY TO MAKE THE MISTAKE OF THINKING PEOPLE HERE ARE IMMUNE FROM TROUBLE BECAUSE THEY LIVE IN

A TOURIST PARADISE, BUT OF COURSE THEY AREN'T. THEY FACE ALL THE SAME ISSUES YOU AND I DO, BUT EXACERBATED BY DISTANCE AND ISOLATION.

Gina had stayed at Victory Church because of her friendship with Esther and the invitation to help out with the children's ministry. For a while, she'd been seduced by the resources available in such a large church. Then she hadn't wanted to leave Esther or the children she taught, but eventually the messages from the pulpit had driven her away. She'd never felt comfortable because of William's focus on promising blessing without mentioning the suffering that Jesus talked about as normal in the Christian life. Leaving had felt like abandoning Esther, but it wasn't long until Esther left too. The church they'd found wasn't fancy, but it was faithful. Stuart preached practical sermons that encouraged her in her daily life.

LORD HOWE ISLAND IS A WONDERFUL PLACE TO SPEND TIME WITH GOD. IT IS SAFE TO WALK ON THE BEACH AT ALL HOURS, AND GOD AND I HAVE LONG CHATS. WILLIAM STILL LOVES TO GO SNORKELLING AND HIKING WITH YOUNG DAVY. I'VE NEVER GOT INTO EITHER, SO I LEAVE THEM TO IT.

I WOULD NEVER HAVE GUESSED THAT FOLLOWING JESUS WOULD LEAD ME HERE, BUT IT IS VERY GOOD. MAY YOU TOO DISCOVER THAT JESUS ALWAYS KNOWS WHAT HE IS DOING, AND TRUST HIM TO LEAD YOU TO PLACES WHERE YOU CAN THRIVE.

YOUR FELLOW PILGRIM ON LIFE'S JOURNEY,

BLANCHE

Gina folded the letter and added it to the pile of others that

Blanche had written.

Lord, thank you for my friends and for giving me encouragers of all different ages to help me follow you. Please help the lady in Tamworth to be well enough to see me, and help me cope with whatever happens.

She'd ring Sister Smith after dinner, and see if she'd be driving five hours north again.

CHAPTER 18

*G*ina glanced over to Tony's hands on the steering wheel, gentle like the man himself. After Gina rang Noelene Smith on Thursday evening and heard her friend was much better, Tony had asked if she'd like him to accompany her. She'd gotten teary and Tony had taken that as a yes.

They'd set off a little later than last week because the girls had to be packed off for camp.

They followed the tail lights of yet another truck in front of them. It was a relief to have Tony share the driving. He'd also arranged two nights' accommodation with some friends who used to go to his church.

It was nearly ten o'clock before the sign for Tamworth appeared.

"Almost there," Tony said.

Tony wasn't coming with her tomorrow, but he'd be there to support her after the visit. He'd promised her a proper date. The guy was a gem. Why did she keep doubting he could be interested in her?

*S*ister Smith was welcoming, and she drove Gina over to the nursing home. It had a beautiful garden outside, but Sister Smith headed straight for the front door and led Gina down various corridors to a single room with an open door.

Inside, a slender woman sat in a chair, reading, her long thick silver hair hiding her face. Her clothes were old-fashioned but she looked ready for a day at the office. Sister Smith went over and touched her shoulder. "I've brought her, Rosalie."

Rosalie hastily put her book down. "Let me see her. Let me see Rehina's child."

Rehina. Was that the name of Gina's mother? It was a name Gina had never heard before. Sister Smith stood aside and drew Gina forward.

Rosalie looked up at her face, tears welling in her eyes, and Gina dropped down into a crouch and placed a hand on the old woman's knee.

"Oh, you look so like Rehina."

Rosalie reached out and cupped Gina's chin in her hand, turning her face side to side as though seeking to memorise every detail.

"Beautiful, so beautiful."

Gina's ankle ached but she couldn't break the moment. Rehina was obviously her mother, but who was Rosalie?

"Noelene, can you pull up a chair so my great-niece can sit down without having to crouch in such an uncomfortable position."

"You're my great-aunt?"

"Yes, your grandmother's sister." Rosalie spoke with some sort of accent. European, certainly, but Gina wasn't sure which part of Europe.

Gina stood up and took the chair Sister Smith had dragged forward.

"Do you want me to stay, Rosalie? Or should I come back later?"

Rosalie turned her head with the elegant posture of a dancer. "Perhaps you could give us some time alone."

Sister Smith nodded. "I'll go and visit some of my other friends." She turned and left the room.

"We both have so many questions it's hard to know where to start," Rosalie said. "Noelene has told me a little about you and how you found me, and she's assured me you're not angry."

No, Gina wasn't angry, but she had equal measures of sadness and curiosity.

"Just let me touch you again so I can believe you're real." Rosalie reached out and stroked Gina's arm. "I'm glad you're not angry. I deserve your anger, and I've lived in regret for too many years to count. I treated your mother very badly."

Gina swallowed. She had always known that this story might be hard to hear. "Before you start to tell me the story, what is your accent? Where are you from?"

"It's Dutch. Right after the war, the Dutch were one of the biggest groups of migrants to Australia." She laughed bitterly. "Mostly because we were acceptable to the White Australia policy and we assimilated quickly. We were also willing to go out and live in rural areas."

"How old were you and my grandmother when you came?"

Rosalie briefly closed her eyes. "I was twenty-five and your grandmother, Anneke, was twenty-two. The government was keen to have young men and women come and work hard. Our parents stayed behind with our brother. They felt they were too old to move, but insisted we must seize the chance to go."

Gina wanted to hear about her other relatives too but first she must hear about her mother.

"Your grandmother married another Dutch migrant and moved back to Sydney. I lived here from soon after we arrived, teaching French and German."

She looked like a teacher. Gina imagined she'd been strict and demanded high standards from her students.

"Your mother was my favourite niece. When my sister contacted me and asked me to take her in late 1966, I couldn't refuse." She sighed. "Perhaps her being my favourite was a problem, because when she arrived already four months pregnant, I admit I was disappointed in her. And when she refused to name the father, I labelled her stubborn."

There were many reasons why a girl might not reveal the name of the father. Out of love. Out of fear. Out of ignorance. Which was it?

"Aunt—" Gina stumbled, not sure what to call this new relative.

"Aunt Rosalie is fine. My days of being called Miss Janssen are long gone. Here I'm just called Rosalie—or Ros, by one particularly cheeky resident."

A Ros she was not. Rosalie suited her.

"Aunt Rosalie, how old was my mother?"

Rosalie shook her head. "Just seventeen and pretty as a picture. I think they sent her here for a number of reasons, but one was that they knew I would help her finish school."

"And did she?"

"She did indeed. I'd finish teaching for the day and come home and coach her on anything she was struggling with."

"So she didn't go to school with other kids?"

"Not until a couple of months after you were born. Then she did another year and a bit." Rosalie shifted in her seat. "Back in the sixties, kids were going crazy with all that rock and roll and protesting against Vietnam. Conservative families like ours lived in dread that we'd lose our kids. A teenage pregnancy was about the most shameful thing we could imagine. Your grandparents were respectable people, your grandfather a church elder. A pregnant daughter was a disaster."

"Didn't they think it might be a disaster for my mother?"

"Yes, but only in the sense that she'd blown her chances for an education and a good marriage. No one really thought of Rehina at all."

Gina's chest tightened. Back in the sixties what type of sex education had kids had? Even in the eighties, Gina's mother had simply shoved a book into her hand and expected her to work it out herself. Had her birth mother been tricked by a more sophisticated man or fallen into a sexual relationship with a boyfriend?

"And I'm afraid your mother was the one we all ignored the whole time. She was sent to me before her pregnancy showed and was expected to have the baby up here, away from anyone else they knew, then give it up for adoption, and return to Sydney in time for further education and act as though nothing had happened. No one bothered to ask her if that was what she wanted."

"So she never had a choice about giving me up for adoption?" Gina asked.

"Girls didn't in those days. They just got steamrolled, and it took a very courageous girl to insist on keeping the baby. That usually only happened if she had a strong boyfriend beside her."

"And did Rehina ever say who my father was?"

Rosalie shook her head, lips tight. "No, and we thought she was being defiant and protecting herself and someone else. It was only later that it occurred to me that she might have been a victim." She brushed away a tear. "A victim whom we further traumatised by our lack of understanding. Like her parents, I was more concerned about my reputation. I was glad she had a different name to mine, and I wouldn't let her leave the house or garden for the last four months of her pregnancy."

Her poor, poor mother. What must it have been like to have been sent away from her own family, then palmed off on an aunt who also cared more about protecting her reputation?

"I've spent the last decades bitterly regretting my attitude. I never bothered to put myself in Rehina's place or treat her as I would have liked to be treated."

"And did Sister Smith know the truth about my mother?"

"I told her early on. She was the kindest of us all, but even she couldn't protect Rehina once she went into labour. Many nurses considered it part of their moral duty to neglect your mother, to punish her for being pregnant before marriage. There was no pain relief for her during labour and little kindness. It was only when Noelene came on in the morning that she made them jump to it and clean Rehina up."

Nausea swept through Gina. This story reminded her of the lack of grace shown to the women in Jesus' day, treated as representatives of 'wickedness' and thus targets for people's anger and self-righteousness. She wrapped her arms around her stomach. She'd always assumed she'd find her mother, but what if she had ended everything all those years ago?

"Is my mother still alive?" Gina asked, shivering.

Rosalie's eyes widened. "I assume so. I've only ever had a few letters from her, the last one telling me she was married. I don't think she has ever left New Zealand."

"New Zealand?" Gina gasped.

"You're getting ahead of the story," Rosalie said. "We were just getting to Neil and Flora."

"Did my mother ever say she wanted to keep me?" Gina asked.

"All the time, but no one ever took any notice of her. It wasn't done." Rosalie brushed away another tear. "I should've listened. We could easily have raised you together, but I was too fixated on what was convenient to everyone else. I wanted your mother to succeed in life and not be burdened with a baby."

Burdened. Had Gina been considered a burden?

"Of course, your mother never saw you, and I kept away too. Deep down, I knew that if either of us actually saw you, we'd be lost."

Or found. It was all a matter of perspective. How might her life have been different if Rehina had been able to make her own decisions and had the support of her family? Why were reputation and education rated more highly than a child being with its mother?

"When Neil and Flora lost their child, it was regarded as a convenient way to solve two problems. Here was a mother distraught at the loss of her baby, and here was an extra child."

Gina wanted to shout, "I wasn't extra," but she liked this woman. Liked her too much to hurt her.

"Of course, I saw later how arrogant we'd been. We treated you as a pawn in a chess game, something to be moved and sacrificed to everyone around you."

"Yes, and my mother was treated as though she was a child who couldn't make any decisions."

Rosalie hung her head. "We never considered that Rehina was already an adult." She paused. "She must have instinctively known when you were handed over, because she began to shriek. I thought she was losing her mind."

Gina's nausea returned and she bent over clutching her stomach.

"Are you okay?"

"No, not really," Gina mumbled. "But please don't stop. I need to hear what happened."

Rosalie took a sip from the glass next to her. As she moved to put it back on the table, her hand shook, and she dropped it. It shattered on the hard floor. Gina stood up.

"Leave it, Gina. I'll call the nurse in a minute."

Gina sank back into her seat.

"I'll never forget her words. I heard her mutter to herself, "She must never forget her mother. Never.' And then she said it again, only louder. 'She must never forget my name, it's Regina.' The last words came out in a yell that reverberated off the walls." Rosalie flushed. "And all I felt was anger because she'd embarrassed me."

"I thought you said her name was Rehina," Gina said.

"It is, but it is spelled with a 'G' and most people pronounced it incorrectly. Your mother got tired of correcting them and switched to Regina, pronounced the Australian way."

"And now I know why I have my name. My Dad only heard, 'It's —Gina.' He always knew he'd missed a bit and said they assumed it was my mother naming me. He didn't know if she'd said Regina or Virginia or something else entirely, but he told my mother I was already named and my name was Gina." She shrugged. "And I've been Gina ever since."

Sister Smith popped her head into the room. "I thought I heard a crash. I'll go and get a broom and mop. I know where they're stored."

Gina looked around. "Thank you, and thank you for giving us privacy. I appreciate it."

Rosalie slumped in her chair, shrunken and old.

"I'm sorry to have tired you out." Gina leaned forward and laid a hand on her great-aunt's bony one.

"I'm not tired. I'm relieved." Rosalie straightened her spine and lifted her chin. "I'm relieved to have lived long enough to meet you. I've longed for reconciliation for the past thirty years, but I've known I didn't deserve it."

"Few do," Gina said, heart in throat. *Lord, do you want me to say something? You'll have to give me the words.* "I'm thankful to have found reconciliation as a teenager, and I'm so glad to have found you. You have no idea what it means to me to know I have a birth family."

"Maybe as much as it means to me to have found you. I always meant to search for you, but I was too afraid. Too afraid you'd reject me."

"You didn't know. How could you? I would never do that." Gina touched Rosalie's hand again.

Rosalie reached into the bag hanging at the front of her walker and pulled out a lace handkerchief to dab her eyes. "It is such a relief to hear you say that. I've lived with such guilt."

Sister Smith came back into the room, and Gina took the broom from her and swept up the broken bits of glass. Once she was done, she turned back to her great-aunt. "I still have questions, would I be able to visit again tomorrow morning?"

"And didn't you say you have a young man?" Sister Smith asked.

"Tony would be delighted to be called a young man."

Sister Smith gave a ladylike snort. "When you reach our age, anyone under sixty is young."

Rosalie sat up straight. "I'm always up early. Would you both like to come at half past nine? Then you could accompany me to the eleven o'clock chapel service. I suddenly feel like going."

"We'd be delighted to," Gina said. "And Aunt Rosalie, if you have time today, would you be able to draw me a family tree?"

Seeing Rosalie so frail and elderly was frightening. What if she died or had a stroke and everything she knew was lost? Gina only had a first name for her mother and the surname for her aunt.

"I've already prepared a family tree for you," Rosalie said. "I'm going to loan you an envelope of things to look at overnight. You might like to photocopy them." She pinned Gina with her gaze. "Make sure you bring them back. Some of these are the only photos I have."

Now it was Gina whose hand shook. It was almost too much that Aunt Rosalie would trust her with things she treasured. What might she find inside?

CHAPTER 19

*G*ina parked the car outside where she and Tony were staying. Her fingers itched to open the folder, but this was something she could share with Tony. He'd been waiting patiently all morning.

He was beside her as soon as she exited the car. "Was it alright?"

Gina turned and burst into tears.

He enfolded her in a hug. "A bit much, was it?"

"Oh Tony, Mum and I have the same name." Gina hiccupped. "Or sort of." She broke out of the hug and scrabbled in her handbag for tissues. "Sorry. It's been quite a morning, but Aunt Rosalie—Great-aunt Rosalie—is terrific." She raised the folder she was clutching in her hand. "I didn't open it, though I wanted to. Aunt Rosalie has let me borrow this overnight."

"Do you want me to hold it for a moment?" Tony said. "We're going out for lunch and a hike, and you might like to get ready."

She scrubbed her face with a tissue. "I'll go and wash my face and change into something more casual." She'd worn slightly better clothes today, having seen the way Sister Smith dressed and not wanting to make a wrong first impression on Sister Smith's friend.

Gina locked the car and they walked into the house together.

"My friends have a photocopier. Why don't I do that while you get ready?"

She nodded, tears welling again. Oh my, this could be a fun afternoon for him. It would prove once and for all if he was afraid of emotion.

*T*hey drove a few minutes through the town, past St Paul's and up towards the heights. The road wound around until they pulled into a carpark.

"It's a beautiful clear day to visit a lookout," Tony said. "And there are several walking tracks here too. I thought we'd have a picnic and look at the documents first. You must be dying to see them."

Gina tightened her lips to prevent the tears welling again. It was so much better having him here than being on her own at a bed and breakfast.

They found a picnic table and sat down. He must have been shopping while she was visiting Aunt Rosalie. Roast chicken, fresh rolls, and salad things, already washed and prepared. He'd even brought a tablecloth.

"What say I make you a roll while you tell me a little about what happened."

"I can make my own."

"I know you can," he said with a laugh. "But let me serve you for once."

Gina got out a tissue, just in case. "This is going to come out all incoherent."

"It doesn't matter. You should see how people send in their tax things to my office, and I manage to sort them out." Tony started making a roll with everything he'd prepared, laying aside the two chicken wings for her plate, knowing they were her favourite.

She told him about Aunt Rosalie, about the kind of woman she was and what she'd said about Gina's mother. Somewhere along the way, Gina managed to eat lunch although she barely noticed what she'd eaten.

"It sounds like it was pretty hard hearing about your mother," Tony said.

Gina nodded, throat tight. "It was really, really hard hearing how she was treated. The whole single-mother-and-adoption thing was pretty tough in those days."

"I knew it happened to Aboriginal mothers, but I hadn't realised it was a general policy," Tony said.

"I'm not sure it was necessarily a policy. I think it was more a societal blind spot. I'm going to do some more reading about it." She wanted to understand what her mother went through.

"And Rosalie has no idea who your father is?"

"No. My mother kept that information to herself." Gina sighed. "I may never know. If she hasn't ever told anyone, why would she tell me?"

"And does your great-aunt think she's still alive?" Tony asked as he tidied up the leftovers.

"Yes, but all I know at the moment is that she moved to New Zealand and married over there. She has apparently written to Aunt Rosalie and her parents a few times."

"That might have been one of the letters in the folder. Do you want to look at it now? I don't want you to burst with curiosity, but I also didn't want you fainting from hunger."

Tony placed everything back in the bag. "Fruit and snacks for our walk."

They'd left the copies in the car, and opened the folder to look at the originals. There was a hand-drawn family tree which Gina ran her eye over. Rosalie and Gina's grandmother and great-uncle were listed. There were several other children too, but some were already dead and it seemed only the two youngest daughters migrated to Australia. Probably because they were still single. The tree went back to Rosalie's great-grandparents, and there were all sorts of dates and place names to investigate another day.

Gina laid the family tree to one side and used her water bottle to weigh it down, in case of wind gusts.

The first photo was of Rosalie's whole family. Gina turned it over. *Kinderdijk, 1947* was written on the back, along with the names of all the family members. She found Rosalie, then looked for the position of a younger sister. She indicated to Tony. "That should be my grandmother." She turned the photo over to see the name. "Anneke. I think that's my maternal grandmother. I'm guessing this photo was taken just before they emigrated."

"And what about your grandfather?"

"We haven't had time to talk about him yet." There'd been so much to talk about. "We need to pray Aunt Rosalie gets a good sleep so she's able to talk to us tomorrow. You're invited if you want to come."

"I wouldn't miss it for the world."

They looked through each photo, searching for clues. There were photos of young Rosalie and Anneke on board the ship, on their own, and with other young people. Perhaps one of them was her grandfather. There was a wedding photo. On the back it was labelled, *Ruben and Anneke's wedding.* Rosalie was one of the bridesmaids.

Gina laid aside several more photos, then gasped. There was a photo of a family of six. Ruben and Anneke were clearly recognisable. Two boys and two girls. Which was her mother? Her hands were shaking so much that she dropped the photo and Tony had to turn it over for her. Regina was the one on the far left. She flipped the photo over and looked at the child. Blonde and about eight years old. The second child in the family.

"Wow," Tony said. "What did you look like at that age?"

"Almost identical," Gina said. "We could have been twins." She took a deep breath. "I'm going to have to stop for a while. It's like someone has been force-feeding me for hours, and I need to process it." She looked over at Tony. "Did you say something about a walk?"

"I did. There's a few on offer." He pulled a folded brochure out of his pocket. "They're nearly all between two and five kilometres."

"You choose, I'm not up to making decisions today."

"Does a five kilometre loop with views sound appealing?"

Gina nodded as she stood. "It sure does."

"I'll stow the picnic stuff and bring the snacks."

Gina accompanied him back to the car, put on some sunscreen, and picked up her hat, sunglasses, and camera. They left the envelope in the car, carefully hidden under a picnic blanket. It seemed safer than taking it hiking with them.

"Mount Flagstaff, here we come," Tony said, leading the way.

The track was dry, but walkers needed to concentrate to avoid spraining an ankle. Gina put one foot in front of the other and powered on, sucking air into her lungs. This morning, she'd known almost nothing about her background. Now she knew not only the name of her mother but her grandparents as well, and that she had all sorts of aunts and uncles. And there was an older generation. Some of the blood flowing in her veins was Dutch. Oh, there were so many questions still to ask and there was no way one weekend would be enough. *Lord, keep Aunt Rosalie and the others alive.*

"What are you thinking?" Tony called back.

"I'm praying Aunt Rosalie stays alive. And my mother, and my grandparents."

"No wonder you're overwhelmed." Tony stopped on the edge of the track, waiting for her to catch up.

"My mind keeps going round and round with all the questions I want to ask."

"Why don't you write a list tonight and prioritise them."

"I'd already thought of that. I'm praying Aunt Rosalie is still able to write letters or handle phone calls," Gina said, walking on.

"That's something to check tomorrow. And did you mention she wants to go to the chapel service? Do you think she might be a Christian?"

"I'm not sure." Aunt Rosalie was of a generation that didn't talk easily about such things. "I did get the impression she hadn't been for a long time."

"Maybe talking to you has helped."

"She mentioned all her regrets, feeling like she had let my mother down. Whatever she felt, it stopped her from ever looking for me even though she knew my parents' names."

"She might blame herself for your mother going to New Zealand."

"I think so."

"There's meant to be a few lookout points along this walk. What say we find one and spend some time praying about tomorrow?" Tony said.

"I'd like that. Praying out loud with you might help me concentrate." Now she'd met Aunt Rosalie, she was less afraid of the older woman clamming up. There'd been a definite connection between them which Sister Smith had commented on as Gina drove her home.

"Sister Smith thanked me for coming up again. Said it was obvious Rosalie has shed a burden she's been carrying ever since my mother left."

"I wonder if she's hoping to see your mother again."

"I would imagine so, but she doesn't look well enough to travel and she doesn't know where my mother is."

"Were any of the letters in an envelope?" Tony said, voice excited.

"One, but there wasn't a return address on it."

"But there might be a postmark."

Gina hadn't thought of checking for a postmark. But with a letter that old, it would be better not to get her hopes up. It was just as likely to be a smudged mess.

They came to a track branching off to the right and soon, another junction. Tony pointed out the other tracks on the map. "Long Gully lookout isn't far ahead."

She'd think for a bit, running through the things she'd found out, and then plan another avenue of investigation. "Now we've seen a picture of Ruben, we can go back to the group photo on board the ship and see if he's in it."

"Good thinking. Even if Aunt Rosalie can't tell us much more, there are all sorts of avenues to explore. There might be a place that has ship records or passenger lists."

"And now we have some names, we can look up the electoral registers. The librarian said they give addresses and occupations."

"We've got plenty of work ahead of us," Tony said.

Gina grimaced. "I'm sorry my search is dominating everything at the moment."

"Don't be sorry. I've always loved mysteries. Maybe this will inspire me to investigate my family history. Isabella mentioned something about having to do a family tree sometime soon."

"Maybe she'll let me help her."

"She might. Now Sophia has talked to you, Isabella probably doesn't feel so torn. It's been difficult for the kids to realise that accepting someone else isn't being disloyal to their mother."

"I understand," Gina said. But understanding didn't make it any less difficult. She'd always prided herself on being able to connect with children and it hurt that she hadn't succeeded this time.

"I'm praying hard about the whole situation, and the guys in my Bible study group are praying too. Did I tell you I went to see Greg for some counselling?"

Gina blinked. Most men she knew didn't go near counsellors.

She'd known a few wives who complained they had to go alone if their marriage was under pressure.

"This was my first visit to Greg, but I wanted to talk about the girls and how to help them through this time, and that's one of his specialties. We all went for a few sessions with another counsellor after Anna died. Greg suggested it soon after we met and gave me a recommendation."

"Was it helpful?"

"Very. It might be something you could consider. I found being asked questions by a wise stranger forced me to stop and really think."

"Ms Jones, the adoptive counsellor, gave me a list of counsellors who specialise in adoption."

"There must be a lot of work for them. There are at least three or four people in our church looking for their adoptive families or children at the moment."

"It wasn't possible in the past but now people like me are taking the opportunity."

"Here's the first lookout," Tony said.

They moved towards the edge. A flat plain of houses and fields stretched away to the distant mountains, a navy blue smudge on the horizon. Tony snapped some pictures of the scenery and insisted Gina be in some of them.

After a few minutes, Tony rummaged in his backpack and brought out two apples. They ate in silence, enjoying the warbling of a magpie and the zephyr of a breeze.

"The wattle thinks it's spring already."

Tufts of golden balls were bursting out all through the undergrowth.

"Let's pray for a while, then keep going to the Mount Flagstaff lookout. According to the map, we're halfway there."

They prayed with their eyes open, looking at the scenery. Gina wasn't afraid to be seen praying in public, but she also didn't want to freak out any other walkers who weren't used to such displays on a Saturday afternoon. They prayed for everyone—Rosalie, Sister Smith, her yet-to-be-found mother and grandparents. And Tony spent a few minutes praying just for her.

Lord, I am so thankful for this man.

She was glad he was here with her. Her journey needed companions and what a companion he'd turned out to be. As Rachel had said several times already, "He's a keeper."

CHAPTER 20

"Sleep well?" their host asked Gina.

"I did. That hike yesterday must have done the trick."
In the aftermath of so much emotion, the fresh air, sunshine and
prayer had settled Gina's heart.

Tony joined them, and they ate a good breakfast and loaded up
the car so they could leave for Sydney directly from the nursing
home.

Rosalie greeted them with a broad smile. "So this is Tony." She
winked. "I hope you know my great-niece comes from quality
stock."

"You and I will get along. We think alike." He chuckled as he
looked around the room. "Where will I find another chair?"

Rosalie gave him directions. While he headed out to find a chair,
Gina settled herself in the same chair she'd used yesterday.

Aunt Rosalie was quite different today. Maybe Tony was right
and her conscience was more at peace.

Gina handed back the envelope. "Thank you so much for
entrusting me with all those precious things. We've taken copies of
everything."

Tony came back into the room carrying a chair and put it near Gina.

Aunt Rosalie clasped her hands. "We've got over an hour. What do you want to start with today?"

Gina pulled out her notebook and handed it to Tony. "Do you mind if he takes a few notes? I'm terrified I'm going to forget something important."

"Not at all. I'm guessing you want to talk about your mother first."

Gina nodded. "And then my grandparents."

"Did you look at the letters your mum sent?"

"Yes, but she doesn't say much. Only that she's married, and the guy's name begins with a P."

Rosalie smiled. "I have a tiny bit more than that, because she rang me once. Just a short call, but she said his name. It sounded like 'Purse' but when I asked for more details, she ended the call fairly abruptly."

"Maybe she doesn't want to be found," Tony said.

"I think that's true."

"Purse," Gina muttered to herself, staring at her lap. "Purse." She lifted her head. "Do you think it might be short for Percival? Like when I was hearing Rehina yesterday and spelling it like it sounded."

"It's a good possibility," Rosalie said. "Didn't one of the letters mention cows?"

Gina drew out her photocopies. "Yes, here it is. There are more cows here than people."

"Maybe Perce is a farmer."

"Do you have the envelopes that came with the other two letters?" Tony asked. "There wasn't a return address on this one and we struggled to read the postmark.

Rosalie shook her head. "I didn't stop to think they'd be important. I guess I always thought she'd keep writing. I never knew that three short letters and one brief call to ask about the details of her parents' place of birth for her marriage certificate, would be it."

"Okay," Tony said. "Then we'll have to work together on the postmark. We thought you might have a magnifying glass."

"I do." Rosalie leaned across to feel into the bag hanging on her walker. "You're assuming Regina would send the letter from within her area?"

"Not really, but we're hoping," Tony said. "It would be great if we had an area to search for someone with your niece's name and possibly married to a Percy."

"It depends on how much she wanted to cover her tracks. Was it just a general idea or an obsession?" Gina said. "Could we please see your letter again, Aunt Rosalie?"

Rosalie opened the big envelope and shuffled through its contents before handing over the letter in its smaller envelope. Then she gave them a magnifying glass.

Gina stood and walked over to the window. Tony joined her.

"The top part of the postmark is completely obscured. Water must have gotten on to it."

"But there are letters curving around the bottom. Gina, do you agree that the last two are KI or KT?"

"Where's the notebook?" Gina said.

Tony handed it over and she leaned the notebook against the wall, and wrote in KI. "KT doesn't sound possible."

"I can't see the letter in front of the KI," Tony said.

"Could it be an A?" Aunt Rosalie said from her chair. "AKI is a common ending in New Zealand."

"I can't see anything in the middle, but the first letter looks like a T or an I," Gina said.

"'I' sounds unlikely," Tony said.

"I still have a set of encyclopaedias," Aunt Rosalie said. "I'd get rid of them except they were a gift from one of my favourite classes. They're over there, in the bookcase behind the door.

Gina crossed the room and moved the door. The encyclopaedias were there along with a French and a German dictionary.

"If you could bring 'N' across and look to see if they have a list of New Zealand place names," Rosalie's cheeks were pink. "I haven't had this much fun in ages."

"Whatever the place, it looks to have seven to nine letters based on the size of those last two," Tony said, his eyes still boring holes into the envelope looking for any clue. He held it up to the light. "I think the last four might be NAKI."

"I've found a list," Gina said, excitement bubbling up inside. She put the book on the closest table and ran her finger down the list. "There's a place called Moeraki, but I think that's too short."

"Let's write it down anyway." Tony grabbed up the pen and notebook.

Gina spelled it and kept looking.

"Here's another. I'll spell it. N-G-A-T-A-K-I."

Tony wrote it down.

By the time she reached the end of the list they'd added: Otaki (too short), Taupaki (probably too short), Whananaki (the right length but a W looked very different to a T).

"I don't think it's any of those," Tony said.

"Gina, was that a list of towns only? What about provinces or regions or whatever they call them," Rosalie said.

Gina flicked back a page. "Yes, the regions are listed. Tony—" Her voice trembled. "Does Taranaki fit?"

She left the encyclopaedia open on the table and took a step towards Tony.

"It fits," he said, voice breathless. "I'm certain that's it."

"And Taranaki has lots of cows," Rosalie said. "I visited there, many years ago." Her voice trailed off. "And there's a mountain, right smack in the middle. I always read Regina's letter as 'mountains' but what if she said 'mountain'? Help me find it, Gina."

Gina grabbed her own photocopies in case she tore them in her excitement. "It's definitely 'mountain', not 'mountains'. Aunt Rosalie, you're a genius."

A nurse poked her head in the door. "Is everything okay in here?"

"It certainly is," Rosalie answered. "We're solving family mysteries."

"That sounds fun. It's good to see you so cheerful," the nurse said as she withdrew.

"Okay," Tony said. "What do we have so far?" He picked up the notebook and sat down.

Gina ticked off on her fingers. "A marriage, possibly to a man named Percy or Percival, possibly in Taranaki, and possibly a farmer or living near a farm. That's an awful lot of possibilities." And too many chances to get things wrong.

"But think of what you know in comparison to yesterday. I'm going to photograph this envelope. I didn't think to photocopy it yesterday."

He took out his camera and took a few photos. Gina checked the three letters her mother had written, then looked back at her great-aunt. "None of the letters have a clear year date on them, only the month. Can you remember what year they came?"

Aunt Rosalie closed her eyes. "I can remember when she went to get the ship, because she went straight down to Sydney from here. That would have been January 1969." She pursed her lips. "It wasn't the first week, but it wasn't the last either. If I had to guess I'd say sometime between the eighth and the twentieth, but I'll check my diaries and see if I can narrow it down. Noelene has them at her place."

"Got that," Tony said, writing a note.

Rosalie looked at the three letters and then reorganised them. "That's the correct order. Perhaps you'd better number them, Gina. Here's a pencil." She passed it over.

"The first must have arrived the same year, the one labelled September third and telling me she is safe."

Gina labelled the letter with a '1' and added the year.

"The next letter was the following year, in March, telling me she was going to stay in New Zealand and asking me to break the news to her parents."

Gina added the note on the second letter. "This third letter doesn't have a date. The one that says she's getting married."

"I'll see if I can find the date she called in one of my diaries."

A tiny carriage clock whirred and struck the half hour. "Is that the time already? All this excitement has made me lose track. Could you ring for the nurse, dear? I need to use the facilities before we go to the service."

"Could I help you, Aunt Rosalie?" Gina asked.

Aunt Rosalie looked her up and down. "Yes, I think you could."

"And I'll make myself scarce." Tony handed Gina back her notebook which she stowed in her bag.

Twenty minutes later, the three of them headed towards the communal area where the chapel service would be held, Tony on one side of the walker, and Gina on the other. Aunt Rosalie greeted everyone she passed.

The lounge chairs were gathered in a double semi-circle, and a middle-aged man with a clerical collar was preparing communion at the front. Aunt Rosalie indicated a trio of chairs. They helped her sit down, and Tony parked her walker off to the side.

"Did you have a Bible you wanted us to fetch?" Gina asked.

"I'm not sure where it is, so don't worry about it."

By ten minutes before the hour, nearly twenty people had gathered. The pastor—or maybe he was a vicar or rector—introduced himself and welcomed everyone.

One of the nurses took her place at the piano, and they sang some hymns. Gina knew them all, but Tony only knew half. His church was a younger age group than hers.

Lord, I don't know where Aunt Rosalie stands with you. Please help the pastor to speak a relevant word today.

The pastor spoke about the lost sheep, and Gina couldn't help thinking about the search that was still ahead of them. Her mother was lost to her family and possibly lost to God as well. *Lord, please help all my family—birth family and adopted family—and Tony's family to one day be found by you.*

Maybe her situation would be the thing that gave all these people the chance to meet Jesus. It was a sobering thought. If she'd stayed with her birth family, would she have had a greater or lesser opportunity of knowing Jesus? As it was, her opportunity had come because her parents had wanted quiet and had trusted the church to step in as carers for those few hours every Sunday. *Thank you, Jesus.*

Gina looked around. Several of the older people were dozing off, but Aunt Rosalie looked as if she was paying attention. *Let your words reach into her heart.*

The sermon was only fifteen minutes long. They sang another hymn, and the pastor launched into communion. He didn't call people up to the front in the Anglican tradition but instead brought the communion to each individual. Aunt Rosalie declined but watched Gina as she took it. What was her aunt thinking? Perhaps they'd have time to talk afterwards. Aunt Rosalie had requested her lunch to be delivered to her room, and Tony was going to pop out and get them something so they could eat with Rosalie.

"*I* watched you both during that service," Aunt Rosalie said once they were back in her room. "You seem to actually believe what the vicar was saying, not like so many young people today."

"We do. Tony has only been a follower of Jesus for a few years." Gina had been about to say 'Christian', but remembered the pointers Joy had given about using terms people couldn't misunderstand. In Aunt Rosalie's youth, most people probably thought they were Christians because they'd been born in countries like Australia or the Netherlands.

"You'll have to tell me his story someday," Aunt Rosalie said.

"I'd love to do that, and mine too. I'm guessing you wouldn't call yourself a follower of Jesus yet?"

"I won't take communion. I'm not a hypocrite, and God and I haven't been on speaking terms for a long time." She peered over her glasses at Gina. "And I suppose you're the kind of girl who will be praying for me. Well, you're welcome to do so, but God won't find me an easy nut to crack." She smiled grimly. "But maybe he already is. I haven't felt I wanted to hear anything about him since Regina left."

"I'm so sorry about all the pain you've experienced," Gina said.

"Humph," Rosalie said. "Most of it is my own fault. I should have tried to understand Regina better and not just assume she was being stubborn. I've done a lot of thinking and reading about trauma since then, and she was showing lots of those signs."

"Like what?"

"Sleep problems, bouts of crying, evasive answers. Do you think my father might have been someone close to the family? There was never any hint of a boyfriend."

Footsteps came down the hallway, and Tony tapped on the door as he stood in the entrance. "Come in, young man. No need to stand on ceremony," Rosalie said.

Before he'd sat down, Rosalie's lunch arrived. Once the nurse had gone, Rosalie said, "I suppose you want to pray before you eat. Don't let me stop you."

Gina bowed her head. "Dear Lord Jesus, shepherd who looks for lost sheep, thank you that you keep pursuing us. Thank you for this food and for allowing us to meet Aunt Rosalie and begin to resolve things from the past. Thank you so much for giving me a new aunt and for letting me hear about my family. In your name, Amen."

Aunt Rosalie wiped the corner of her eye, but she looked pleased. Before they left, Gina arranged how they'd keep in touch over the coming months. She wasn't going to neglect this new relationship. Not when her great-aunt so clearly needed Jesus.

CHAPTER 21

*G*ina handed Rachel a cup of hot chocolate. "It feels like an age since we've actually talked to each other."

"I'm not sure who is busier. You and Tony with your detecting, or me and my wedding preparations." Rachel curled her feet under herself on the armchair. "Everyone says wedding preparation is hectic, but I've always managed to keep out of it up to now."

"Have you found the marriage preparation classes helpful?"

"I have. When Pete told me they'd be for six weeks, I thought it sounded excessive but it's been great to have an outside person asking us direct questions and making us talk about issues we hadn't necessarily talked with each other about before."

"The questionnaire looked long enough."

"Wanting to get prepared?" Rachel said with a gentle tease in her voice.

The heat rose in Gina's neck.

"It seems to me that you and Tony are going great guns," Rachel said.

"I guess so," Gina mumbled, not confident enough to say more.

Rachel unfurled her legs and put down her mug. "Look, a man doesn't invite you to see his parents unless he's serious."

"That didn't go too well."

"Yes, but Tony didn't expect it to. He was letting his parents know early so they'd be prepared."

"You sound far more confident than I am."

"Unfortunately, I know much more about men than you do. The men I hung around with weren't ever going to invite me around to visit their family." She sighed. "That part of marriage preparation hasn't been fun. Stuart and Anne haven't probed for details, but I've felt about an inch high at times."

"It is hard to accept that we've been forgiven, isn't it?" Gina said.

"Forgiveness is all very well but it doesn't mean the past has no impact. I sometimes react badly to Pete because of my past, and he does the same to me. That may never go away."

"But surely being aware of what is happening helps?"

"It does, but there is so much more underneath the surface that we have no idea about yet."

"Like an iceberg," Gina said. Her search was beginning to reveal some of that below the surface stuff too. "And are you glad you chose to do the classes with Stuart and Anne?"

"We are," Rachel said, curling her feet up and taking up her mug again. "They're really down to earth. It helps that they've made their own mistakes and aren't afraid to talk about them. That makes it easier for us."

"Will you go to Pete's church after you're married?" Gina's heart squeezed at the thought. There were so few people anywhere near her age at church and after losing Esther, she didn't want to lose Rachel as well. Not that marriage was the same kind of losing, but sometimes it felt like it.

"One of the reasons we're doing the classes with Stuart and Anne is that Pete has always felt like a spectator at his parents' church. That was fine for a while, but he wants to find another church."

"And?"

"We've clicked with Stuart and Anne and can see they'd appreciate some help with so few people in our age group."

Gina grinned. "I, for one, would love it if you were both at our church."

"It will certainly be much more convenient when we're living here." Rachel looked across at Gina. "Have you decided when you'll move?"

"That's one of my pieces of news. My tenant is moving out this week. The agent said the place needs painting because the tenant used tape to stick pictures all over the walls."

"People can be so inconsiderate," Rachel said with a frown.

"Yes, but it's perfect timing. Tony has volunteered to help me paint. We don't need to paint the ceilings, only the walls."

"See, another tick." Rachel made an exaggerated tick with her left hand.

"What do you mean?"

Rachel took a big mouthful of her hot chocolate, put down her mug, and held up her index finger. "One, Tony has taken you to see his parents." She held up another finger. "Two, he's helping you with your search even though it meant a trip to Tamworth. Three, you've not only been introduced to his children, but you're regularly going to his place for meals. And now, he's helping you paint."

"I'm not sure I put as much emphasis on these things as you do."

"No? Well, you should. Especially meeting his children. You know he wouldn't risk them getting hurt."

A little flicker of excitement ran through Gina, like a flame to paper.

"And wait until he sees you at my wedding. It will scatter any wits he has left." Rachel picked up a photo she'd had face down on the table beside her. "Mum sent me a photo of what she's done with the dresses."

"She said something about embroidery," Gina said.

"They're absolute masterpieces. I've told her she must enter my dress in next year's Royal Easter Show."

Gina took the photo and whistled.

Rachel handed her the next photo, a close-up of the details along the hem.

"That must have taken her hours and hours. All those tiny wattle and flannel flowers."

"She asked me what flowers I wanted. A bright red waratah wasn't appropriate with a white dress, so Mum suggested paler greens and yellows."

"Using the Australian national colours."

"But thankfully not as bright." Rachel sighed. "I struggled about whether to wear that dress. One, because it was Esther's and she never got to use it, and two, because it's white, and I'm not the least virginal."

Gina gave Rachel a long look. How should she put this? "You are, from God's point of view."

Rachel lowered her eyes.

"Once Jesus has forgiven you, you're washed clean, as though you have no past to be ashamed of. You know that," Gina said, her voice gentle.

Rachel nodded. "It's hard to grasp. I still fear what others will say."

"The only ones who know your past are your parents, Pete, myself, and your matron of honour."

"And Pete's parents as well as Stuart and Anne know a little. And Joy."

"Do you think any of us are likely to bring it up?"

"No. None of you are those kinds of people." Rachel paused and then lifted her head. "Talking of my matron of honour, I'd like you two to meet soon."

"Aren't we supposed to arrange a kitchen tea or something?"

"Normally, yes," Rachel said. "But Pete and I have decided we already have most of what we need. My parents and his three are going to club together to buy a bedroom suite and bedding for Gran's room."

Naomi had only ever had single beds in the house, as she'd moved here well after her husband's death.

"Maybe Tony and I can contribute towels. Naomi's old towels are looking a little threadbare."

"Actually, that is something you could help me with. I'd like to go through the whole house and write a list of what we need. We're both happy with the colour scheme and Gran kept this place immaculate, but we do want to put some of our own touches on it to make it ours."

Would painting her place with Tony give him an idea of her tastes and vice versa? It would be interesting to see what colours he'd go for and whether he liked having a feature wall. Was it possible that one day she might have input into his home? Gina's stomach somersaulted at the thought.

"Mum is so excited. She's going to come two weeks before the wedding to help with various things." Rachel grinned. "We finished the invitations and sent them out while you were up in Tamworth. It won't be a big wedding. Binh and three others are coming from Perth. Everyone from work, and a few from both of our churches." She pursed her lips for a moment. "It's about forty in total, but I like the fact that it will be small. Mum found us the reception place and we loved it when we saw it. Looking out over the beach at Narrabeen."

"A far cry from what your parents would have been used to," Gina said.

"Yes, Dad used to officiate at weddings with five hundred at the ceremony and several hundred at receptions. My wedding will be a cinch for Mum, which is good. I want her to enjoy it."

"So would it make sense for me to move out in about a month?"

"There's no rush. It would probably be easier if you were still here the night before. Mum and Dad will book a hotel, although Mum might stay here beforehand too."

Gina got up and went to her room to get her diary. She asked Rachel for the details of when Blanche would arrive. "Looking at the timing. I think I'll move most of my stuff into my place, so I can go straight home after the wedding."

"That makes sense. We won't have a heap of expensive wedding presents, so it doesn't matter if the house is empty. The neighbours will keep an eye on it."

And Gina would make sure to clean it thoroughly and stock the fridge ready for their return. That was the kind of wedding present that Pete and Rachel would appreciate.

"No more talk of weddings," Rachel said. "I'd love to hear what you've found out, if you're happy to talk about it."

Gina was more than happy. Talking about what they'd discovered would help her sort things out in her own head.

"I'll get my folder." She went to her bedroom, scooped up the folder from next to her bed, and returned to find Rachel had already washed up the mugs. Gina put the folder on the coffee table and used the family tree and photos to introduce Rachel to the family she'd only just started to discover.

"It's amazing what you've already discovered. What's next?"

"I'm going to try and find which ship my mother went to New Zealand on. We know the week she left, and maybe even the exact day."

"How do you do that?"

"I'll try the State Library first. They should have microfiche records of the *Sydney Morning Herald* or places that list ship arrivals and departures. They might even have passenger lists."

"Are you sure she didn't fly? It would have been about then that flying became more common."

"Aunt Rosalie says not. Regina didn't have enough money to fly, and she told her aunt she'd bought a boat ticket."

"Funny to think of sailing being cheaper than flying." Rachel picked up the photo of Gina's grandparents. "What about looking for them?"

"Aunt Rosalie and I both agree we should look for my mother first. If I don't succeed, then I'll ask Rosalie to contact them and go from there."

"Does this mean a trip to New Zealand?"

Gina sighed. "I'll have to wait until school holidays."

"And the October ones aren't long enough. Not if your search takes longer than two weeks."

"No, but I'm due for some long-service leave. I should have taken it last year, but I just couldn't face the planning. Esther's death knocked me around a bit."

"As it did us all." Rachel swallowed. "How much leave can you get and what are the rules for taking it?"

"Our chat has made me decide to apply now. I have to give them three months' notice. I don't want to use all of it if I can avoid it."

"Just in case?"

Gina flushed again. Why must people of her colouring always do that? Yes, just in case Tony proposed. Any marriage would be a big adjustment, but adding in three children would likely make things much harder.

Rachel counted on her fingers. "So you could get to New Zealand in November?"

"Yes, if I apply tomorrow."

She'd do it. She'd never forgive herself if her grandparents died while she was trying to make up her mind. She could talk about it with Tony when they did the painting, but she'd get the application in first.

CHAPTER 22

*G*ina climbed one of the two ladders Tony had brought over.

"Here's the paint." Tony handed her the container. She dipped the dry brush in it and ran it carefully along the top of the wall.

They'd agreed with minimal discussion to keep the original colours, off-white on three walls with one sunflower-yellow feature wall.

"It's cheerful and makes this space seem bigger," Tony said.

Bigger was good for a one-bedroom apartment. It was going to take some time to adjust to the cramped space. At least she had a small balcony where she could grow a few flowers and herbs.

Gina had come in on Thursday afternoon to wash all the walls down with bleach and fill the few slight cracks with filler. Last night she'd only needed to sand back the cracks and put on the undercoat. Today was warm enough to do both layers of paint.

"Good job," Tony said. "I knew you were the right person for the cutting in."

"And you'll be better using the roller, I find it too tiring to use on the top parts of the wall." Gina squinted, focusing on not putting any paint onto the white ceiling.

"Good thing the tenant was too short to stick things to the ceiling," Tony said.

"I was thinking the same thing. I was cross enough about the walls, as I'd painted the whole place not long ago."

"It looks cute, but where is your furniture?"

"Pete found a small corner at the nursery for the few things that wouldn't fit at Rachel's when I moved in with her."

"That was kind of him. Perhaps he was buttering you up, knowing he was hoping to move into where you're staying now."

Gina used her forearm to rub her nose. "I certainly think he was interested in Rachel well before she was willing to get to know him better."

Climbing up and down the ladder all day was going to give her a workout. Now she was on the long part of the wall, away from the corners, she only had one line to paint next to the ceiling and the matching line along the bottom of the wall. Tony had already set the ladder up at the next corner.

"We've got a second brush, haven't we?" Tony said. "I can do some of the cutting in too."

Gina stopped, paintbrush in hand. "I was keeping the second brush for the feature wall, so I didn't have to wash the first brush multiple times."

Tony laughed. "I'll do the clean-up. It's pretty easy with these water-based paints."

Gina didn't enjoy clean-up. All she ever wanted to do at the end of the job was jump in a hot shower and wash off all the paint.

The first coat for the three walls of the living area only took an hour, then they moved on to the bedroom. The job was easier this time without any furniture in the house.

Last time she'd had to paint on her own, but it was more fun with someone else. Like much of life, really. She'd been solitary, but not by choice.

Gina finished the cut-in work in the bedroom while Tony washed the second brush and went out to the balcony to stir the paint ready for the golden feature wall. Soon he was back with the brush and paint.

"Thanks, Tony. This is so much easier with you."

"They do say that many hands make light work." He grinned. "The Bible study guys came and helped me paint all the girls' rooms last year. The girls are too young to do it, but once they're a few years older, I'll have a workforce."

Gina laughed. "They might have some opinions about that."

"I'm already meeting some of those opinions with Sophia, but at least she seems to be coping better when I talk about you."

Gina had been concentrating her prayers on Sophia.

Tony positioned the ladder for her again. The hardest part of the feature wall would be going down the two ends of the wall and not getting any paint on the still-wet white walls.

"Greg suggested that I book the girls in with a colleague of his to talk specifically about how they're going and anything related to you."

Gina's hand wobbled and painted a bright yellow streak on the ceiling. "Bother. Can you please hand me that damp cloth on the kitchen counter?"

Tony went to get it. "Sorry. I shouldn't have mentioned it just when you needed to concentrate."

"It wasn't your fault." Gina carefully wiped the paint smears off the ceiling. "Do you know what kinds of questions the counsellor will ask?"

"I asked Greg, and he said things they're afraid of or worried about at the moment. Or whether they've noticed any changes in me since you've come into my life."

A large splodge of paint dropped off Gina's brush and onto the plastic covering the floor.

"I don't think I should be talking about this while you're doing that wall. I'm distracting you, and I've still got a wall to finish in the bedroom. I'll help you move the ladder, then I'll go and finish my bit."

Gina let him help and got back to work. Tony was a good father and spoke of the girls with such pride but with three already, would he want more children? And could she even have children? Not everybody could, and who could say whether she might be one of them.

Tony had brought a simple picnic, which they ate on the balcony away from the strong scent of new paint. After they'd eaten, they checked the first wall they'd painted.

"It's dry already," Gina said. "It was genius to bring both the fan and blow heater."

"It helps that it is a surprisingly warm day for early August and your place has a good cross breeze."

They got to work, painting as a team who'd already found the best rhythm to get the job done. Tony put a small battery-powered radio in the doorway of the bedroom and sang along to the popular musical numbers in a tuneful tenor. Gina joined in on the songs she knew.

Tony came out of the bedroom. "That's done, and the second coat on the feature wall will only take a jiffy. Using the roller covers the wall so quickly. It's very satisfying."

Gina stood watching him as he finished. He moved in an easy rhythm, no movement wasted.

Tony stood back to check the wall, then laid down his roller and came across to her. "Do you know, you have a little drop of paint on your nose." He touched it. "And your cheek." His finger touched that too. "Rather cute." He swallowed. "In fact, Miss Gina Reid, I'm rather enamoured of you altogether and I'm hoping you might be of me."

He dropped to one knee. "This wasn't exactly where I expected to do this."

Gina put her hands up to her face.

"—but I find myself feeling rather impatient. Gina, would you marry me?"

To Gina's embarrassment, she was blinded with tears and when she tried to speak, only a croak came out.

"My darling, I'm sorry to overwhelm you," he said, voice vibrating with emotion.

She cleared her throat. "I want to say yes …"

"But?"

"But I don't feel I can until I find out who I am."

"Gina, dearest Gina, don't you know who you are?"

"No," she sobbed. "No, I don't."

He stood up and stepped towards her, gathering her into his arms.

Oh, it felt so good to be there, but it was too soon. What if she found out things that were normally hidden? She wanted to come to him with joy, not fear and shame. She'd feared rejection all her life, even when she couldn't put her finger on the emotion. Her mother's coldness after the birth of the boys had cut deep, and finding out she was adopted had only made her feel more insecure.

Tony stroked her hair. "I asked too soon. I'm sorry."

She broke out of his hug and tucked some stray hair behind her ear. "The problem isn't you. You're wonderful. The problem is here." She touched the left side of her chest. "Here, there's still a hole." She patted her pockets for a tissue, and he pulled a handkerchief out of his own. She took it and blew her nose. "I know Christians shouldn't feel a hole like that, but I do, and I don't want to marry you while I feel this emptiness."

He reached out and cupped her chin in his hand. "You do know we've all got holes in us?"

She nodded. "But mine feels more like a crevasse."

"Then we'll have to find that mother of yours and pray she talks."

"But she might not." Gina wrapped her arms around her waist. "I'm not a fool. I know this isn't necessarily going to end well."

"We'll keep praying that it will." He took her hand. "Let's sit down for a moment."

She laughed nervously. "I can't even offer you a seat."

"The floor is fine." He sat down, his hair and clothes covered in misty spatters of paint. "I'm guessing you want to go to New Zealand. It's a pity all this kind of searching still has to be done in person. Someday soon, this information might be available on the internet."

"Imagine how much work it will be to put all the records and newspapers there."

"Yes. It will be no small task." He touched her shoulder. "How long do you think you'll need to go for?"

"I was going to tell you today. I've applied to use a month of my long-service leave."

"And when will you go?"

"The earliest possibility is November."

He sighed. "Then November it is. But aren't there things we can do from this end?"

"I'm going to try and find the ship she left on and talk to Aunt Rosalie some more," Gina said.

"And should we start looking for your mother's parents and siblings?"

"I guess we could look at voting enrolment records. Those seem to be available but marriage and birth information isn't just given out to anyone, not for living people anyway."

"That makes sense, and it might not be appropriate to contact your grandparents just yet."

She'd known he would understand. "Aunt Rosalie says we should look for Mum first and go from there. That's why I need to go now. I can't leave it in case I miss the chance to meet my grandparents altogether."

He nodded. "So be it. I'll wait. But I intend to help you as much as possible." He grinned. "For my own selfish reasons, of course. It gives me more time with you, and I would like you to become Mrs Agosto as soon as possible."

Gina swallowed the lump in her throat, as her eyes welled up again.

"And let's pray right now, that God goes before you in this journey. Then you can go and shower while I clean up." He chuckled. "Although I am quite fond of the paint-spattered version of you in the daggy clothes. I think I'll invent a whole lot of painting tasks to keep us occupied."

"Don't you dare!"

CHAPTER 23

On Tuesday, after school, Gina rang the National Archives. The local library had been helpful and given her a list of places to look for shipping records and electoral rolls.

"Good afternoon, I believe you're the place I might find records for ships departing from Sydney to New Zealand in the 1960s. Is that right?"

"We do have records. Which year are you looking for?" a woman answered with what sounded like an Irish accent.

"January 1969."

"Just give me a moment while I check our index."

Gina nibbled the end of her pen while she waited. She'd already checked several places which didn't have the records.

"Hello, are you still there?"

"Yes."

"Yes, we do have those records." Excellent. She'd found the right place.

"Are they written records or on microfiche?"

"We have both."

"And are you open on Saturdays?"

"No. We're open Wednesday, Thursday, and Friday, from ten until four."

"Oh," Gina said. "That's tricky. I'm a teacher, I'll have to see if someone can stand in for me for a few hours on Friday afternoon."

One of the advantages of having been at one school for a while and almost never taking any sick days was that she was much more likely to be granted a bit of leave.

"The system doesn't work like a library. It's better to book a time slot and put in a request for the records, and we'll have them ready for you. Advance requests take five days, and you can request five records per visit."

Five days? She'd have to wait for the following Friday.

She put in her request and booked a one-thirty slot. The plan had been to look for shipping records first, but time was running out before Rachel's wedding. She'd go to the State Library on Saturday and look at the electoral rolls.

---

*O*n Saturday morning, Gina got off the train at St James station. It was a little longer than going from Martin Place station, but this way she could walk through a corner of Hyde Park with its gnarly old trees and views of St Mary's Cathedral. She strolled along the path, basking in the sunshine, then walked more quickly along Macquarie Street past the Hyde Park Barracks.

She'd often seen the sandstone and colonnaded facade of the State Library of New South Wales, but she'd never been inside. Daunted by the size of the place and afraid of missing out on finding something because she didn't know what questions to ask, she'd phoned ahead and explained what she was searching for. A librarian was expecting her at ten.

She walked up the wide outside stairway and opened the big glass doors. She was early because she'd had some idea that the place was vast—it was—and realised it might take her a while to find where she was supposed to go. It did.

The main room had level after level of bookcases, stained-glass windows, and a glass roof. Impressive. Dragging her focus back to her task, she found a plan of the building and located the desk she'd been told to find. She let them know about her appointment, and a few minutes later a young man approached her.

"Good morning, Ms Reid. I'm Douglas. If you'll follow me, I'll take you to where you'll find the electoral rolls."

He moved rapidly along the hall. "All the information related to family history is now in the State Reference Library Reading Room in the Macquarie Street wing. I'll point you towards the original electoral roll books, as they're much easier to read than microfiche."

Gina trotted along behind him, clutching her bag.

"Here we are," he said. He looked at her bag. "That bag is small enough to take in but we ask that you leave the room if you need to drink, even water."

Once in the reading room, he led her over to the bookcases and pointed to a long row of similarly bound books. "The year is printed on the spine."

"And does each book contain the whole state?"

"Let's look at one. Any preference for the year?"

"What about Tamworth, 1967?" Gina said.

He was obviously familiar with the shelves. Even before Gina found the correct part of the shelf he'd already pulled out a large volume. He flipped to the index and found Tamworth and then located the page. "The entries are listed alphabetically. Can I help you with anything else?"

Gina thanked him, and then moved to the nearest clear desk as fast as possible without actually running. She scanned the pages and found Aunt Rosalie with occupation 'teacher' and her address. Gina reached into her bag and got out her notebook and pen and jotted down the details. Then she flipped back to the index and found the Sydney pages, where she searched for Ruben and Anneke. Her grandparents were listed as living on Badminton Road in Croydon. Her grandfather was an engineer, and her grandmother was listed as a housewife.

She closed the book. Next step? Perhaps the earlier years before looking for the years after 1967. She'd go in five-year hops.

Over the next hour and a half, she moved back to the very first mention of her grandparents in the early 1950s. They'd lived in one house all that time. Aunt Rosalie had been remarkably stable too, staying in the same house from her fourth year in Tamworth until she moved into the nursing home about two years ago. Perhaps she'd lived in boarding rooms in her early years as a teacher. Gina had heard about those living arrangements from an older teacher at her school.

The wall clock said it was nearing lunch. Tony was going to meet her outside to eat and take a walk in the Botanic Gardens. The first phone call after she'd said "not yet" to his proposal had been hard. He'd talked as though he'd never asked, and she'd felt it might have been easier if he'd given up on her. He was such a fantastic man. How could she not have said yes immediately? She sighed as she gathered her things together. He'd said he was willing to wait, but that didn't mean he'd wait forever.

*T*hey'd had lunch and were walking close to the waterfront where they'd climbed trees with the girls. Waves slapped the wall, and they paused on the way back to watch a yacht raising a multi-coloured sail. The wind whipped Gina's hair and she pulled up the hood of her anorak to keep it under control.

"Tony, I do have some good news," Gina said.

He turned to look at her.

"The school has asked if I can combine my long-service leave with the October school holidays. Then I'll only need to be away from school for three weeks."

Tony beamed. "That's great. Now we need to keep praying that God leads you straight to your mother. I have a vested interest in this search succeeding."

CHAPTER 24

"It is so good to see you all," Gina said, looking around their living room at Blanche, Joy, and Rachel, and newcomer, Alice.

"I love being on the island, but this group is the thing I've missed most," Blanche said.

"Are you sure that's the truth, Mum?" Rachel said. "I'd have thought craft shops might have edged us out."

Everyone laughed. The laughter of a family happy to be together again.

They chatted and drank tea and ate the scones Gina had made. Blanche had arrived two days ago to help with the final wedding preparations. She was in charge of decorating the church and working with the reception centre for the last flourishes. Rachel had been more than happy to hand those tasks over.

After they'd finished their tea, Rachel gently dinged her teaspoon on her mug. "I was keen to have us gather together before the wedding to share what God has been doing and to pray for each other." She gestured towards Alice. "And I especially invited Alice because she hasn't had the privilege of knowing any of you yet.

Back in the days when I worked at David Jones, she never gave up praying for me and telling me how fantastic it was to follow Jesus."

Alice flushed.

"And I paid not the slightest attention to her," Rachel said, winking at Alice.

"But you did remain friends," Joy said.

"Yes, she was very persistent," Rachel said. "I didn't do friends back then."

Yet look at her now. Rachel used to stay in her room during their Bible study and prayer times. Now she was the host.

"Why don't you go first, Mum?"

"As the oldest, you mean," Blanche said with a laugh.

"No, as my mother and the most beautiful," Rachel said.

Blanche reached across and squeezed her hand.

"Most of you know William and I have been on Lord Howe Island all this year. We're loving it, but we're praying about what the Lord might want us to do next." She outlined some of her ministries. "The most exciting thing has been a retiree who came to the craft group. She asked me a couple of questions and I was terrified I'd mess up. But I remembered you, Joy, telling us that any story is better than no story, so I told her the story of the woman washing Jesus' feet with her hair." She looked at Joy. "That was the only story I could remember off the top of my head. The next week she asked me for another story." Blanche laughed nervously. "I hadn't expected her to ask for another, so I wasn't prepared and had to stumble my way through the Prodigal Son."

"Were you ready the following week?" Joy asked.

"I certainly was, and I'd done a lot of praying too."

Gina leaned forward. "And did she keep wanting more?"

"She did. I remembered Esther learning Old Testament stories, so we did five of those. In fact, some weeks she's come and asked me for an extra story. And I've told her a heap of testimonies too."

She looked across at Rachel. "I hope you don't mind that I told yours?"

"If my story is helpful, please use it," Rachel said.

Blanche smiled. "As I was telling the stories, it struck me over and over how much God has done not only in but through our family. I'm so thankful."

"I haven't thought about telling Bible stories to adults," Alice said. "What stories have you told and what stories are you telling now?"

"I told the Adam and Eve story from Genesis, then one about Abraham, and two about Moses."

"Which two?" Alice asked.

"When God sends the plague of hail and then leads the Israelites out of Egypt after the first Passover," Blanche said. "Then the Christmas story from Luke, and the story of the paralytic man from chapter two of Mark."

Alice had pulled out a piece of paper and scribbled furiously. Blanche waited for her to catch up.

"Then I was going to tell her about Lazarus being raised from the dead, and finally a crucifixion and resurrection account." Blanche looked up, eyes shining. "But guess what? She insisted on becoming a Christian after the Mark story. I told her, 'But the stories aren't finished yet!'"

Gina giggled. "Sounds like God's timing isn't yours."

"I barely knew what to do but she said, 'I guess I need to say sorry for my past and then ask Jesus to forgive me and give me a new start.' I just nodded, and Carol launched right into prayer. She didn't need me at all!"

Gina flinched. It felt like she'd been struck in the chest. Even though Aunt Rosalie had clearly left a little crack open, Gina had only prayed for her. There'd been two opportunities in their phone calls to say something, yet she'd let them pass by convincing herself she wasn't any good at telling others about Jesus. She'd begun to shift the responsibility for talking to those who were good at it. People like Esther and Joy.

"As God told Moses when he said he wasn't any good at public speaking, 'Who made your mouth?' In other words, it's not our weakness that matters but God's strength," Joy said.

"I always felt I failed with Rachel," Alice said.

Rachel grinned. "And yet look what God did through your prayers."

"Prayer is a total mystery, isn't it?" Blanche said. "Naomi—that's Rachel's grandmother," she said as an aside to Alice, "Naomi prayed for over thirty years for William and Rachel and our family before God saved us. Why didn't God answer earlier?"

"Only God knows," Joy said. "And that's good. He's much greater and wiser than us."

Gina needed to be reminded of this as she prepared to head off to New Zealand. Being adopted didn't look like the best option for any child, but what if more people came to know Jesus through her adoption? Her brothers had already been beneficiaries, but she must redouble her prayers for her parents. And she needed to believe God would work, instead of putting things in the too hard basket. And Aunt Rosalie? She couldn't push that responsibility off onto someone else. Tony was unavailable this weekend, but there was no reason she couldn't make the drive to Tamworth.

"Would someone pray for Mum?" Rachel asked.

Gina raised her hand, and they all bowed their heads. "Heavenly Father, thank you for giving us this chance to meet again and for bringing Alice to join us. Thank you that we're family because we know Jesus." They might be different ages and racial backgrounds, but this group felt like a circle of sisters. "We're so excited that we have a new sister we've never met. Give Blanche your words as she helps Carol learn how to follow Jesus day by day." She prayed a little longer for Carol and Blanche and especially for Blanche's role in the wedding preparations. "Lord, Blanche's story has reminded me of what I'd been forgetting—you use the weak because through us you get the most glory. I confess I've been using excuses to not tell others about you. I'm sorry I've been content to enjoy the benefits of being your child, but I haven't given that opportunity to others. Please forgive me."

"Amen," everyone said at the end of her prayer.

Alice shared about her family and some challenges with one of her children, and Joy prayed for her.

"Rachel, what about you?" Blanche said.

Rachel updated them on the wedding and how much she'd learned through the marriage preparation classes. "I'd like to pray for a few things. For Josh in particular. We don't want him overwhelmed by being a groomsman. We'll have the wedding practice next Thursday evening, and we're going to be a bit more thorough than usual for his sake. And could you pray—" She flushed. "For the honeymoon and settling into marriage. There are still many things we both have to work through."

Blanche prayed for Rachel and then said, "Who's next, Joy or Gina?"

"Gina," Joy said.

Gina didn't even know where to start. Joy and Alice wouldn't know anything about what had been happening unless Rachel had told them.

"Well, I've been on a bit of a detective journey," Gina said. She summarised what had happened and then said, "The upshot is that I'm booked to fly out on the twenty-sixth of September for four weeks."

"And if you find your mother more quickly than expected?" Alice asked.

"Then I can probably change my flight home. There's a lot I have to play by ear."

"Meantime, she has terrific Tony praying she'll get home as early as possible," Rachel said with a wink.

Alice prayed for Gina. Alice might have been a stranger, but her prayer got below the surface.

"May Gina know that whether she finds her mother or not, whether her mother accepts her or not, that Gina is your much-loved daughter. You will never leave her or forsake her …"

That was the thing that Gina's heart kept forgetting. No matter who else had abandoned her, God never had and never would. *Lord, help me to believe that, deep, deep down. Help me not to react like a hurt child to Tony or anyone else.*

The three of them who knew Joy well looked at her with expectation. She always had something worthwhile to say.

"You might remember that last time I asked you to pray for Esther's cancer specialist."

Gina, Rachel, and Blanche nodded. Joy took a minute to tell Alice about the situation.

Dr Webster was another person who'd slipped off Gina's prayer list because she'd thought him beyond the reach of God's grace. Why was her faith so feeble? Rachel always prayed for him when the two of them prayed together on Sunday evenings. Judging by the look on Joy's face, there'd been progress, yet Gina's own unbelief meant she hadn't been part of it.

"I don't see Dr Webster much at work," Joy said.

Cleaners usually started work early and passed unnoticed by most people.

"But I kept praying, sensing a real spiritual battle was going on. I do know he kept reading Luke because he sent me a letter asking some questions and I answered as best I could."

Having experienced Joy's wisdom over the last two years, Gina was sure that not one word of Joy's response would have been written without prayer.

"He's had a tough few months with family-related things but each one made him confront issues that he needed to think through."

It was obvious that Joy knew more of the details but was trying to respect the man's privacy.

"We've recently had a good talk, and it's clear he's become a Christian." She laughed. "He just wasn't sure he'd done it properly."

"So he was on his own?" Rachel said. "Do tell us what you can."

"Well, he finished reading Luke and started John, then went on a solitary walk in the Snowy Mountains."

"That sounds potentially dangerous," Alice said.

"He's a careful man and experienced in the mountains, but a whole lot of things went wrong. He had a scary time and nearly got lost in the dark. He called out to Jesus and finally became convinced Jesus was real. Back in his hotel room, he couldn't sleep and got out the Bible he found in the drawer." Joy raised an eyebrow. "He said something about an organisation that puts Bibles in hotels and prisons."

"Gideons," Gina said.

"That's right," Joy said. "He read their explanation of how to become a Christian and prayed the suggested prayer, but he wasn't sure if he'd done everything correctly, so he came to find me."

"And were you able to help him?" Rachel asked.

"He needed to know he truly was a Christian and not to doubt because his conversion didn't feel spectacular."

"Not all of us have experiences like Rachel or William," Blanche said.

"We also had a talk about his mother, who had just died," Joy said. "He was worried that she didn't know Jesus. I told him his concern was an excellent sign that he'd become a Christian."

"Were you able to calm his fears?" Gina asked.

"I mostly assured him that God loved his mother and would have given her every chance to believe. He has discovered the father he's been estranged from for years is also a Christian."

"How wonderful," Blanche said. "And are you going to keep meeting with him?"

"He wanted to meet with a man and had apparently gone to your church."

"Oh," Rachel said. "I think he turned up a few weeks ago. I thought I recognised him. He turned up with an older man."

"He mentioned that he'd taken his father to your church," Joy said. "Anyway, I've called Stuart and told him to expect a call."

"Let me pray for him now," Rachel said. "And for that other friend of Esther's who was doing Bible study with Dr Webster."

"He's apparently decided not to follow Jesus," Joy said.

"All the more reason to pray," Rachel said, closing her eyes.

*A*t bedtime, Gina got on her knees next to the bed, something she rarely did, and whispered.

"Jesus, thank you for tonight. I needed a good kick and you've delivered it. I've really let evangelism slip off the agenda. I guess I shouldn't be surprised, as Satan doesn't want any of us thinking about it or praying. Praying with Tony is good. Great, really, but I can see I need to meet with other women. Please help Rachel and maybe Joy to be willing to start meeting again after Rachel's honeymoon and my trip to New Zealand. I need their support and encouragement."

Gina shifted her knees unused to this prayer posture. "Please help Aunt Rosalie to be clear in her mind if I go up this weekend. It's a long drive, but I feel you're urging me to go. I don't want her to die without me at least trying to talk with her. Prepare her heart and give me courage and your words to share. And I want to pray for my parents too, and Tony's. This will be a long prayer tonight, but I know you won't mind in the least …"

CHAPTER 25

*G*ina and Tony were sitting in the living room after dinner, dishes, and making sure the girls had gone to bed.

Tony leaned back with a contented sigh. "Gina, thank you for coming over early to cook dinner. The girls loved the change from my limited repertoire."

"And Sophia is saying more during the meal."

"She's a good kid, and there have been plenty of us praying for her."

"I need a group like yours. I'm going to ask Rachel and our friend, Joy, to meet up again after I get back from New Zealand."

"I don't know how I would have survived the first few months after Anna's death without them."

Something felt different. Anna. He'd mentioned Anna and for the first time, it hadn't bothered her. *Thank you, Jesus.* When had that bitter poison of the comparison game shifted? Maybe the prayer time she'd had last night had helped.

"I had a really special evening last night with Rachel and her mother and two other friends."

"I'd love to hear about it."

She swivelled in her seat to look at him. "I love that about you. You are truly interested in others. It's not just an interest in me. I've seen you do the same with my friends too."

"Before I became a Christian, there was only room in my life for work and my family and close family friends. Anna's sickness made me see work wasn't nearly as important as I'd thought. The girls and their needs have grounded me. I still have a long way to go, but they're quick to let me know if I'm not spending enough time with them."

"How do they do that?" Gina asked.

"Elissa cries or gets clingy. Isabella gets sulky, or tells me outright, and Sophia withdraws."

"I find the differences between siblings interesting. Our school is small, so I often teach multiple children from one family. I quickly learned to treat each family member as an individual and not assume that a child would be clever or bossy or sporty because their older sibling was."

"I've done some reading on how birth order affects children. It certainly seems to be true in my family—for myself and my siblings, and for my girls." He grinned. "You and my oldest sister have a lot in common. You're organised but tend to worry about the rest of us. As the youngest, I was content to let others do things for me and to cruise along."

He pulled up a footstool and put his feet up. "That's better. Now, weren't you going to tell me why you enjoyed last night?"

"Well, apart from the sense of comradeship and that we're all united towards a common goal, I heard two really encouraging testimonies of what God has been doing and they really impacted me." She told him about the lady in Blanche's craft group becoming a Christian and Esther's cancer specialist.

"The guys in our group have started regularly sharing testimonies like this. Greg suggested we all read some books. We've read this one on sharing our faith." He picked up a book on the table next to his chair and handed it to Gina. It wasn't a book she'd read before and she read the blurb on the back. "I could lend it to you when you go to New Zealand."

"That would be great. God convicted me that I've been excusing myself from introducing Jesus to people." She sighed. "And unfortunately, as I did that, I also lost the urge to pray for them. Perhaps I didn't want to be the answer to my own prayers."

"We've been praying for our families together," Tony said.

"Yes, but I've been avoiding the topic privately. I didn't realise I was, but that's the reality. Last night showed me what I've been missing out on." She curled one foot under her so she could turn towards Tony. "Blanche was radiant with joy after seeing God work. That's what I want. It's scary, but I remember how much Esther changed as she conquered her fears and spoke with people."

"People like Anna."

"Anna wasn't the only one. She also spoke to her specialist, and a lady at work, and a science teacher who was also having chemo."

"It's interesting you're being convicted on this subject, as the guys and I spent last night here brainstorming ideas for sharing our faith. The second book we read was *A Fresh Start*. It isn't a book about doing evangelism but rather a book to give to non-Christians." He passed it across. "In a lot of ways, I liked this book even better. It got me fired up and it seems perfect for this country because it's written by an Australian who communicates really simply."

"I'll look forward to reading this one too."

"Oh, I don't want you just to read it, I want you to help me give it away."

She narrowed her eyes. "What do you mean?"

"We're buying a box of one hundred between us. We're going to have a competition to see who gives away the most."

"You do have interesting ideas." She'd never considered running a competition to encourage people to share their faith.

"Yes, but there are rules. We're not allowed to give one away unless we've had a conversation with the person first and they've shown an interest in reading something."

"Tony." Gina grasped his arm. "God convicted me about going to see Aunt Rosalie on Saturday. Do you think your copies will be here on time? I want to read it before I give it to anyone."

"You bet. Greg was dropping into the bookshop after work and picking up the first fifty. He's going to swing by and give me ten copies tonight."

"Before I leave?"

"We'll check the letterbox as we go out to your car."

"Let's look now," Gina said, jumping to her feet.

Tony laughed and pushed his footstool aside, before standing up beside her. "Come on then."

Outside the chill in the air made her cough but she wrapped her scarf around her mouth and went towards the letterbox.

"Good thing it's oversized." Tony held up a large plastic bag. "Just as promised." He looked towards her. "We'd better get inside, or I'm going to forget my intentions and kiss you. You're a beautiful woman, my love." He turned to walk back towards the house.

Gina swallowed. Sometimes she wished he'd forget his good intentions, but she respected him for them. What would she know about kissing, having never been kissed except in the school playground when she was six? All she remembered was she'd said, "Yucky," and wiped her mouth. The boy had been eating peppermints, so maybe that had something to do with it.

Back inside, Tony said, "Would you like to pray for a while?"

"I would. There are so many of our friends and family who don't know Jesus."

"Have you asked Rosalie if it's okay to go up?"

"I'm planning to call her and Sister Smith tomorrow. It will be my last chance before I fly to New Zealand."

"Have you got time to go shopping next week for Rachel and Pete's present?"

Gina nodded. "I can do it any day after school. Did we agree on two sets of towels?"

"Or four? I'm happy either way." He looked towards the stairs. "Sophie must have turned out her light, because here comes her faithful follower."

Pirate came down the stairs and across the kitchen area, claws clicking on the wooden floor. She came into the living room and settled down with her head on Tony's feet.

"No more footrest for you," Gina said.

"I'm more likely to stay awake sitting upright." He closed his eyes. "Dearest Lord, thank you for tonight. Thank you that the girls are beginning to connect with Gina. We ask that they grow to love her."

They prayed back and forth, each praying for one person or couple who needed Jesus. For Tony's parents to come to understand that Jesus' death and resurrection were the central thing, not a church or traditions or their familiar way of doing things. "Free them from fear, give them assurance," Tony prayed.

"And for my parents, give me courage to talk to Dad. I've been afraid to risk our special relationship. But he needs you. Please prepare his heart and give me courage ... and for Mum. She's bound by her own anxieties. Please reach into her heart and give her peace ..."

Prayer had its own intimacy. Two people with heads bowed, coming into the presence of the King of the Universe and asking for his divine intervention.

"... Amen, and amen," Tony said, looking up at her with a slow smile. "Thank you. That was special." He sighed and then opened the plastic bag they'd brought in from the letterbox. "Why don't you take four and I'll keep the others."

"Are you sure you're not cheating?" Gina said with a laugh.

"I call it using my brain. I'm sure the Bible encourages teamwork."

"Well, pray I find people to give them to."

"I will. Sister Smith and Aunt Rosalie for starters." He raised a finger. "But only if you have a conversation first."

She saluted him. "Yes, sir."

CHAPTER 26

Gina drove into the carpark at the National Archives. There'd been no problem getting a few hours off. Her car was packed and ready to head straight to Tamworth. Sister Smith had said Aunt Rosalie was excited she was coming. The receptionist took her bag, allowing her to keep a camera and her notebook. She wasn't even allowed her pen, and was given a pencil instead.

As promised, the shipping records were waiting for her. Since they were relatively new records, there was no need to wear gloves, although the place was filled with cameras and the attendants kept a careful eye on her. There were only five others in the main room. Two were looking at massive books that had to be supported on small beanbags. One researcher had a map unfurled. She'd have loved to browse, but time was tight and it wasn't that kind of place.

Gina carefully opened the book and looked at the index. There were hundreds of listings, but they helpfully included the ship's name and destination port.

Pencil in hand, she jotted down any possible ship's names. She concentrated on the North Island ports, especially Auckland and

Wellington. Aunt Rosalie's clear recollection of the date that her mother had left Tamworth meant she was able to focus on two weeks of departures. There were six possibilities.

Gina found the passenger lists for the first ship. Aunt Rosalie had written out Regina's full name but there was no Regina Vermeire there. Ships two, three, and four were the same. Gina rolled her shoulders and arched her back. Five resources per visit now seemed a sensible idea. It wasn't easy searching for a single name among hundreds.

She found the passenger list for the fifth ship. Still nothing.

Again she stretched. If she couldn't find the name, she'd have to review the whole lot again or go back to the index and add ships sailing into the South Island. She glanced at the clock on the wall. She'd already been here an hour. Her finger ran down the columns. Nothing. And nothing again. Had Aunt Rosalie been wrong? Gina closed her eyes and laid her head on her hands. She'd been so sure she'd find her mother. Why wasn't she here?

She'd definitely arrived in New Zealand by August, as they had the first letter. Could she have gone much later than planned or had she lied about her name?

Gina's head jerked up. She hadn't checked the ship's crew but perhaps, just perhaps, her eighteen-year-old mother had decided to get a free trip by working her way. Only forty minutes left until closing time. Thank goodness she'd left a clean sheet of paper as a bookmark in each list of passengers. She flipped back to the first bookmark and scanned the crew for the first ship. Nothing. Already another five minutes had gone. She turned to the second ship. Nothing.

Thirty minutes to go. Gina's gaze swept down the list. There. What was that? She slowed down and read the name. It looked more like R Vermeer. She'd nearly missed it because she was concentrating on first names and the surname had been misspelled. Her mother was hidden among the serving staff on this third ship.

With an eye on the time and with trembling hands, Gina took out her camera, made sure the flash was off, and photographed the page multiple times. Then she jotted down the details. The ship had left Sydney on January fourteenth. It would only have taken three days to reach Wellington. On the maps that Gina had photocopied in her lunch break at school, passengers from Wellington either caught the ferry to the South Island or headed north.

A bell rang and the receptionist called, "Ten minutes to closing. Please close the records and leave them on the desk."

She'd only found one new detail, but it fleshed out her mother's story. Add the date and port she arrived at in New Zealand to the possible spouse's first name and a marriage in 1970 or 1971, and there would be a good possibility of finding her. If her mother had fled to England or the United States, maybe not, but New Zealand had a population of less than four million. Surely it was possible.

Gina closed the shipping records, remembering she'd prayed for opportunities to talk to Aunt Rosalie about Jesus over the coming weekend and she'd prayed for an opportunity here. She'd even put two copies of *A Fresh Start* in her bag. But she'd forgotten once she became engaged in the hunt. *Jesus, sorry. I need to learn to leave more margins in my life.*

Leaving the main research room, Gina went back to the locker where she'd had to deposit her bag and water bottle. She leaned down to insert her locker key and tried to turn it. It jammed. She gave it a little wriggle, but it was immovable. She straightened. Now what?

She stuck her head out the door. The receptionist from the research room was locking the inner door.

"Excuse me." Gina waved to get her attention. "The key is stuck, and I can't get the locker open."

The woman walked over to her. "Sorry about that. It's happened several times lately, but I've been shown the trick."

She came into the locker area, pushed the key in and gave

another wriggle. The key came loose immediately, and she was able to remove it. She squatted down and took care to insert the key exactly parallel to the ground. It turned and the door opened. "There you are."

"Thank you so much." Gina removed her things, and the two women walked out together towards the carpark.

"Did you find what you were looking for?" the woman asked.

"Yes, thank you I did. I was looking for the ship that my mother travelled on to New Zealand."

The woman paused and looked at Gina. "We don't usually have people coming in to look for such modern history."

"I only recently found out her name, and I'm pushing every door I can."

"You're adopted?" The woman stopped walking and looked at her. "I've always thought that would be hard."

"Yes and no. My adoptive family were great." Mostly great, but she'd never expected perfection in a family. *God, could this conversation go somewhere? I don't know how to move on to talking about you. You'll have to help.*

"Did you ever feel—" the woman flushed. "I probably shouldn't ask you something personal."

Gina smiled. "No problem. Ask away."

"Did you ever feel abandoned?"

"I think every adoptee has to work through that issue." *God give me an in.*

"What helped you work through it? Counselling or something else?"

Fear washed over her. All she wanted to do was say something innocuous and run. *Help, Lord. Give me the words.*

Gina swallowed. "Actually, the biggest help was knowing I've been adopted by God. I have a heavenly Father who cares for me whether my birth mother accepts me or rejects me."

"I've never been religious."

Reading *A Fresh Start* last night had primed her for this conversation. "I'm not religious either."

The woman raised an eyebrow.

"Jesus wasn't keen on religion because it was man-made. He doesn't want people to follow a set of rules. He wants us to follow him."

The woman squinted at her. "I'm not sure I get the distinction."

"I'm sure I'm not explaining it well but if you're willing to read a book, I've got one right here." She drew out the book from her bag.

The receptionist didn't look annoyed, so Gina handed it over. The woman turned it over and read the blurb and the first page. "This actually looks quite good, but you don't have to give this to me. I'm happy to pay for it."

Gina grinned. "Jesus freely gives me so much, I'm happy to do the same."

The woman blinked. "Thanks. I have a quiet weekend ahead, and this looks like a quick read."

"Have a good weekend," Gina said as she turned towards her own car.

The woman waved as she drove off.

Gina got into her car, heart singing. Once she'd prayed and requested God's help, she'd been given the words she needed.

CHAPTER 27

Sister Smith handed Gina a bowl of brown sugar. "Rosalie is looking forward to seeing you any time from half past nine. She knows you're planning to drive back to Sydney today."

Gina sprinkled the sugar on her porridge. She wouldn't normally eat porridge, but that was what Sister Smith offered. It had been a lovely surprise when she'd been invited to stay.

Gina put down the sugar and added milk. "It's more tiring to drive back today, but I've really missed being at my church with all the busyness of late."

"Ah, yes, I picked you for a churchgoer. Your great-aunt used to go with me every week."

So was Sister Smith a Christian or merely a churchgoer? "Aunt Rosalie mentioned that she hadn't been much since my mother left. I've been praying about that."

"So have I." Sister Smith shook her head. "I tried to find out what was bothering her, but she told me to leave it alone, so I did. I've been praying that you turning up might have a positive impact on her."

Gina ate a few spoonfuls of porridge. Should she say something to Sister Smith about Aunt Rosalie asking her and Tony to take her to the chapel service? No, not now. That was Aunt Rosalie's news to share. *God, give me a chance to say something today.*

"Rosalie has been much brighter my last few visits," Sister Smith said.

"I'm so glad. I feel like I've already won a prize during my search. Meeting you both, I mean." Gina yawned.

"I kept you up too late last night talking but I was so interested in what you'd discovered."

"Did you know my mother well?"

"I did. I was the only person your aunt asked to visit during the last five months of the pregnancy."

"Aunt Rosalie must have trusted you."

Sister Smith smiled sadly. "Yes, but not enough to tell me why she stopped going to church."

Gina took a piece of toast from the rack and spread it with what looked like homemade marmalade. "How did you become a Christian?"

"Nothing dramatic, dear. My family were Christians, and I assumed I was until I got to nursing school. We had an excellent Christian fellowship group. I went along to make friends and stayed long enough to work out that being a Christian wasn't a genetic inheritance." She laughed. "I don't even remember the person who explained what I'd misunderstood, but I remember the joy that flooded my heart afterwards."

"That's the joy Aunt Rosalie needs." Gina folded the crisp linen napkin she'd been given. "I came up here this weekend because I hope to be able to say something to her about Jesus."

"Oh, that would be wonderful. She might be more willing to listen to you."

"I would value your prayers." Gina had prayed on and off during the five-hour drive yesterday. "I'm not very good at talking about my faith, but Tony and I have made a commitment to pray consistently for opportunities and to keep our eyes open."

"That sounds like something I could be doing too. It's never too late to try something new."

"Sister Smith—"

"No more of that Sister stuff. It's Noelene."

"Noelene, would you be willing to pray with me about my visit?"

"It would be a privilege. Let's do it before I clear the table."

"I'll help with that."

"No, no, dear. I know where everything goes, and I don't want you to lose a minute with Rosalie. She'll chew me out later if I keep you."

———

*G*ina knocked on the door of her aunt's room.

Rosalie looked up and her smile stretched from ear to ear. "Oh, you came. I was so afraid you'd change your mind."

Gina walked in, kissed her cheek, and presented an African violet wrapped in pink paper.

"There's a perfect spot for the violet near the window," her aunt said. "Then come and sit down. I just want to look at you."

After depositing the violet, Gina pulled the second chair up close to her aunt.

"I've been so excited, knowing you were coming back. It's a long way, and I know you're busy getting ready for your friend's wedding."

"Thankfully, Rachel is super organised. Her mum has arrived and is in her element organising all the stuff Rachel doesn't enjoy. It's not going to be a big crowd."

"Would you send me a photo in your bridesmaid dress afterwards?"

"Of course."

Rosalie's cheeks were pink. Perhaps she hadn't had anything to look forward to for a long time.

"And tell me what you've discovered. Did you find the ship?"

"I certainly did."

Gina told her all about yesterday at the archives. Rosalie asked intelligent questions and wanted all the details of the search, not just the results.

"Yes, I'm not surprised to hear that Regina worked for her passage. I was puzzled when she said she'd bought a ticket, because I didn't think she had any money." Rosalie cleared her throat. "Until I received that first letter, I was terrified she might have lied and gone on the streets to earn money."

Gina shivered. What a sad thought. If her mother hadn't written, would Aunt Rosalie still be afraid that had happened?

"And tell me about your plans for your trip," Rosalie said, drawing her shawl more closely around her shoulders.

"I'm flying to Wellington because that is where m—Regina went."

"It is hard to know what to call someone you've never met."

"I can't call her Mum, yet constantly saying 'my mother' sounds weird."

"Then calling her Regina makes sense," Rosalie said.

"I'm fairly certain I won't be allowed to look for a marriage certificate in the Births, Deaths, and Marriages registry. So my plan is to go straight up to Taranaki and visit the main library in New Plymouth and see if they have microfiche or actual copies of the newspapers from 1970 and '71."

"Have you got accommodation sorted out?"

"Tony has found me a place to stay the first night. Then I'll catch a bus up to New Plymouth. It won't be peak tourist season, so I'll just go and see what happens. If I can find a marriage announcement, that might give me a clue as to where to go next."

"Sounds like quite the adventure."

It would have been better if she could have taken someone with her, but neither Tony nor Rachel were available and her brothers didn't know she was on this quest. Actually, they didn't even know she was adopted. Yet more people to talk to in the near future.

"Would you like to go for a walk, Aunt Rosalie? Out in the gardens, perhaps?"

"That would be lovely. If you're willing to let me hold onto your arm, I should be able to manage with just a walking stick. How cold is it out there?"

"About twenty, I think, and the sun is shining."

Gina helped Aunt Rosalie get ready and they headed out into the grounds.

"Oh, this is wonderful. I seldom come out here because I'm not confident on my own and don't want to trouble Noelene."

Gina squeezed Rosalie's arm. "I don't think she'd mind. As a nurse, she'd know the sunshine is good for you."

Lord, I have no idea how to start the conversation about you. Please help me see a way to bridge into the topic.

As they toured the winding paths and stopped to view the blossoms and new flowers, Gina kept sending up arrow prayers in between exclamations at the beauty. *Lord, help her see past the beauty of the created world to the Creator of everything.*

"—tell me your stories."

Gina turned to look at Aunt Rosalie. "I'm sorry, I missed the first part of what you said." Here she was, praying for opportunities but too busy to listen.

"I suggest we sit down, and you tell me how you and Tony became Christians."

Thank you Jesus.

They found a sturdy garden bench bathed in sunlight. Gina made sure her aunt was comfortable, then told her own and Tony's stories as simply and clearly as she could. As she talked, there was constant chatter in her head telling her she was doing a bad job and Aunt Rosalie wouldn't be interested. The book she'd been reading had a chapter on how to deal with this negativity. She reminded herself that God delighted in using the weak and pressed on, trusting that God would use her words and the way she said them even if she didn't do a great job.

When Gina finished, Aunt Rosalie was silent for a long moment. A fairy-wren flitted in and out of the shadows cast by a nearby bush, its brilliant blue and glossy black mantle flashing in the sunlight and a cortège of family members close by.

"I used to go to church," Aunt Rosalie murmured, "but I haven't been since Regina was here."

Lord, help me keep the conversation going. A question slipped into Gina's mind and she asked it. "Do you think there's a link between the two?"

Her aunt nodded. "I felt ashamed, having Regina here, and it was easier to stay away." She gave a long sigh. "After Regina left, I was embarrassed because I felt I hadn't shown the mercy and grace that I should have."

It sounded like Aunt Rosalie had some Biblical background.

"And the longer I stayed away, the easier it was to continue to do so."

What could Gina say in response? *Help.* Her mind was blank.

"I like to think shame kept me away," Aunt Rosalie murmured. "But perhaps it was just pride. I didn't want to have to admit my failures to God. It felt humiliating, and I've never been into humiliation."

"Is anyone?" Gina asked.

Aunt Rosalie gave a rueful smile. "Probably not. Talking about it now, it all seems rather pathetic. Noelene did her best to talk about things, but I wouldn't let her." She shook her head. "Stupid, really. She's always been a good friend, and I know she's kept praying for me."

Gina swallowed. "How do you think God would have responded if you'd come to him?"

"I know all the correct answers, dear. He would have welcomed me, but there was something that made me not want to admit I needed him." She swatted at an insect. "I've always been independent, and submitting to God seemed too hard."

Lord, help me say something useful. Aunt Rosalie said she knew the answers, but how could Gina lead her closer to Jesus? Joy or Esther would have already thought of an appropriate story to share but Gina's mind was one big blank. Starting with Genesis, Gina did a mental scroll through the Old and New Testaments but came up empty.

"… need to rethink."

She'd done it again. Been so busy trying to think what to say that she hadn't listened. *Forgive me, Lord.*

"I'm sorry Aunt Rosalie. I missed the first part of what you said."

"I was saying I want a second chance with your mother."

"I have to find her first. Tony and I are praying I will, and that she'll talk to me."

Aunt Rosalie chuckled. "I haven't prayed in a long, long time, but that is a request I can get behind. Meeting you again has been the best thing to happen to me in a long while."

"I've loved finding you too."

A tear glistened in Aunt Rosalie's eye and she patted Gina's cheek.

Gina reached over and gave her a little hug.

"Thank you for driving all this way to see me. You've given me so many things to look forward to recently."

Apart from the African violet, Gina had also brought a second gift—the book. She was acutely aware of it sitting wrapped in her handbag alongside a card. She'd hoped for a better conversation about spiritual things, so it would be natural to give it to her aunt. *Lord, help me know whether I should give her the book.*

A dark cloud drifted over the sun and Aunt Rosalie shivered. "Ready to go back in?"

Aunt Rosalie nodded and stood, and they went inside to have lunch together.

---

*O*nce Gina was back in the car driving home, she replayed the visit in her head. It was easy to beat herself up over the way things had gone. Why couldn't she come up with Bible stories in the same way as Joy did? But maybe it was just practice. She seemed to remember Esther saying the more stories she told, the more she improved. Perhaps Gina needed to prepare some stories and have them ready.

Aunt Rosalie had thanked her for coming and had been happy to be prayed for at the end. Looking back, God had answered prayers even if the visit didn't come up to Gina's expectations. Had she really been hoping she could lead her aunt to Jesus in a single conversation? Gina snorted. Silly, really. If her expectations had been to see her aunt move a step forward, then the visit had been a success. Even better, right at the end she'd dared to mention that she and Tony had prepared another small gift, but she wasn't sure if Aunt Rosalie would appreciate it. Aunt Rosalie had insisted on seeing what was on offer. Gina had taken the trouble to wrap the book and make a home-made card with the words "Jesus cares for you," and her aunt seemed to appreciate the gesture. Gina had prepared a little spiel to recommend the book and Aunt Rosalie had said she'd love to take a look at a book written by an Australian.

Lord, help Aunt Rosalie to read it. It can say things much better than I ever will.

CHAPTER 28

 he music for Pachelbel's Canon started and Gina turned
to Josh. "Ready? Nice and slowly, just like we practised
last night."

Gina put out her right foot to walk down the aisle. It would
have been easier if she'd been leading the way down the aisle alone,
but Josh had absolutely insisted he wanted to walk in too. After two
failed attempts to convince him otherwise, Pete had shrugged and
agreed.

Gina scattered red and white petals towards the left and Josh,
frowning with concentration, scattered petals on the right.

Halfway down the aisle, Gina started to relax. The repeated
practise at the Thursday night wedding rehearsal had obviously
been enough. She looked towards the men at the front. Pete was
going to be bowled over by Rachel. Blanche had outdone herself
with the wedding gown and flowers, and Pete had rarely seen the
polished Rachel who used to sell makeup at David Jones. That
Rachel had little connection with the Rachel who worked with dirt
and plants.

A camera flashed and Gina blinked. Tony. She didn't dare to

look at him. If Tony looked at her with anything like Pete's expression as he gazed behind her to where Rachel would be standing with her father, she'd lose it completely.

Rachel had made a late decision to let her father walk her down the aisle, but had made it easier on herself by having her mother there too.

Gina and Josh reached the front more or less at the same time. He almost followed her to the left, but Binh, as the best man, called him over to the men's side. Gina turned to see Alice halfway down the aisle, with Rachel and her parents at the back ready to follow. She blinked back tears. She'd probably be doing that a lot today. This wedding represented so many miracles God had done in people's lives. And it reminded her that she'd turned Tony down. But that was something she was determined not to think about today. This was Rachel's day. Rachel and Pete's.

Alice joined Gina at the front and they turned to watch Rachel and her parents make their way forward. The super-nervous Rachel of last night was gone and she was all smiles with her eyes locked on Pete's. Gina swallowed the lump in her throat as Josh jumped up and down and clapped, making everyone laugh. He could sense how important this was for his friends.

The bridesmaids and groomsmen were allowed to sit in the front row, while Pete and Rachel remained standing. As part of the service, they took the chance to thank their parents and give them a thank you gift. Binh was nearly overwhelmed by being included. Gina tucked the idea away to use for her own wedding. She swallowed. If she hadn't totally blown her chance. Tony said he'd wait, but for how long?

Rachel had initially refused Pete, and said last night that she regretted that. She should have trusted him with her doubts instead of pushing him away because she was afraid to get hurt. Was that what Gina was doing? Was it fear that had made her say no? She'd have to think about that. There'd been times in recent days when Gina had wanted to reverse her earlier answer to Tony's proposal, but she still wanted to have answers for the questions Tony's parents would ask. And she wanted Tony to have the best. Not some woman who didn't even know who she was. What if Tony's parents were right and there were significant medical issues in her birth family? Or what if she was the daughter of a monster?

Gina forced her thoughts back to the wedding. Today was a day to be savoured.

Stuart commenced the wedding vows, and Pete and Rachel made their promises, their voices quavering with emotion. Gina had arranged for a box of tissues to be sitting ready at the end of the row. Blanche and Alice were already dabbing their eyes and blowing their noses.

*G*ina couldn't stop herself taking mental notes. There were so many things she liked about this wedding. The intimacy, the size of the venue, the informality, the flowers.

After the service, Tony drove her, Alice, and Josh to the reception venue so they could be part of the photo session on Narrabeen Beach. The weather had been unseasonably warm, and the sky was bright blue with huge white puffy clouds.

Tony made himself useful by looking after people's things while the photographer snapped photo after photo on the beach and in an adjoining park. Rachel insisted that Gina have some photos on her own and with Tony. "He can hardly keep his eyes off you," Rachel whispered with a wink.

Gina blushed. It felt strange to finally be at a wedding with a boyfriend. Strange, but nice. It was just a pity that she couldn't sit with him the whole time because she was a bridesmaid.

Josh was soon clowning around, and the photographer snapped

away as they laughed. They were going to have an amazing collection of informal photos to enjoy later.

As the first guests arrived, Gina and Alice headed up to the surf lifesaving club to welcome them. Blanche had prepared a guest book with handmade paper for everyone to sign. Josh helped by carrying presents, and placing them carefully on the table ready for them.

Behind them was a complete wall of floor-to-ceiling windows. The guests happily drifted out onto the balcony to enjoy the beach views of golden sand stretching all the way to the headland.

Inside, the best of the flowering plants from Kloppers Nursery were placed in strategic positions. The bridal table was at the far end of the room, with seven round tables set up in front. As Gina handed over the special pen to the next person to sign the guest book, she could hear someone oohing and ahhing over Blanche's masterpiece of a cake.

Tony came over with drinks for them all, and Josh recruited him to help carry presents. He and Josh were soon talking like old friends. Tony's ease at making friends was yet another characteristic Gina loved about him. And she did love him. It was becoming increasingly obvious that she didn't want to be apart from him. So what if he came with three daughters? God would give them the wisdom and strength they needed.

Pete and Rachel came in from the beach and shook the sand out of their shoes before mingling with the guests.

After the meal came the speeches. Rachel had asked Gina and Blanche to work together on a speech. Blanche concentrated on Rachel's early years and offered some marriage advice. Gina talked about how she'd gotten to know Rachel and some humorous pointers for Pete in living with Rachel.

Dirk, Pete's father, gave a warm speech full of godly wisdom. Then Binh stood up.

"I don't know of anyone else in my position who has had the

privilege of being best man at his son-in-law's wedding. As you can imagine, today is a bittersweet day for me." He took a sip from the glass of water in front of him. "Our family has faced lots of tragedy. In the days when I was Buddhist, it would have been too hard to handle."

Rachel had told Gina some of Binh's story, his dramatic escape by boat from Vietnam, coming to Australia as a refugee with only his daughter still alive and not knowing his wife's whereabouts.

"Buddhism gave me no hope at all, but with Jesus, I've seen over and over that he is with us in everything, even the worst of days, and he brings not only hope but joy as well."

Gina sent up a prayer for the employees at Pete's nursery, that they'd hear enough to pique their curiosity so Pete and Rachel would have future opportunities to speak about the difference Jesus made in their lives.

"Today it is my great pleasure to welcome Rachel into our family. I never expected to have another daughter, and I am delighted with this gift God has given us. I will continue praying for you both and hope that a plane regularly carries you over to visit me in Western Australia."

Pete stood and reached over to shake Binh's hand and thank him, before turning to stand in front of the microphone.

"It's traditional for the groom to give a speech on his wedding day but this wasn't the easiest of tasks. There are many things I won't speak about today. Not because they're not important, but because this shouldn't be a day of too many tears. But I believe it is traditional to say something about the bridesmaids and my bride. I am sure you all noticed the intricate needlework on the dresses. That is the work of my gifted mother-in-law, Blanche. I know it must have taken hours and hours of stitching, and I'm cheering you on to take out the grand prize at the next Easter Show."

Pete turned and gave Rachel a look that left Gina breathless.

"And to my wife. It is so amazing to call you my wife. You've made me wait longer than I'd hoped, but the extra preparation time has been worthwhile. We've had issues to work through, but God has made our relationship so much richer in the process. Thank you for making me a very happy man. At last I will not only be working with you, but living with you in the home that means so much to you. I am so glad I met your grandmother and Esther, and I look forward to getting to know my new in-laws, William and Blanche." He half-bowed towards them. "Their enthusiasm for their current home has convinced us to go and honeymoon on Lord Howe Island. William, thank you for your suggestion of a place to stay." He grinned at William. "Not too close and not too far from where you are."

Gina was proud of Rachel. She'd been writing a letter a week to her father. Two days ago, they'd had a teary reunion at their home. Gina had kept out of the way and prayed hard while she dealt with the dishes. Rachel had said it had gone far better than she could have believed possible. God was truly doing a miracle in that long-term broken relationship. Rachel had given her a model of how to forgive and take things slowly. Hopefully Gina would have the same opportunity with Regina and other members of her family.

The speeches finished with a list of thanks to all who'd helped with the wedding. Then Rachel and Pete cut the cake and visited each table to talk to guests. The photographer took a final group photo from the balcony, then everyone farewelled Pete and Rachel as they left for their hotel.

Tony whispered in Gina's ear. "I'll take you home whenever you're ready."

It wouldn't take long to finish up here, and the last of her things from Rachel's place were already in his car. Tonight, she'd move back among her familiar furniture in her newly painted apartment. In a few days, she'd be off to New Zealand. Were the answers she longed for waiting to be found?

CHAPTER 29

*G*ina stared out the window as the plane took off over the red-tiled roofs of Sydney. Next stop, Wellington. The plane turned east and she watched until they left the cliffs behind, then settled down to read over all the notes she'd taken.

"First trip to New Zealand?" the man next to her said.

She nodded, not sure if she wanted to encourage conversation.

"I work in Sydney, but I always love going home. Time to see the folks and get away from the snakes and all the creepy crawlies." He turned to peer at her over his glasses. "What are you going for?"

"I'm hoping to find my mother."

"Estranged?"

"Sort of. I'm adopted, and I've discovered my mother left Sydney in 1969 and hasn't been back."

He chortled. "Fell in love with all the sheep."

"Not sheep, but perhaps somewhere with cows."

"Well, we've got lots of those too."

If the man was determined to talk, perhaps she could get some information. "I want to get to New Plymouth tomorrow by bus. Do you know which company to use?"

She'd planned to ask at the accommodation Tony had found for her.

"That will be the InterCity. There's a couple of pick-up points in Wellington. The closest will depend on where you're staying."

She debated whether to tell him. He seemed harmless enough but maybe axe murderers did too. "I'm staying in Thorndon."

"Oh, I'll be driving right by there. Can drop you off if you like. And you can walk from there to the central train station. That's where the buses go from."

Gina hesitated.

"You don't need to be uptight. My mother's coming to get me. She's safe enough." He slapped his knee. "As long as she's remembered her glasses. Blind as a bat without them."

He chatted all through the meal, giving her all sorts of practical advice and pointing out places she should pay attention to on the bus trip. "It's a cracker country, but too cold and not enough work. Every time I come home, I don't want to leave again."

If the rest of the people here were this friendly, she'd have no difficulties. Had her mother loved being here all these years, or was there a reason she couldn't leave?

---

*T*he man from the plane was as good as his word. He and his very friendly mother dropped her off at her accommodation. There was an envelope tucked under the doormat with her name on it. Opening it, Gina read,

---

GONE FISHING. KEY UNDER FLOWER POT. YOUR ROOM IS LAST ON THE RIGHT DOWN THE HALL. MAKE YOURSELF AT HOME. TEA AND COFFEE ON THE BENCH, MILK IN FRIDGE, FRUIT ON TABLE. WE'LL

BE HOME BY DINNER. FEEL FREE TO EAT WITH US—HOPEFULLY
FISH AND CHIPS.

Since she was only staying one night, she didn't unpack her
backpack but she took out her toiletries and stowed her pyjamas
under the pillow. A folder on the desk contained maps and tourist
brochures. Taking some fruit off the table, she set off to explore the
waterfront and the museum, Te Papa. She also spent a pleasant half
hour strolling through the Bolton Street Cemetery and seeing
graves from the earliest days of the city in the 1840s.

Later in the afternoon she walked wearily up towards her
accommodation just as her hosts backed their small boat into the
driveway. Her hostess held up a bucket. "Fish for tea."

She was soon swept into the family like some long-lost relative.
She'd have plenty to write to Tony about.

Her host settled down with a beer and the evening paper, and
her hostess accepted her offer to help prepare the meal. Gina was
handed a bowl of washed potatoes, a knife, and a chopping board.

"Can you cut these into chips? Broad chips are best. We don't
bother to peel them."

Gina chopped the first potato according to her hostess' instructions, then settled down to hear about their fishing trip. "Choppy
out there ... the fish were biting, and we've got enough to freeze."

When her hostess eventually ran out of steam, Gina told her
about her quest and asked about buses.

"There's an up-to-date bus timetable in the folder on your desk.
I'd ring now and book a seat."

Gina got up from the kitchen chair.

"New Plymouth, you say. I've got a cousin up there. She'll look
after you."

And without any trouble on Gina's part, she'd found accommodation for at least one night.

"If you book a ticket from the central bus station at around midday, you could fit in a trip to the archives and confirm that your mother did arrive here and precisely when. It's only a short walk between the archives and the bus station."

That would work as she'd only brought a backpack and it wasn't heavy.

---

*T*he archivists were helpful, but all Gina found was confirmation that her mother had definitely arrived in Wellington on 18 January 1969 as a temporary member of the crew.

The midday bus set off on time for the six-hour trip. She spent the whole trip looking out the window, absorbing the views of the sea and farmland. As the bus passed, the lambs would rush towards the protection of their mothers, long tails wriggling ecstatically as they headbutted her udder to get milk flowing as fast as they could drink.

They crossed a river at Wanganui and she soon glimpsed what must be Mt Taranaki. The slopes became increasingly clear, but the top of the mountain disappeared into a fluffy crown of clouds.

Her new host, Alison, was waiting at the bus stop and promised her an evening meal. Gina told her story and was advised to ring the local library first thing in the morning.

"But you'd better stick around because the local trampers are doing the Whitecliffs walk the next day, and you don't want to miss that."

Pride in their local area seemed to be a feature of this country.

---

*I*n the morning, her phone call confirmed what Gina and Tony had predicted. The other libraries in the area were too small and all the microfiche and original papers were stored in the main library in New Plymouth. She'd come to the right place.

Alison dropped her off on the way to the shopping centre and Gina was soon set up in front of the microfiche machine. She delicately eased the first microfiche page out of its folder and inserted it between the glass plates.

She jerked the controls, and the images scrolled by in a blur. Okay, a delicate touch was needed with this machine. It took her a few more minutes to discover where the births, deaths, and marriages were in each issue. She started with the *Taranaki Herald*, as it covered all the areas. If she could find a wedding notice, it might mention a place and she could go from there. Aunt Rosalie's diary had pinpointed the date she received the letter mentioning the upcoming marriage as 15 August 1970.

By the end of the first thirty minutes, she'd worked out a system. Since weddings were traditionally on Saturdays, the wedding notice tended to be early the following week. This allowed her to skim over the other days. If only this had been a weekly rather than a daily paper. It would have saved her a heap of time.

By lunch time, she'd reached the end of October and still hadn't found a notice. She left the library, and bought a salad to eat in the sunshine. If her mother had married in 1971, this task wasn't going to be done in a day. She munched for a few minutes, staring at the clouds racing overhead. What if she wasn't doing this the most efficient way? By now, she should have learned that asking the librarian could speed things up, but being in a new country had knocked that out of her head.

After lunch, she stopped at the main desk and waited until a librarian was free. Her name tag revealed her name as Barbara.

"Good afternoon, Barbara. I've come across from Australia to search for my birth mother and we think she might have married in Taranaki."

"Do you have any of their names?"

"Her name was Regina Vermeire." Gina said her mother's first name with the 'g' sound and then spelled the surname. "We don't know her husband's name, but the first name might be Percival and he might have a job that's something to do with cows."

"That doesn't narrow things down around here. Taranaki is a dairying area. What year are you looking for?"

"I'm guessing sometime within twelve months of August 1970."

"If your man is a dairy farmer, he'd be more likely to get married between May to July because that's the off season. They'd have time to go on a honeymoon, although it would be rather cold. If you'll just give me those details again, I'll write them down." The librarian tore a piece of paper off a pad.

"I noticed you were trawling through the papers on microfiche. If you're looking for marriages, there's a more efficient way."

Gina's heart rate sped up.

"In the years you want, we had a monthly photo news. Engagements and weddings and local events were its mainstay. I'll go out the back and get the boxes for 1970 and 1971. Anything you find, we can photocopy."

The librarian disappeared, and Gina took a deep breath. Could she be mere minutes away from seeing a picture of her mother's wedding?

The librarian emerged carrying a medium-sized box. "This is 1970 to 1972. The magazines are in order. I'll give you these gloves to protect the pages, as they're a valuable social history."

Hands shaking, Gina pulled on the gloves and took out all the magazines from 1970 and 1971. She laid aside the first five, but opened June 1970 to see if there was an engagement. No, but it wasn't really a surprise. If Aunt Rosalie had received the letter about the engagement in mid-August, then a July engagement was the most likely.

The magazines were only about twenty pages. The pages were dingy but the photos clear. Each photo had a typewritten label.

She flipped the papers of the July magazine. There were reports on the local Scout troops and the snowfall on Mt Egmont, obviously the old name for Mt Taranaki. The wedding and engagement photos were scattered throughout the magazine rather than being all together, perhaps an indication of the technology where each page had to be set up by hand and was probably done week by week.

There were five engagement notices on the right-hand side of page ten. She ran her gloved finger down the entries. There. She squealed and looked around. An older man glared at her, but no one else seemed bothered.

The five photos were all large headshots, and accompanied by their names.

CRAWFORD-VERMEIRE. REGINA, OF AUSTRALIA CURRENTLY RESIDING IN INGLEWOOD TO PERCIVAL, ELDEST SON OF MR AND MRS P CRAWFORD OF STRATFORD.

Her mother had a cute, short hairstyle with carefully manufactured waves and a scooped neckline blouse, à la Jackie Kennedy. Percy—they'd got that name correct—was in a black suit and tie.

Gina stared at the photo. Like all the photos on the page, they were smiling for the camera. Aunt Rosalie and Noelene were right. She was obviously her mother's daughter. The eyes, the mouth, the chin. But not the nose. Her nose was quite different. Did that mean she should go searching for someone close to her mother in the 1960s who had her nose? It would be an impossible search without more clues. The photos were black and white, so she didn't know if she'd inherited her hazel eyes from her mother or her father. Her mother would only have been twenty.

The librarian drifted over. "You found them?"

"I've found the engagement."

"Would you like me to photocopy it for you?" the librarian asked.

"I'll wait and do them all together. It's still three hours until you close. I'm hoping to find more information in the wedding report."

It took another hour to search from August 1970 to May of 1971. As the librarian had predicted, the wedding was in the beginning of May.

The photo included two bridesmaids and a flower girl. Once again, her mother's parents weren't listed but 'of Sydney' had made it into the details. Why had she left her parents out of both announcements? All the other wedding entries clearly stated the names of the parents on both sides. Had the magazine only printed what was submitted to them?

CRAWFORD-VERMEIRE. AT ST ANDREW'S PRESBYTERIAN CHURCH, STRATFORD, REGINA MAY, OF SYDNEY, AUSTRALIA, TO PERCIVAL JOHN, ELDEST SON OF MR AND MRS P CRAWFORD OF MONMOUTH ROAD, STRATFORD.

The other members of the wedding party and the photography studio were listed too. If the studio still existed, she might be able to get a proper print of the photos.

Now she had the wedding date, 1 May 1971, she quickly found the wedding notice in the *Taranaki Herald*, but it didn't add any more information.

Gina collected the two photo magazines and took them across

to be photocopied. The librarian enlarged the snippets for her and peered at the photos. "You certainly look like your mother." She tapped her finger on the engagement notice. "The *Inglewood Record* was published up to 1969 and was replaced by the *Times Record*. They're both weekly papers. Inglewood only has about three thousand people nowadays, and it would have had less then. That's lucky for you, because they'd report on even small events like a school sports day or a Country Women's afternoon tea. You might find your mother in there."

She glanced down at the photocopies again. "I'll bring you 1969, 1970, and 1971 for Inglewood. From 1960, Stratford had its own newspaper."

"Thank you."

"Actually, you might be better going to the Stratford library for those. We have them, but if the Crawford family are farmers, which is likely, they'll be well-known in the district." She hesitated. "But then again. I'm guessing that they don't know you're coming. Perhaps you should do the research here. It will stir up less curiosity."

"That might be wiser." Especially as Percy might not even know of her existence. She wasn't going to go tramping into what could be a delicate situation with steel-toed boots. She might only get one shot at this, so she had to get it right.

Gina looked at her watch. "Could I look at the Inglewood newspapers today and come back tomorrow or the next day for the Stratford ones?"

Barbara headed into the back rooms again and Gina went back to her desk. *Lord, thank you for introducing me to Barbara. She's been a big help. If you want me to talk to her, I'm ready. But you know me, Lord. I'm not very good at this. I'll need you to open the conversation.*

It took all the remaining time to go through the Inglewood papers. Along the way she found four more photos of her mother and a few mentions: attending several dances, a photograph of her soccer team, captioned 'Fighting Fit Female Footballers', and a photo of her laughing with a group of people on skis. One of the people in the photo was Percy. Perhaps that was how they'd met.

Barbara helped her photocopy the relevant pages, and Gina thanked her. "I'll try to get back here tomorrow afternoon, but my hostess insists I go with her and some friends to the Whitecliffs walk tomorrow. She said something about having to do it at low tide."

Barbara laughed. "That's right. Part of the walk is on the beach and it is scary to get caught by the tide. You're much safer with locals, and you'll love it."

CHAPTER 30

*K*nock, knock, knock.

"I'm awake, Alison." Gina threw back her covers. It was still dark, but her backpack was ready, and they'd made their lunches last night. She dressed quickly without turning on the light, then carried her pack and boots into the kitchen. Tony had advised her to take her boots, and he'd been right.

"Here you are." Alison handed her a cup of tea. "Help yourself to whatever cereal you want, and there's plenty of stewed rhubarb."

Stewed fruit seemed to be a thing here. Alison had proudly shown her a pantry full of bottled peaches, nectarines, quinces, and feijoa, a fruit Gina hadn't had before. "All off my own trees."

The backyard was crammed with vegetables and fruit trees. Only the front, the part open to the public, had flowers.

"Perfect weather, and you're in for a treat the minute the sun rises," Alison said.

What treat did she have in mind?

Twenty minutes later, Gina laced her boots and went out to the car. Her breath steamed in the crisp air.

"It'll be a beaut day later," Alison said as they climbed into the car. "But we're setting off early because I'm taking you on a slight detour first."

After a short drive, Alison turned right and parked somewhere. Alison had asked Gina to close her eyes five minutes earlier, so Gina had no idea where they were. Instead, Gina undid her seatbelt and waited for Alison to come around her side of the car. The door opened.

"No peeking now." Alison helped Gina out of the car and turned her round. "Now you can look."

Gina opened her eyes and gasped. The smooth cone of Mount Taranaki rose in front of her. The upper third gleamed pink as the sunrise reflected off the snow. "It's stunning." She pulled out her camera and took a few shots. Tony said he'd been to New Zealand once before but only the South Island. From what she'd seen so far, they'd want to come back when the girls were older.

"If you're in the area long enough, you'll come to know her moods. The mountain is often covered in clouds, but every time she shows her face it's worth it."

"Thank you so much for taking the effort to show me and for everything else, walks and meals. I was worried about having to come and find my own way, but it's been easy so far."

Alison flapped a hand. "It's my pleasure. Come on. You'll like the girls. We've been tramping together almost every month for thirty years."

They were soon parked at the start of the walk. A motley collection of four-wheel drives and station wagons were already there. The ladies were chattering like starlings, and Alison had to shout to make herself heard. She introduced Gina as her Aussie guest. Gina was welcomed and they did a head count before setting off.

"The walk isn't officially open for two more days because of lambing season," Alison said. "But one of our members knows all the farmers and so we always walk it when we're the only ones. We'll do the beach section first to fit in with the tides and come back via the farm track at the top of the cliffs. Keep your camera handy."

They were soon walking along sand packed hard by the retreating tide. The easy walking allowed Gina plenty of time to take photos of the white cliffs and the ripples on the sand. Conversation ebbed and flowed around her.

They stopped for a drink and a snack at ten, then made their way up the cliffs, the only steep bit of the walk so far. It was easy walking although Gina's feet would be happy for a break by the end of the twenty-plus kilometres. It had been a long time since she'd hiked this far.

Three women asked what she was doing in New Zealand and she gave vague answers, not mentioning her search. This area was too small. She couldn't risk the news getting to her mother or Percy.

They ate lunch sitting on emerald-green grass so wet that she sat on her raincoat. On one side, the sea stretched thousands of kilometres towards Sydney and on the other, the impossibly beautiful mountain strained towards the sky. Perfect and serene.

"Don't be fooled," the woman next to her said. "It's dangerous. The weather changes quickly, and there have been plenty of deaths up there. It doesn't look high, but it's killed over eighty people that we know of. That's second only to Mt Cook."

Looking at it today, it was hard to believe.

"It's best to only go up there with locals."

"I'm not a mountain climber," Gina said. "I'll stick with admiring it from afar."

"Oh, no, you must do some walks. Go to Wilkies Pools and do some of the walks on the side of the mountain. You'll love it. On a day like this, you should be able to see Taranaki's three sisters in the centre of the island: Tongariro, Ngauruhoe, and Ruapehu."

After lunch, they finished the last hour of the walk. The sheer beauty made Gina long to be doing this walk with Tony. He'd told her he'd done a lot of hiking before Sophia had been born.

***

*B*arbara had three boxes of the *Stratford Press* waiting for her.

Gina's heart sank. "That looks like a lot of work."

"I have a suggestion," Barbara said. "We have a volunteer here this afternoon and not much work for her to do. Would you be willing for her to help you?"

"That would be great." Gina said.

"I know it looks like a lot, but I'd concentrate on the personal notices after the wedding date and see if they announced the births of any children. If you think Percy is a farmer, check out the local show reports. It's not a common surname, so something should turn up. I'll send the volunteer over." Barbara headed back into the office and Gina prepared for the next three hours of work by laying the boxes on a larger table.

After quick introductions, they got to work. By the end of the afternoon, Gina had found the births of four children, two boys and two girls. She had half-siblings. It was overwhelming to think of these children growing up in a different country, never knowing she existed. She checked the birth dates. They were born between 1974 and 1983, so the youngest two were still at school. It was highly unlikely she'd get to meet them any time soon. If she was their mother, she'd want to shield them from this whole story.

The volunteer had found information confirming that Percy was a dairy farmer and had probably bought or inherited the farm just before his marriage. His cows regularly won awards at the local shows. Gina thanked the woman for her help and went to photocopy some of the items.

Barbara came out to help. "Found what you want?"

"Yes, thank you, but I'm not going to look any more. It feels like stalking. It's time to actually travel to Stratford and try and contact my mother."

"Good luck," Barbara said.

There was her chance again. It was so much easier to let the comment slide, but she'd been praying for Barbara and Alison for the last two days, so she couldn't stay silent. She had five copies of *A Fresh Start* in her luggage to give away.

"I'm not someone who believes in luck, but I have been praying pretty hard for wisdom to do this in the right way."

Barbara's eyebrows rose towards her hairline. "I didn't think people your age actually believed in prayer."

Help, Jesus. I can't see where to go with that comment. Her mind ran to several possible comments. "I've seen too many prayers answered to doubt God is listening and that he cares."

"Like what?"

"Like all the help I've received on my search. If I hadn't met my great-aunt, I would never have seen the letters my mother sent from here."

"Couldn't that just be coincidences combined with helpful people?"

"Maybe, but it's unlikely all the answers were coincidences." Why was it that when she talked about things like this, she always felt stupid? As though she was an intellectual simpleton who was easily fooled by outdated beliefs. *Help, Lord. Keep this going.*

"I'd love to believe that prayer works."

Lord?

"Is there something that you need help with?" Gina said gently.

Barbara glanced over her shoulder before saying sotto voce, "My daughter's got some mysterious disease and the doctors can't work it out. I'd do almost anything to have her well. She's all I've got since my husband died."

"Could I pray for her now? I promise I won't close my eyes or speak loudly."

"As long as you're quick," Barbara said.

Keeping her eyes open, Gina said. "Dear heavenly Father, thank you that you love Barbara and her daughter. You know them inside out. You even know how many hairs they have on their head and you know what is wrong with Barbara's daughter. Please show the doctors what is wrong. While Jesus was on earth, he healed many, so please heal Barbara's daughter too. Amen."

Barbara pulled out a tissue and blew her nose. "I don't know if I believe in prayer but thank you. That made me feel warm inside." She leaned towards Gina. "You seem like an intelligent person. Do you really believe all those stories about Jesus?"

"So you've heard some of the stories?"

"Oh yes," Barbara said. "We had to go to the Bible in Schools programme, but the teacher didn't seem to believe what she was telling us."

"That's sad, but yes, I do believe the stories. I've lived my whole life on the basis that Jesus knows me and he truly rose from the dead."

"I thought that was some sort of metaphor. Do you mean you think it actually happened?"

"I certainly do." Did she dare to give this woman one of her precious copies? *Lord, is Barbara one of those that you've prepared?*

"Just a second. I've got something in my bag that might help." Gina picked her bag off the floor and pulled out one of the books. "I brought five copies of this book with me to New Zealand because I think it does an excellent job of explaining why it's worth taking a look at Jesus. I'd love for you to have one."

Barbara took a step back, "Oh, I couldn't."

"I've been praying that God would show me five people he wanted me to give the book to while I'm here and I think you're one."

Barbara still hesitated.

"You can always put it in the library collection or give it away if you don't like it."

Barbara reached for the book. "I guess I could. Thank you. No one has ever given me a book like this before."

"*T*ony, I couldn't wait any longer to ring, so much has happened," Gina said, using the first of four phone cards she'd bought. Each would give her about forty minutes of conversation.

"I've been praying for you. Not only that you'd find your mother, but that you'd enjoy yourself."

"Oh, I have been enjoying myself. My hostess took me on a twenty kilometre hike this morning, and she's going to drive me to Stratford tomorrow and make sure I find a safe place to stay."

"Sounds like God has answered our prayers for accommodation."

"It's been amazing, and I've just given away the first book." She told him about Barbara at the library. "And I'm hoping my hostess will accept one too."

"Don't forget to give them your address so they can write to ask questions."

Gina clicked her tongue. "I didn't think of that. Maybe I could write a note for the librarian and drop it in on my way out of town tomorrow. Have you had any opportunities to give away books?"

"I gave away my first today to a client who always seems stressed about his monetary affairs. I asked if I could pray for him. After he got over the shock, he accepted. I told him a little about how I deal with fear. After that, it was easy to give him the book."

"Have any of the other guys given away books?"

"We're thinking we might have to order another fifty next

month. Once they knew you and I were working as a team, they've all recruited a family member too. It's created quite a buzz."

Gina tucked her feet under the chair. Alison was out at a committee meeting somewhere, so she could talk without restraint. "Do you think God has opened up these opportunities, or have they always been there?"

"I've been asking myself the same question. I think that people are far more open than we realise—"

"Yes but we don't pray. Instead, we go rushing by doing our own thing."

"Exactly. When a client comes in, I'm making a conscious effort to give them more time and leave space for God to show me things besides their accounting needs."

A little voice spoke in the background, and Tony covered the receiver with his hand. Gina sat, thinking about what she'd write in her note to Barbara.

"That was Elissa, she has a stomach ache, and I've promised to go and get her a hot water bottle. Can you call again in a few days?"

"I'll call once I'm settled in Stratford. I've found the address of the farm and need wisdom for the next step."

"You know I'll be praying."

She sure did.

CHAPTER 31

When it reached half past ten and Alison still wasn't home, Gina went to bed. As she lay down, she kept herself awake by whispering her prayers. She prayed for Tony and each of the girls. She prayed for Rachel and Pete on their honeymoon, that they'd be having fun and adjusting to each other—not so easy with Rachel in her forties and Pete not far behind.

Lastly, she prayed for Alison. "Lord, she has been so generous, taking me in, making most of my meals, and taking me hiking. Lord, bless her for her generosity and help her to receive the greatest blessing of all, getting to know you. We haven't had time to talk much about her life, but it would be great if we could talk in the car tomorrow. Please help her to be willing to accept a copy of the book."

Not much later, she'd fallen asleep mid-prayer.

In the early morning, she got up and wrote a thank you card, leaving a blank space for a Bible verse. She wasn't sure yet which verse would be appropriate. She made sure to write her Sydney address on the envelope.

"*I*'ve made us some lunch," Alison said. "It's forty kilometres to Stratford, and I'm planning to take you to a park first. It's got one of the best views of the mountain in the area."

"Alison, you don't have to do all this for me. I could catch the bus."

Alison waved aside her objections. "I've enjoyed showing you around. I can too easily just end up frittering away my time watching soap operas."

Gina hadn't seen many photos around the place. Did Alison have a family?

"Have you got everything?" Alison asked as they finished breakfast. "I always seem to leave stuff in the bathroom whenever I stay somewhere."

Gina checked again, but there was nothing.

It was another beautiful day, and a circlet of clouds draped around the mountain leaving its head poking out.

"I'm planning two side trips. The first one is a stunning little walk with views. Everyone loves Lake Mangamahoe and the view of the mountain with the lake in front has featured in many calendars."

"Sounds beautiful."

It didn't take long before they were parked in the carpark. "It's only an hour around the lake," Alison said. "Are you up to it?"

Gina nodded. "I'm in no hurry. My only goal for today is finding a place to stay, somewhere I can use as a base. I can't just drop in at the farm. I'll have to write and let my mother decide if she wants to see me."

Gina took photos from the tourist spot. As they started round the lake edge between stands of pine trees, she prayed. *God, it's up to you to get the conversation going.*

They'd only walked a short way before Alison spoke. "Would you be willing to tell me the full story of your search for your mother?"

Lord? Do you have a plan with this?

Gina started right back at the beginning, when she discovered she was adopted. At every stage, Alison asked questions about how Gina had felt. Had she felt abandoned? Had she hated her mother? Gina answered as best she could, then continued on with what had finally prompted her to start searching.

"I'm grateful to Tony's mother, because she gave me the impetus to get moving. I'm afraid I would have left it too late and Aunt Rosalie might have been gone before I started. Then I would never have known about New Zealand."

"Do you think the nurse would have told you?"

Gina paused. "It would have depended on whether she felt my aunt wanted to keep the secret or not."

Alison turned and gave her a long look. Long enough to make Gina squirm internally.

"And how do you feel about your mother now?"

"It's complicated and it changes from week to week. I sometimes ask myself what was wrong with me that she gave me away, but the more I look into the history of adoption and listen to what my aunt has had to say, the more I realise it's not that simple. My mother was under considerable pressure to adopt me out." Gina stepped around a log. "In today's context, I probably wouldn't have been given a chance to live. Girls in my mother's position would be pressured to have an abortion. I'm grateful that she gave me life, and I'm grateful I went to a good family."

Alison sighed, a sound of deep sadness. "That's what I've always feared, that my boy went to a bad family."

Gina kept quiet and prayed that Alison would say more.

"My boy—he'd be a few years older than you—born on the 5

September 1965—eight pounds, four ounces." The initial words were so faint that Gina had to strain to hear them.

"I was only fifteen, and my boyfriend and I had no idea about life. There was no sex education in schools, and my parents weren't the type who would ever sit me down for a birds and bees talk." She laughed. "I didn't know I was pregnant until I was four months along, and then my Dad gave me the walloping of my life." She grimaced. "It didn't seem to affect the baby though."

"What happened to your boyfriend?"

"My parents wouldn't let me tell him and I never saw him again. I was packed off to the Salvation Army home for unwed mothers in Auckland. They weren't unkind, but it was pretty tough." She wiped her eyes. "Lonely and all that."

"And what happened?"

"I had the baby and had to sign papers to give him away. My parents made it quite clear I couldn't go home if I didn't do that." She sniffed. "I've got nothing. No photo, no name, no knowledge of where he went. When I went home, my parents didn't speak to me anyway, so it was all for nothing."

"And your boyfriend?"

"He was gone. I did ask a former school friend once and she said the family had moved away but he was pretty mad at me before he went." She kicked a stone in front of her. "Probably thought I'd rejected him."

By the looks of things, Alison had never married. She'd said she had no family when Gina had asked yesterday.

"Thank you for trusting me with your story," Gina said. "It's likely my mother had little choice in what happened to me either."

"Yeah," Alison said. "But listening to what you've said, I'm wondering whether I should try to search."

"It's much easier to do now," Gina said.

"Easier to find him, but I doubt it's ever easy to make those first steps. I'd expect him to be angry and resentful, especially if his adopted family wasn't too good. That thought has haunted me. If I'd known my parents would never make me feel welcome at home, would I have kept him?"

Gina waited and prayed that Alison would keep talking.

"I still don't know the answer to that question. Would he have been better with me or not?" Alison stopped walking and turned to look at Gina. "What would you do in my place?"

"I'd look for him. I've had to deal with that fear that I might make things worse, but it might make things better. Not necessarily for both of you, but for at least one of you."

Gina walked towards the lake edge and Alison followed. A cool breeze ruffled the water surface and brought the smell of pine needles.

"I am preparing my heart for the possibility that my mother might not want to see me. I think the whole experience was pretty traumatic for her. She's had a new life here for a long time, and she's got four more children from high school age and up."

"How do you prepare your heart for something like that?"

Gina's chest tightened. "One thing I've done is journal my emotions." She laughed. "There's been a lot of them. I've also got a few good friends I can talk things through with, and we've prayed a lot together."

"My parents prayed. They used prayer like a weapon to attack me."

Gina put her hand on Alison's shoulder. "I'm sorry to hear that. Jesus had strong words for those kinds of people. He called them whitewashed tombs. Pretty on the outside but full of stinking corpses."

Alison chuckled. "I like his style. I called them a lot worse in my head, but never dared to say it out loud. Bad language would have cost me my next meal, and I was determined to stick it out until I finished the school year. The minute I had a proper job, I was out of there."

Gina went back to the track and they continued walking.

Lord, this is a woman who has been hurt by those who claim to be your people. It makes me angry. Maybe she should tell Alison that, instead of keeping her thoughts to herself.

"What you said about your parents makes me so angry," Gina said. "It's the opposite of what Jesus would want anyone who claimed to be his follower to do."

"You certainly seem different. And to be fair, the people at the Salvation Army home weren't nearly as harsh as my parents."

The path was wide enough for them to walk side by side.

"What was the home like?"

"There was a set routine and we all had jobs to do, but I put that down to the kind of place it was. There were even a couple of staff who made me feel welcome."

Thank you Lord, that you had some of your servants in that maternity home. And thank you that Tony and others are praying for me back home. Give me words to say to this hurting lady.

Mentally Gina rehearsed a few lines. What got to the heart of the issue and was short enough to say without Alison switching off? Something personal?

"There is something Jesus once said that helps me differentiate between people who claim to be his followers and those who really are."

Alison kept walking, her eyes on the path in front of them.

"He talked about a tree and its fruit. You could tell what kind of tree it was by how tasty its fruit was. So if an orange was sweet and juicy, the tree was good. If the fruit was tiny and bitter, the tree was no good."

"I'm not sure I get you," Alison said.

"If someone claims to be a Christian, they'll behave like one.

When you tell me about your parents and the way they treated you, I can't help doubting if they really knew Jesus. Jesus would never have treated you like they did."

"So the Salvation Army ladies who treated me kindly, you'd say they knew Jesus?"

"It certainly sounds like it."

Joy would tell a story at this point, but which one? There was the adulterous woman in John 8, or the woman at the well, or the woman who washed Jesus' feet with her hair. Too many choices and she didn't know any of them well. *Help, Lord.*

"You know, this reminds me of a story I once heard about Jesus," Alison said. "It must have been at Bible in Schools. There was one lady when I was about ten who told us lots of stories."

"Can you give me any clues what the story was about?" Gina asked.

Alison stopped. "Let me think." She squeezed her eyes closed. "Something about a woman and a jar of perfume." She opened her eyes. "Does that ring any bells?"

"It sure does. Could I tell you the story as best as I can remember?"

Alison nodded and started walking again. They were now about three-quarters of the way around the lake.

"Okay, it starts with Jesus being invited to the house of a religious leader for a meal. During the meal a woman came in and stood near Jesus. She began to cry. As her tears dropped onto Jesus' feet, she wiped them with her hair. Then she brought out a very expensive jar of perfume and poured it on Jesus' feet."

"Sounds a bit weird," Alison said.

"Well, the religious leader was pretty upset about the whole thing because he couldn't understand why Jesus would let such a 'sinner' touch him." Gina did air quotes. "She was probably a prostitute. The religious leader's opinion was that if Jesus really was God, as he claimed to be, then surely he'd know what the woman did for a living and would have nothing to do with such a person."

"My parents were like that, seeing me as unclean and spoiled."

"How did that make you feel?" Gina asked.

"Lower than low." Alison swore. "And angry. I wanted to punch my father right on his self-righteous nose."

Gina laughed. "Sounds like he deserved it. Do you know how the story ends?"

"I can't remember."

"Jesus said, 'Two men owed a debt, one a small debt and one a much bigger one. Neither could repay the debt and so the king forgave them both.' Then Jesus asked, 'Simon, which man would love the king more?' What do you think, Alison?"

"The one with the bigger debt."

"Yes, and Simon, the host worked that one out too. Jesus told a similar story elsewhere about a man who was forgiven a huge debt. The forgiven man went out the door and spotted someone who owed him a tiny amount of money. He grabbed hold of the man and demanded the debt be repaid. When the man begged for mercy, the forgiven man ignored him. Instead, he had the debtor thrown into prison."

"Whew. The guy didn't understand what the king had just done for him."

Bingo. *Thank you Lord.* "And Jesus made that exact point. He said to his host, 'Today, when I came into your home, you did not give me any water to wash my dusty feet, but this woman has washed my feet with her tears. You did not anoint me with oil, but this woman has used perfume. Her many sins have been forgiven, for she who is forgiven much loves much.'"

Alison took a few quick steps to get ahead of Gina and didn't say a word.

Now what Lord? Am I supposed to say anything? Gina prayed for Alison, that the story and words she'd said might have an impact.

Lord, help me not to add to the hurt she has already experienced. You love this woman. Help her to feel it.

A quiet joy seeped into Gina's heart. Esther had told her about the joy she'd felt whenever she'd talked about Jesus with someone, but Gina hadn't understood. *Lord, I think I do now. The person doesn't have to become a Christian on the spot. It's enough for me to know I've spoken up and you gave me the words I needed.*

They got back to the car, and Alison still hadn't said anything. They went to Inglewood, where Gina's mother had lived and worked before her wedding. As Barbara at the library had said, it was a small place. Alison drove up and down the few streets.

"Your mum might have worked in a shop or the pub or the dairy factory. It was here until the early nineties."

Gina took a few photos.

"I want to thank you for listening this morning," Alison said as they approached Stratford. "I haven't ever told anyone my story, and like you said, we need other people. I've cut myself off from anything besides work and community stuff." She slowed down as they approached the outer town limits. "Would you be willing to stay in touch? I think I'd like to start looking for my boy, but I'll need help."

"I'd be happy to help where I can, but I don't know how different the New Zealand system is to Australia. The first thing I had to do was find the government agency that handles adoptions. They weren't able to get me started on my search because there doesn't seem to be an original birth certificate but they were helpful in talking about the process."

"What did they say?"

"They gave me some guidelines for how to make the first contact with my mother. I've got them in my backpack." Gina indicated over her shoulder. "They suggest writing a letter, which is what I plan to do tonight."

"Could we photocopy those, so I have a copy?"

"If you can find the library."

"I know where that is. Shall we go there first, then go and check out the two bed and breakfasts recommended to me?"

"That's fine," Gina said.

It only took them forty-five minutes to choose a place for Gina to stay. She chose the one with the friendlier feel and a view over King Edward Park. After she'd dropped off her things, been given a key, and paid for her first two nights, they went out into the park and found a table for lunch.

The bees were busy among the azalea and rhododendron blooms.

"This park is worth strolling around," Alison said. "There are paths along the river."

"Thank you for all you've done over the last few days. You've gone well beyond anything I imagined."

"I should be thanking you. I feel quite different after talking this morning."

They finished their lunch and Alison got to her feet. "I took a card from your accommodation. Would you be happy for me to ring you with questions, as I begin my search?"

"Of course. I'll give you my contact details in Australia too."

"I do want to know what happens with your search."

"Don't worry. I'll let you know." Gina had popped the second copy of the five books she had to give away in her daypack. Would Alison take it?

"I had a small gift for you, but I don't know if you'd appreciate it."

"I normally appreciate gifts."

"It's a book, and I like it so much that I've brought five copies to give away." She looked across the picnic table at Alison. "It upset me to hear of your experiences with your parents. The Jesus I've been following all these years is so different to what you've described. Lots of people have found this book helps them to sort out the truth from the lies they've heard." Gina held the book so Alison could see it.

"I'll read it," Alison said. "And tell you what I think."

Gina laughed. "And knowing you, you'll be completely honest."

Alison took the book. "You can depend on it."

CHAPTER 32

*I*t wasn't until the next morning that Gina had time to compose her letter, as settling in had taken longer than anticipated.

Her room had a lovely window looking out on the flower garden with a small desk positioned right in front of it. Gina had already laid the folder the adoption counsellor had given her on the desk. The pages inside were highlighted with numerous notes in the margins. They'd been invaluable. Someone or more likely, a group of social workers, had taken the time to think through the whole process from the point of view of the adoptee and the birth mother, and provided a list of questions to consider.

She flipped through the pages of the questions she'd answered so far:

---

    * WHY DO YOU WANT TO FIND YOUR BIRTH PARENTS?

      * WHAT ARE YOUR NEEDS AND EXPECTATIONS?

      * WHAT MIGHT HAVE BEEN YOUR BIRTH MOTHER'S EXPERIENCE DURING PREGNANCY?

* WHAT CHOICES MIGHT SHE HAVE FACED?

She'd written page-long answers to some questions, but for others, there had been multiple pages. Pages with words smudged with tears. The handouts had encouraged her to write down how she was feeling, and she'd not held back.

She'd photocopied all the questions for Alison and suggested she start working through them.

Last night, Gina had told Tony about Barbara and Alison, and they'd committed themselves to pray for both women while she was in New Zealand. They were typical of people in both countries who were anti-Christian even though what they were reacting against wasn't the real deal. The strong opinions of Gina's workmates on what they called 'iniquities of religion' had kept her quiet for all the years she'd been teaching. Could it be that even at her school there were hearts more open than she thought?

Gina looked down at her highlighted sections. One quote she'd highlighted said, "Most mothers reported that losing their child was the most painful experience of their life."

The handouts strongly recommended against turning up on someone's doorstep, because it didn't give the person who'd been found any time to prepare. The advice made total sense. Gina had been searching for months and had had time to process each new piece of information. It would be unbelievably difficult if she sprung herself on her mother. And what if Percy or one of the children opened the door?

Calling was discouraged for the same reason. Gina had her mother's phone number and she'd imagined calling, but it would be unfair. A letter was obviously going to be best, but the disadvantage was that Gina would have to hang around, waiting for an answer.

This morning she'd gone to a newsagent and bought blue-coloured notepaper, matching envelopes, and a map of the local area. It could be a long week with no guarantee of success.

Gina laid the first sheet of notepaper on top of a magazine. *Jesus, help me to do a good job of this.*

Taking out her pen, she wrote,

DEAR

—then stopped. She couldn't write mother or any such thing. Even Regina sounded too personal.

She added Mrs Crawford, next to Dear. Then she nibbled her pen. There was no way she'd get this right the first time. She went back to her backpack in the bottom of the wardrobe and got out some scrap paper she had left over from the New Plymouth library. She'd write a draft and edit it before writing on the notepaper.

It took two hours and six false starts but eventually she'd finished her letter.

DEAR MRS CRAWFORD

MY NAME IS GINA, AND I WAS BORN AT TAMWORTH BASE HOSPITAL ON THE 2 APRIL 1967.

I BELIEVED NEIL AND FLORA REID WERE MY PARENTS UNTIL I WAS IN MY EARLY TWENTIES. THEY KNEW NOTHING ABOUT MY BIRTH PARENTS, AS THEY WERE ONLY STRANGERS PASSING THROUGH TAMWORTH WHEN FLORA WENT INTO PREMATURE LABOUR AND LOST HER BABY. THEIR BABY'S DEATH TRAUMATISED THEM SO MUCH THAT THEY DIDN'T ASK MANY QUESTIONS WHEN THEY WERE OFFERED ME.

THEY HAVE BEEN GOOD PARENTS, AND I HAVE TWO YOUNGER BROTHERS.

Having heard about Alison's main fear the day before, she'd wanted to reassure her mother that she had been looked after and not neglected in the Reid household. She'd debated whether to write about her adopted parents as "Mum" and "Dad" as felt natural, but opted for using their names instead.

I AM A KINDERGARTEN TEACHER AT A SMALL SCHOOL IN SYDNEY AND LIVE NEARBY. I'M NOT YET MARRIED BUT HAVE A BOYFRIEND, TONY. WE WENT TO TAMWORTH AND FOUND AUNT ROSALIE. SHE DEEPLY REGRETS HOW SHE TREATED YOU AND LONGS TO MAKE THINGS RIGHT. I HAVE NOT CONTACTED YOUR PARENTS, AS I WANTED TO CONTACT YOU FIRST.

I FLEW TO NEW ZEALAND NEARLY A WEEK AGO, AND IT TOOK ME A WHILE TO FIND OUT ABOUT YOUR MARRIAGE AND YOUR ADDRESS. AUNT ROSALIE STILL HAD ONE OF THE ENVELOPES FROM YOUR LETTERS, AND TARANAKI WAS VISIBLE ON THE ENVELOPE.

She'd debated about what to say on this issue but decided the truth was best. Better than letting her mother think that Aunt Rosalie or someone else had given her away.

I AM STAYING ON PAGE STREET.

She added the house and telephone numbers.

My flight home is in three weeks, and I plan to wait in Stratford for the next week. I hope you might be willing to see me.

Sincerely,

Gina

Ending the letter had also led to some pen chewing. She found she couldn't write "your daughter" in case she'd somehow got this completely wrong or if someone other than her mother opened the letter. She'd pray that wouldn't happen.

Gina put the letter in the envelope, sealed and addressed it, and added the stamp. The post office wasn't far away.

As Gina gathered her things, another thought occurred to her. Her host had told her she was welcome to borrow their bike. She grabbed the map. What if she headed out and did a loop up Opunake Road via Cardiff and over to Pembroke School? It didn't look further than six kilometres, and it was a lovely day. She could cruise past the farm and drop the letter in the letterbox. Most farms had their letterbox a long way from the house. No one would see her, and it might speed up the whole process.

Stuffing the map, letter, and water bottle into her daypack, she went out to the kitchen. Her hosts were relaxed and had given her fridge and pantry space. She packed a picnic to enjoy on the way.

She was soon out of town and cycling up Opunake Road. It was hard work because she'd forgotten that Stratford was at the base of the mountain, so any roads heading west went uphill. Oh well, she could always get off and push. There was only an occasional car and she always heard them coming and could pull off onto the grassy verge. She stopped at various gateways and noted the cows. Most were caramel brown or black and white, their udders hanging half full, presumably because they were in between the morning and evening milkings. She'd have to ask her host when those were done and see if it was possible to visit a farm.

At Cardiff, she turned right and headed around the base of the mountain. The wind was a little chilly, but it was fine as long as she kept moving. She had extra layers in her backpack. A cow lowed off to her right. There was a pleasant smell of warm grass and mud, and everywhere was green, green, green. The emerald green of the grass, the mid-green of the trees, and the darker green of the hedges.

Eventually she came to a crossroad with a school in front of her. She didn't know whether the farm she was seeking was up to the left, closer to the mountain or down. Rather than turn downhill and then discover she had to climb again, she turned uphill and rode past the first two farms, checking the numbers. No, the numbers were increasing. The farm she was seeking must be downhill.

She turned her back on the mountain and coasted down the road, past the school, and further on down the road, careful not to ride too fast. She'd hate to meet a tractor on a corner or come off her bike out here where farms were hundreds of metres apart.

There was a driveway ahead, and she slowed. Not this one but perhaps the next on the left. She coasted down another two hundred metres, and there it was. She put on her brakes, stopped, laid the bike off to the side and got out the letter to put in the box. As she'd predicted, the mailbox was about one hundred metres from the house, which was a low, one-storey home running perpendicular to the road and on a little hillock. There was a cluster of sheds off to the right.

Gina popped the letter into the box. As she turned to go, a car drew up and turned into the driveway. She stopped breathing, keeping her head down.

"Can we help you?" the man driving the car called.

"I was just dropping something in the box," Gina said, voice low and head down. *Horrors.* It was almost lunchtime. She'd assumed they'd be at home, tucking into a nice cooked lunch.

"Well, since you're there could I ask you to get anything out of the box? It will save my wife getting out of the car."

Gina turned away. *Lord, help, help, help. I never intended for them to see me.* And she wasn't even wearing a hat. She opened the mailbox and got out a small pile of letters. She slipped hers to the bottom and handed them in through the open window, while trying to keep her face turned away.

"Perc, oh Perc," said a woman's voice, high and stretched thin.

Gina flicked her eyes past Percy into the wide, staring eyes of her mother. The blood had drained from her mother's face and her mouth was open in an O.

Gina took a step back and Percy looked towards his wife.

"What's wrong?" and then louder. "What's wrong?" He touched her face. "Are you okay?"

Gina felt like throwing up. This was exactly what she'd meant to avoid, and now her cursed curiosity and desire to be doing something had thrown her into this nightmare.

"I'm sorry," Gina said, backing away. "So sorry."

"Take me home, Perc," her mother croaked.

Percy leaned out the window. "I don't know what this is about, but don't come back," he yelled.

Gina fled, stumbling towards her bike, tears streaming down her cheeks.

CHAPTER 33

"Tony," Gina said into the phone handset. Her voice trembled.

"What's wrong?" Tony asked. She'd never rung him at work before.

"I've m-made a t-total mess of things." Her teeth chattered and she hugged one arm around her body.

"Take a deep breath." She could hear someone talking in the background.

Oh, no. He had a client. Of course he did. She hadn't thought about the time. Hadn't thought that he could be embarrassed and inconvenienced. She'd just put the bike away and staggered into her room, thankful her hosts were out.

"Take a few deep breaths, and I'll ask my client to go and get a cup of coffee."

She heard him place the phone on the surface of his desk, the creak of his chair, and some murmured conversation.

Her face burned, but she took the breaths he'd suggested. One, two, three. She shivered again, and reached for the quilt on the bed to wrap around herself.

"Gina, what's wrong? Are you hurt? Have you had an accident?"

"N-no." She shook her head. "I'm okay, but I've … I've messed up big time."

"Take it slowly, and tell me what's happened."

It took her several minutes to tell him because she broke down twice. She had to get up and bring the whole toilet roll from the bathroom to wipe her nose.

He listened while she finished the story. "And then I was shaking so badly that I fell off the bike and vomited."

"But you're back to your room now? Is anyone there with you?"

"No. I had to use my key to get in."

"Can you ring me again in fifteen minutes? I only have a few more things I need to say to this client, and he's travelled quite a way to see me. Then I'm free to talk."

"Sorry for ringing. I didn't think."

"It's not a problem. Promise me you'll ring again in fifteen minutes."

She promised.

"Love you, make sure you remember. Fifteen minutes."

Gina sat in her room, staring at a tiny imperfection in the paintwork. Maybe a previous guest had bumped the wall. Time passed, but she didn't know how long. She'd forgotten to look at her watch when she put the phone down.

A motorbike buzzed along the road outside, and the phone rang. She jumped and picked it up.

"Gina, you didn't ring back."

"I lost track of time." She moaned. "I was so careful to do everything right, and now I've wrecked everything. He was so mad at me."

"Percy? Think about it logically, darling. He had no idea who you were or why his wife was reacting so strangely. He was worried and scared—like I would be if anything happened to you. He was trying to protect her from an unknown threat."

"But her f-face. Her face was terrible."

"If she knew who you were, it must have been like seeing a ghost."

"She must have known. There's no other explanation for her reaction."

"I agree, but it might not be as terrible as you're assuming. Like the social worker said, meeting your relative for the first time can be a shock, and she had no warning you were coming."

"Aunt Rosalie wasn't like this."

"No, but Noelene went to see her first, so she had several days to get used to the idea. Besides, she's your great-aunt, not your mother."

"I doubt I'll ever meet my mother now, and I have no one to blame but myself." She sighed. "My cursed curiosity. I just wanted to see where she lived the last thirty years. I thought I'd timed it right. I was stupid." Gina thumped the bed.

"Honey, stop!" Tony's voice was sharp.

She gulped. He'd never spoken to her like that.

"Gina, you are not to beat yourself up for making a genuine mistake."

"I just wish I hadn't been so impatient."

"Impatience is understandable, as you feel like you've been searching for ages. What's done is done, but who do we serve?"

"Jesus," Gina hiccupped, tears welling again.

"And what do we know about him?"

She knew what Tony was getting at, but she couldn't get the words out.

"He's in control, isn't he?" Tony said gently. "Jesus wasn't napping when this happened. He's in control. Whether it turns out well or not, he'll help you deal with it."

She cried some more, and Tony let her cry.

As she calmed down, he said, "Tell me about the letter you wrote."

Gina opened the clear folder on her desk. "I have a copy here."

"Read it to me then."

She read it through. It seemed so long ago that she'd written these words. She'd had such high hopes for the outcome.

"It's a great letter, and your mother has it now."

"She might throw it in the rubbish."

"She might, but let's pray she doesn't. Let her absorb it, and we'll pray that she is able to process all the emotions inside her. Just because Percy was angry doesn't mean he isn't a good husband. He might be able to help her."

"And we can pray she has some good friends like Rachel, Joy, and Blanche to help her."

"That's my girl," Tony said, warm pride in his voice. "You've had a big shock. Let's pray together. Then why don't you go and make yourself some tea or coffee with extra sugar. An early night might help."

"Thanks Tony, I hope I didn't mess up things with your client."

Tony laughed. "Don't you worry about him. He calls me the best accountant in Sydney. I don't think a ten minute wait will change that opinion, especially since I saved him ten thousand dollars. Do you want me to pray first?"

"Please," Gina said. She doubted she'd be able to pray at all.

"Dear heavenly Father, we thank you that you know everything before it happens and nothing happens outside your control. You know what Gina feels right now and all the confusion and pain in her heart. Please comfort her. Please help her to sleep well tonight and be able to look at things differently in the morning. Help Gina's mother not to throw the letter away and help her to recover from the shock she had at seeing Gina. Not that Gina is at all shocking to look at."

A giggle burst out of Gina.

"Lord, you know I think she's beautiful, but don't let me get distracted. We pray that Regina has some good friends or her husband to help her process her emotions. We don't know if she knows you, Lord, possibly not, but we ask you to be close to her tonight and in the coming days. Please help Gina to be able to get out and about and enjoy your creation without worrying."

He prayed for another minute or two. "And we ask that Regina might be willing to talk to Gina. It probably won't be an easy conversation, but Lord, we ask you to make it happen. Encourage Gina, and we thank you for all the opportunities she's had to talk about you recently. Please help Aunt Rosalie to be growing in her understanding of you and thank you that Noelene is such a good friend. Help Barbara and Alison to read the book and move closer towards you. In the name of your son, Jesus, who is king over everything, even over people who make mistakes. Amen."

"Thank you," Gina said. "I do feel much calmer."

"And what are you going to do now?"

"I'll go and make a cup of tea and enjoy a nice hearty soup for dinner."

"And feel free to phone again tomorrow."

"But at a better time," Gina said.

"Yes, evening would be better," Tony said, with a teasing tone. "Although I love to hear your voice anytime."

The phone clicked and Gina hung it up. *God, thank you for that man. He keeps my eyes focused on you.*

CHAPTER 34

*G*ina woke with the word, 'fool' bouncing around the echo chamber in her head. The sun was shining outside, but inside her head was as bleak as a day on a windswept moor in the pouring rain. Fool. You ignored the advice you were given, and now you've probably blown the whole process. She hunched down and pulled the blankets over her head. If only she could shut out the voice as easily. Its accusations stuck barbs in her quivering flesh. And flesh she had plenty of. Tony had assured her he didn't like skinny women, but he was only being kind. This morning, even memories of that kindness felt like he was pitying her and pity she could do without.

God, help. I feel useless, fat, and lonely. I'm here, far from home with no friends, no one to pray with, and I feel miserable. What are you going to do with that? I can't seem to get out of the doldrums.

What was it Rachel often said? "Get out of bed, have a shower, then re-evaluate." It didn't sound like much of an accomplishment, but getting up and having a shower sounded possible.

Gina swung back the bed covers, and stumbled to her feet. The image she caught in the mirror as she gathered her clothes wasn't inspiring. Even her hair looked straggly, as though it needed positivity to gain body and bounce.

She turned the bathroom fan on and the water volume up and scrubbed her scalp and body vigorously. Maybe Rachel's pointers had some truth in them. Rachel had assured her that during her months of depression, her shower routine had kept her sane and allowed her the energy to accomplish one other thing that day.

Gina turned off the water and towelled herself dry. Her skin tingled. There was something else Rachel had said to her recently, but the words eluded her at the moment. Maybe it would come to her as she blow-dried her hair with the dryer provided in one of the drawers.

The dryer roared in her ears and Gina lifted the layers of hair to dry underneath. That was it. Rachel had been uptight the night before the wedding, convinced Pete could have done so much better for himself. Gina had hugged her and said, over and over, "Pete knows your past, and you know you're forgiven."

"My head knows," Rachel had said through her tears. "But not my heart. Gina, you've got to help me sword fight."

"Sword fight?" Gina had never heard the term before.

"It is something Pete got from his father. When he told me about it, I realised that Gran did it all the time."

"Did what?" Gina still hadn't got it.

"She took God's word and used it to attack Satan's lies."

"Like what?"

"Tell me some of the promises that God makes about forgiveness." Rachel wiped her eyes. "The barrage of lies is so strong this evening that truth has been smothered."

And so Gina had recited verses like Psalm 103:12.

As far as the east is from the west, so far has he removed our transgressions from us.

And 1 John 1:9.

IF WE CONFESS OUR SINS, HE IS FAITHFUL AND JUST AND WILL FORGIVE US OUR SINS AND PURIFY US FROM ALL UNRIGHT-EOUSNESS.

Rachel had asked her to repeat some of the verses four or five times. Gradually she'd calmed down and begun to respond and add stories and verses of her own.

Sword fighting. That was what Gina needed to do. She brushed her hair, tied it up, and gathered a few things together. She'd go out for a walk and find a place to sit down with her Bible and journal.

The main part of town wasn't large. Gina avoided the main road by walking the street parallel to it. Many of the houses were painted wood and to her amusement, nearly every street was Shakespearean. She spotted Hamlet, Portia, and Juliet. After seeing all those names, she'd guessed there'd be a River Avon, but there wasn't. Maybe someone had put their foot down about the Shake-spearean theme extending beyond the street names.

Alison had recommended walking the river section of King Edward Park. The river rushed busily over and around rocks, then lingered in the deeper pools. Gina took a deep breath. *Thank you for getting me out of the house. Out here, it's so much easier to believe that you're with me, that you care, and that you're in control of everything that happens.*

The path wound along the side of the river, then came to a bridge. In the middle of the bridge, she looked down. The tops of the lower trees under the bridge, overshadowed the water. The water wasn't brown, but clear. She could see the individual rocks and even some good-sized fish in the bigger pool. She took a deep breath, drawing the clean air deep into her lungs. This was much better than being curled up and miserable in bed.

She crossed the bridge and kept walking along the slightly muddy path. Shafts of sunlight pierced the leaf canopy and danced between the tree trunks. She stopped to admire the light for a few minutes before setting off again. The path wound down towards the river, and there was an open area right next to the water with a tumble of rocks just perfect for sitting on. She used her hands to scramble down, and found a flat rock where she could spread her raincoat. Her Bible, pen, and journal were soon out of her daypack. Time for battle.

Jesus, show me the root issues. I want to fight the right battle. So often when she had a frustration or failure, the attacks became personal, and she ended up feeling overweight and unattractive. She drew two circles in her journal. In one she wrote,

---

Is God really in control?

She nibbled the end of her pen, then added more words.

Of everything?!?

Even yesterday's disaster? She stared at the river twinkling in the sunlight. A small fish leapt out of the water and splashed down again.

In the second circle, she wrote

LOW SELF-ESTEEM

She stared at the words for a long moment. Was that really the issue, or was it a symptom? Maybe that circle should have another question. She bracketed the first answer she'd written, looked back at the first question, and then wrote,

DID GOD MAKE A MISTAKE WHEN HE MADE ME?

Below that, she wrote.

WHO AM I?!?

Stating the problem as a question made it clearer. She opened her Bible and turned to Psalm 139. She read the whole psalm slowly, whispering the words to herself. Then she went back to the beginning and read verse by verse from verse one to twelve, jotting down answers to the first question in her journal. She'd come back to those later. The verses she wanted to think about now were verses thirteen to sixteen.

FOR YOU CREATED MY INMOST BEING; YOU KNIT ME TOGETHER IN MY MOTHER'S WOMB.

She giggled. She knew 'knit' meant put together, but for a

second she'd had an image of God sitting there with a big set of knitting needles and a frown of concentration on his face as he knitted her together. If she had the drawing skills, it would make a delightful cartoon.

Did her mother know Jesus?

It was amazing to think that whether Regina's pregnancy had been planned or not, God had still been in control. He could have prevented the pregnancy, but he didn't. Gina read verse fifteen.

MY FRAME WAS NOT HIDDEN FROM YOU WHEN I WAS MADE IN THE SECRET PLACE, WHEN I WAS WOVEN TOGETHER IN THE DEPTHS OF THE EARTH.

Would she have chosen to be born to an unmarried teen? Or to be given to the Reid family to raise? No, definitely not. Yet God had still taken the trouble to weave her together in her mother's womb. He hadn't seen her mother's shame and decided Gina wasn't worth wasting any effort on.

Gina shivered. *Thank you, Jesus, for bothering with me. For not concluding that I was unimportant.*

Jesus had been the son of an unmarried teenager. He understood.

Verse sixteen said,

YOUR EYES SAW MY UNFORMED BODY; ALL THE DAYS ORDAINED FOR ME WERE WRITTEN IN YOUR BOOK BEFORE ONE OF THEM CAME TO BE.

She wrote the final long phrase in her journal and drew an

arrow across to the first circle. If every day of her life was known to God, then yesterday's bungle was no shock to him. He'd known Gina would get impatient. He'd known she would put the letter into the Crawfords' letterbox. He'd known her path would connect with her mother's, despite all Gina's plans to avoid such an encounter. And since God had been running the universe since its creation, surely he was more than capable of untying the knots she'd tied with her thoughtless actions. *Please, Jesus, help my mother to work through the hurts I caused. Help her to want to see me.*

Gina stopped. It sounded like she was trying to tell God what to do again.

Jesus, you know what is best. Please do it. No, she stopped again. Did she really need to ask for this or could she simply thank him? *Thank you that you always do the right thing. Thank you that my thoughtlessness won't prevent your plans from succeeding. Please comfort my mother and help me to have patience as I wait. I'm not good at patience. I want things sorted out, and sorted out right away. Help me to accept that your timing might not be anything like mine.*

She reread the four verses. They were already familiar, so it shouldn't take long to memorise them.

Gina read the first line out loud and murmured it back to herself several times. She only needed to glance down at her Bible twice to check she had it right. Then she added the next line, murmuring it on its own three times before going back and saying the first and second line together.

It didn't take long to have the four verses right, but past experience had taught her that she'd need to say them again to herself, morning and evening, for the next couple of weeks for them to be rock solid in her mind. She grinned to herself. The best part was that every time she said them to herself, the truths would dig themselves deeper into her heart.

A floating stick came down the tiny rapid about four metres from where she was sitting. Gina stood up and hunted around for some suitable stones to act as missiles. She lobbed one and missed. By the third stone she hit the front of the stick. She and her father and brothers loved to do this. By the time the stick was out of range, she'd hit it four times.

She was a bit like that stick. Satan had scored some hits in the last twenty-four hours, but thanks to her heavenly Father holding her up, she was still floating. She sat and rummaged deep in her bag for the apple she'd put in there.

Finding it, she took a big bite. The crisp juiciness of the apple reminded her of how many gifts she received every day. *Thank you Lord, for apples and rivers, for sunshine and rain, for beauty and friends. Thank you that I am fearfully and wonderfully made and that my worth isn't based on weight or brain capacity or any worldly standard. Thank you Lord, for making me, me.*

There'd been a song with those last words, back in her primary school days. Gina hummed a few notes. She couldn't remember all the words at the moment, but maybe she could teach it to Elissa.

When she returned to her accommodation, she checked the letterbox. Nothing. Gina's spirits slid towards her toes. "Buck up, Gina," she muttered to herself. It wasn't as if she really expected her mother to get in contact so soon, but the empty box reminded her that she might have lost the chance. Would she ever get the opportunity to apologise to her mother for yesterday's mess? Maybe, maybe not. Gina went into the house, reciting the words she'd just memorised.

CHAPTER 35

"*Y*ou won't believe who called me today," Tony said.

"No idea." Gina put her feet up on the bed to be more comfortable.

It was the fourth day since she'd dropped off the letter and there'd been no response. No letter, no call, no visit.

"Your Aunt Rosalie," Tony said. "She rang me because she didn't have your number."

Gina had given Aunt Rosalie Tony's number in case there was any reason they needed to contact Gina.

"Is anything wrong?" Gina asked.

"Not at all. I think things are rather right actually. She's finished the book and wanted to know what to do next."

Gina's heart did a little skip of joy. "What did she think of the book?"

"She said she found it simple and clear, and it reminded her that she'd chosen to follow Jesus long ago, but she'd allowed things to get in the way."

Like her guilt and shame about how she'd treated her niece.

"She said the book made it crystal clear what to do, and she wanted to tell you that she's able to pray now and she's praying for you and, of course, your mother."

Gina's stomach fluttered with excitement. "Oh, Tony, that's fantastic news. I sensed she was beginning to open up on my last visit. I've been praying for her every day."

"And I've been praying for those you've met in New Zealand."

"I've got some news about Alison and Barbara, but please tell me what you advised Aunt Rosalie first." There was a loud breathy sigh at the other end of the phone line. "Is Pirate there?"

Tony chuckled. "I'm glad you know that wasn't me. She's here with her head on my feet. Thinks I need a foot warmer. Pirate, can you hear Gina?"

There was the sound of a tail beating on the wooden floor.

"Can you hear her agreeing?"

"I can."

"Let me remember what I said." He paused. "First, Aunt Rosalie asked what she should be reading in the Bible. I suggested that she read from Genesis 1 to Exodus 20, then Luke and Acts. I also suggested she talk to Noelene. I'm guessing Noelene will either accompany her to the chapel service in the home or work out how to get Rosalie along to her church."

Good thinking. Aunt Rosalie would need someone to encourage her fragile faith.

"And I've promised we'll go and visit once you're back."

"You're a good man, Tony Agosto."

"You keep saying that. Now come back to me as fast as you can, but first, tell me what's happening at your end."

She told him about the lack of contact with Regina, her follow-up with Alison and Barbara, and her scripture memorisation and subsequent reflections. Tony then updated her on how the girls were going.

"Isabella asked when you were coming back," Tony said.

"She probably just wants my cooking."

"Don't underrate yourself. I'm happy she asked, and they all seemed to be listening to the answer. Even Sophia, although she pretended she wasn't."

Gina heard Pirate give a moist yawn.

"I hope you're not just sitting inside all day, waiting around," Tony said.

"Not at all. I've been out on the bike twice. There's a beautiful river park here, and Alison just rang and asked if I wanted to go hiking on the mountain tomorrow as the weather looks promising."

---

*A*lison picked Gina up at ten, then drove back to Monmouth Road and straight up the mountain. "May as well use this road, since we're here. I don't get onto this side of the mountain much."

They drove over a cattle grid and left the farmland behind. Dense undergrowth pressed in on both sides of the road, with the occasional tree fern thrusting through to reach for the light.

"We'll go to the carpark and look at the view before walking around a section of the mountain to Wilkies Pools. Did you bring everything I suggested?"

Alison had told her not to be fooled by the pleasant weather. She always took extra layers, rain gear, gloves and beanie, plus snacks.

The carpark was half full. After they parked, Alison led the way up the path towards where Gina could glimpse ski lifts. "We won't go all the way up, but I wanted to give you the best view."

Gina concentrated on placing her feet carefully on the shifting stones of the path. Off to each side were pockets of snow in the shadowy areas near rocks. In front of her, Alison turned around. "Now look."

Gina turned. The mountain dropped steeply below her to the flat plain filled with emerald-green fields, scattered farmhouses, and sheds as far as she could see. Some of the fields had tiny specks of cows clumped together.

"And can you see the outline of the mountains on the skyline?"

Gina looked in the direction Alison was pointing. Sure enough, there were three mountains there, one with a beautiful cone.

"The big one is Ruapehu, with the multiple peaks. The cone is Ngauruhoe, and the other one is Tongariro," Alison said.

Gina took a few photos.

"We'll head down when you're ready. I want to take you on my favourite walk," Alison said. "It's less than four kilometres of walking but you'll love it."

She drove back to where Gina had travelled on the bike. At Cardiff, Alison turned west to continue up Opunake Road. Once out of the car, Alison got her pack and a climbing pole. Within minutes they were immersed in a world of cold moisture, moss, and ferns. Gina couldn't resist snapping close-ups of the heart of the ferns.

"It's stunning."

"Wait until you see the pools. If it was summer, I would have told you to bring your swimming togs."

Gina shivered. She was cool enough already.

Alison turned to look over her shoulder. "I've started the process."

Gina scurried to catch up. "To look for your son, you mean?"

"Yeah, I made some phone calls and discovered the first step is to fill in a form. I sent it off yesterday."

"What's in the form?"

"I had to put all the details I have about date of birth, place he was born, etcetera. Then I have to wait. Thankfully he's over twenty, or I wouldn't be able to search at all."

"Interesting, but it makes sense. They're trying to protect the children. If my mother had come looking for me before I was twenty, it would have been a huge shock. I didn't even know I was adopted at that point." Gina stopped talking while she negotiated her way around a muddy spot. "What happens after they receive the form?"

"They'll go looking for me and check whether my son has a veto against giving out information. They say it happens, but sometimes the child has written a letter to explain."

"I'll be praying that doesn't happen."

"I'm not convinced praying will help," Alison mumbled. "But you do what makes you feel better."

God, give me a chance to talk more about you with Alison. She needs your healing touch in so many aspects of her heart.

"I've been praying a lot lately," Gina said. "I managed to mess up my approach to my mother." She told Alison what happened. "I don't know if she'll get in touch."

"Waiting must be hard."

Gina nodded. "It is, but getting out to hike is a good distraction."

"It seemed such a pity for you to be seeing so little of our beautiful country. If I have to go somewhere further afield for my interview and you're still here, I'll make sure to call and invite you on the drive."

"I appreciate that," Gina said. "How are you feeling about things so far?"

"Scared," Alison said. She walked a few more paces. "Excited … a mix of scared and excited and more."

"It's terrifying, isn't it?" Gina said keeping pace. "Whether you're the child or the parent, both sides fear rejection."

"And that the other has had a terrible time and is angry and resentful."

"Yeah, that too."

They kept walking. As they climbed higher, Gina could just see the snow-capped peak of the mountain rising above them. The sound of rushing water grew louder.

"Here we are," Alison said. "It's great to have the place to ourselves."

A small waterfall rushed down a water-smoothed stone chute and gushed into a pool of clear green water.

"Keep climbing," Alison said, leading the way. "There's a whole series of pools."

They continued their way to the top. Gina bent to feel the water. Within seconds the icy coldness gave her hand pins and needles. She withdrew it and rubbed it vigorously. Definitely not the day for a quick dip.

At the top, they found a spot for a cup of tea. Alison had brought a thermos. Below them, the series of falls plunged into pools of all shapes and sizes.

"It must be packed here in summer," Gina said.

"It is, which is why I tend to come in the off season."

After stopping for twenty minutes, Gina had to get to her feet and jog on the spot to keep warm.

"Come on. Dawson Falls is at the other end of the loop, just before we reach our car." Alison put away the thermos and cups and they started walking. Ten minutes later, she said, "I guess you're curious about whether I've read the book you gave me."

Gina made a small sound of assent but didn't say anything further. *Please Lord, keep her speaking.*

"I will say it's easy to read and I like the author's sense of humour. I didn't expect to enjoy reading it."

"So you believe all Christians are boring?"

"Or manipulative, self-righteous prigs," Alison said. "Not that you're like that, but I have avoided Christians as much as possible."

Not too surprising, with the parents she'd had.

"I've skipped the first bit at the moment. It seems like Part Two is more appropriate for me."

Part Two was written to non-Christians to consider such issues of whether the New Testament was history and if its accounts about Jesus could be relied upon.

"And what do you think so far?" Gina asked, skirting another puddle.

"It's not too bad. There's lots I need to check up on." Alison cleared her throat.

"Yes, don't just take the author's word for it. It's always best to read things for yourself."

"If I was to get a Bible, where would you suggest I start?" Alison said.

"When we get back to where I'm staying, I'll show you in my Bible," Gina said. She might end up giving her Bible to Alison so her desire to get one didn't remain a good intention. There was sure to be a Bible in the second-hand store she'd spotted in town. "What has impressed you so far?"

"Well, I never considered that Jesus was God. The author seems to think that not only can we know a lot about Jesus but that there is plenty of evidence that he's God." Alison shook her head. "If he's God, I'm not sure he's done a good job of managing this world."

"Has the author written some things about that?"

"I did skim ahead and that's coming up. I might even get to it tonight."

Lord, please help her to do so.

Gina took a few quick steps to keep up with Alison's longer strides. "It's not easy for us humans to understand how God works, because we're more interested in a God who smooths the way and wipes out all suffering."

Alison chuckled. "That sounds like my sort of God."

"I've been wishing all week that God would erase my mistake with my mother." Gina took a few more steps. "But there are so many stories in the Bible about people who went through suffering, and it was the suffering that opened them up to what Jesus had to say."

"Like the woman you told me about. She'd had a tough life, but the religious leader hadn't. He seemed to think Jesus was just a good kind of guest to invite for a meal but never thought of him as anything more."

"Spot on," Gina said. *Thank you Lord, that she's kept thinking about that story. Is there another story I could tell her?*

"Have you got any more stories like that one?"

Gina's heart sped up.

"You know, more stories of people Jesus met but others didn't like."

"Do you know the story of Zacchaeus?"

"Zach who?"

How was it that a woman who'd grown up in a church-going household knew so few Bible stories? Had she never heard them, or had her experiences made her block them out of her mind?

Gina explained a little about why people hated Zacchaeus, then told the story.

"Now I hear this, I do remember something about a very short man," Alison said. "But I have no idea what Jesus means when he says that Zacchaeus is a 'son of Abraham.'"

"Do you remember anything about Abraham?"

"Wasn't he the guy who lived a long time but didn't have a son until he was ancient?"

So Alison did remember something. Gina summarised the Abraham story and discovered Alison knew Abraham was known as the Father of Faith. From there, Alison worked out what Jesus had meant, and they had a good discussion about the word faith and what it meant to be lost and found.

Wouldn't it be amazing if her whole search for her mother—her very own lost and found story—was part of God's plan to impact other lives along the way? Perhaps that had been God's plan all along, to bring her here so that people like Barbara and Alison could be introduced to Jesus. A chain reaction which had started when Gina discovered she was adopted, and was now impacting many others.

CHAPTER 36

*T*here was a letter on the breakfast table, leaning against the marmalade jar. Attached was a note from her hostess.

I FOUND THIS IN THE LETTERBOX THIS MORNING. I THOUGHT I HEARD A CAR STOP OUTSIDE LAST NIGHT. MUST BE IMPORTANT IF IT WAS HAND DELIVERED.

Gina's heart pounded as she picked up the envelope. She took a clean knife off the table, slid it into the top corner and slit the envelope open. The sheet inside was folded in three. She unfolded it and smoothed it out.

DEAR GINA,

I AM SORRY FOR MY SLOW RESPONSE TO YOUR LETTER. I HOPE YOU'RE STILL HERE.

Just last night, Gina had decided it was time to move on, but hadn't known whether she should see something of New Zealand or change her plane ticket and go home earlier. She had planned to leave a forwarding address just in case.

As you can imagine, seeing you and reading your letter was a shock. I have often wanted to look for you but my fear of your slamming the door in my face has prevented me. My husband knows about you, but none of the children know of your existence or anything other than 'Mum is from Australia'. I guess I've tried to wipe out my first eighteen years.

Gina shivered. What had happened that her mother had run away?

I have never forgotten you. I don't think it's possible for a mother to forget her child. If you'd been born during this decade, I like to think I'd have chosen to raise you myself, but it was the sixties. I wasn't given that option. It was assumed by everyone—my mother, my aunt, and all the hospital staff—that adoption was the only option.

She'd already known her mother had to have been under huge pressure, but it was good to hear it from her. The letter was only one page. Gina's stomach cramped. Was her mother going to agree to meet with her?

PERCE SAYS TO SAY SORRY FOR HIS ANGER TOWARDS YOU. HE THOUGHT I NEEDED PROTECTION AND WENT INTO 'SHINING KNIGHT' MODE.

HE WILL BRING ME TO THE MEMORIAL GATES AT VICTORIA PARK (ON THE CORNER OF FENTON AND ORLANDO) AT 1 P.M. THURSDAY, IF YOU WANT TO MEET. IF YOU'RE NOT THERE, THEN I'LL ASSUME YOU'RE GONE AND WILL WRITE TO YOUR HOME ADDRESS IN SYDNEY.

Thursday was today, and the clock on the wall said nine fifteen. Sydney was two hours behind New Zealand time. If she rang Tony now, he'd still be getting the girls up and out the door. He'd want to be praying.

Breakfast forgotten, she went back into her room. Tony only had a few minutes, but she was able to read the letter to him and he prayed for her.

At ten to one, Gina was standing impatiently at the Memorial Gates. At 1 p.m. on the dot, a car drew up and parked across from the gates, and her mother got out. She leaned into the car to say something, presumably to Percy, then she checked both ways and walked across the street. Gina walked towards her. Her mother gave a hesitant flicker of a smile as she approached.

"Hello," they both said together. Then they both laughed, a mixture of embarrassment and relief.

"Awkward, isn't it?" Gina said.

Her mother nodded.

There was a long silence as they looked at each other. Several times her mother raised a hand as though to touch Gina but lowered it again, just as quickly. Maybe they should have hugged when they met. It would have been awkward, but so was this.

"It's hard to start, isn't it?" Gina said. "Should we walk or find a place to sit down?"

"Walking might be easier." Regina led the way. "There's a good track around the lake and we'll find plenty of places to sit."

"Won't we see people you know?" Gina had been surprised Regina hadn't suggested meeting somewhere further away. She'd been prepared to call a taxi if necessary.

"That's why we're here at one. Country folk tend to have a cooked lunch and then a nap. If we see anyone, don't be surprised if I claim that you're the daughter of a school friend."

Her mother had it all sorted out except knowing how to bridge the chasm that yawned between them. They were related by blood but separated by thirty-one years of non-shared history.

"Regina," Gina said it the way Aunt Rosalie pronounced it. "I think I'd better call you that."

"Yes-s, you certainly can't call me Mum," her mother said. "But perhaps with a hard j-sound, as everyone here says it like that."

"Would it help if I told you how I found out about you and traced you here?"

Her mother nodded. "Hearing some of your story might prepare me for telling some of mine."

As they walked, Gina shared the day she found out she'd been adopted and the various stages of her search. Regina asked clarifying questions and sometimes for more detail.

When Gina was finished Regina said, "Let's sit," and led the way to a table overlooking the lake. She sat down on the same side of the bench as Gina. "If I look at you, I'll cry."

Lord, help Regina speak. She has probably kept all this inside of her for years. Gina put her bag in a handy place, ready to grab the tissues she'd brought.

"I was sixteen when I discovered I was pregnant."

Gina clenched her fist on the bench next to her. This story was obviously going to skip the precipitating factor. She'd suspected for a while that this wasn't a boyfriend-girlfriend-going-too-far kind of story.

"I was terrified." Her mother took a deep, shuddering breath. "I struggled on my own for a while, but it was getting harder and harder to cover up my thickening waistline and lack of interest in food." She paused for a long moment. "My parents were good people, and I knew they'd be devastated."

Regina wrapped her arms around her middle and rocked back and forth.

Help her, Lord.

"I walked out of school in the middle of the day to tell Mum. I had to do it while she was alone at home." Rock, rock. "After she cried, she sprang into action. I just sat there, numb."

Gina put an unopened bottle of water in front of her mother and Regina grabbed it like a lifeline. She unsnapped the top and gulped a mouthful, coughing and having to gasp for air.

"I begged her not to send me to one of those places I'd heard about, one of those 'homes' for people like me. I didn't know Aunt Rosalie well, but I preferred to go to someone I was familiar with. I didn't expect her to be warm and loving, but I knew she'd be fair."

Her mother had been a good judge of character.

"I didn't want loving. It would have made me fall apart." Regina took another, more careful, mouthful of water. "I was packed off by the end of the week. I don't know what excuse they gave to take me out of school and send me up there. I don't know what my father suspected, and I have no idea what my siblings thought."

"Did you keep in contact with your family?" This was a question Gina had been wanting to ask for months.

"Aunt Rosalie made me write every week and tell them what I

was learning at school. Writing lots about school was a way of avoiding talking about anything else."

"But you weren't at school that year."

"No, but Aunt Rosalie was an excellent teacher. By the time I entered the final year, I wasn't behind at all. I did surprisingly well in the Leaving Certificate."

"Which meant you worked hard."

"Well, study was my way of not dealing with what had happened." For the first time she turned her face towards Gina. "I guess you want to hear about your birth?"

Gina nodded. The need to hear the story in her mother's words almost overwhelmed her concern about the cost of the telling.

"To tell the truth, I don't remember much about it. I remember a tunnel of pain that went on and on, and being left in the labour room alone and without pain relief. I remember wanting to hold you but not being allowed." She flushed. "When you were born, a sheet was put across me so I couldn't see. One of the nurses told me that getting to hold the baby wasn't for the likes of me."

Bile filled Gina's throat. How dare they? Gina reached across and gripped her mother's hand. "I'm so sorry you had to endure other people's prejudices."

"There were lots of jibes like that. I later realised my experience was typical for unmarried mothers. I was lucky to get some pain relief in the end because Sister Smith came on duty and they all snapped to attention. The jibes were one of the reasons I left Australia. I couldn't bear the thought of a lifetime of snide remarks and being snubbed in the supermarket."

"So you never saw me?"

Regina shook her head slowly. "I don't think so. From the moment I knew I was pregnant, everyone said you must be given up for adoption. I wanted Aunt Rosalie to take you or to help me care for you, but she insisted adoption was the best thing for everybody." She blew out a gusty breath and took another mouthful of water. "The pressure was relentless, and the week after you were born passed in a haze. I was probably drugged, but I only found that out recently. Apparently, it was common practice to drug girls like me. It made it easier for them to take our babies."

"Because you didn't know what was happening and couldn't make a fuss."

"I did make trouble twice." Regina gave a grim smile. "I insisted on seeing Sister Smith and asking whether you were a boy or a girl. I found out later that she wasn't supposed to tell me. There was a belief that if we didn't know anything and were kept sedated, the whole thing would seem less real and we wouldn't grieve."

Anger curdled Gina's stomach and rose in her throat. "So unfair."

"Yes, it was, but Perce reminded me of two things this week that have helped."

"What were they?" Gina asked.

"That the people of that generation were acting in what they thought was in your best interest and I wasn't alone."

"I'm not sure it helps me to know that many others went through this. I know about the stolen generations but I never knew that these experiences were common throughout Australia."

"Probably not just Australia."

No. Alison had faced similar things here.

"I'm puzzled why you ended up being named Gina," Regina said. "I wasn't allowed to name you—yet another thing that was discouraged. I don't know why they bothered with all the rules, as I never had a choice. I didn't even get to sign any of the papers."

Gina explained about the name and then said, "What happened next?"

"Aunt Rosalie carried on as if nothing had happened. I believe I had two weeks off from studying. Then it was back to work. She made me exercise until there was no outward sign that I'd given birth, and then told some convincing story to get me enrolled at school. I was supposed to pretend that nothing had happened."

"That must have been soul-destroying."

"Hmm," Regina mumbled. "I don't think I had any idea how soul-destroying it was until I arrived in Wellington. I spent the first month partying, then woke up one morning and thought, this isn't how I want to spend my life. I came up to Taranaki because there was a job advertised in the paper."

"In Inglewood?"

Regina raised an eyebrow.

"I found some photos in the old Inglewood papers at the New Plymouth library."

"I did waitressing to start with, then I worked in a real estate office. The boss encouraged me to get my licence and I've been doing that ever since. Not full-time, but it helps pay the bills."

"How did you meet your husband?"

"They used to have monthly dances. He asked me to dance, and we went from there."

"And when did you tell him about me?"

"That took me a long time. I was afraid I'd lose him, but once he proposed, I couldn't continue to say nothing. He was shocked, of course, but he went away to think about it for a week, and then came back to me. He's been my rock."

"I'm glad. Glad you had someone like that."

Regina was quiet for a few moments. "Tell me about your family. I used to get nightmares about where you might have ended up."

Gina had come prepared. She pulled out some photos taken at her brother's wedding and introduced each family member. As she talked, she could sense a burden rolling off her mother's shoulders. Like Alison, her mother had feared that Gina might have had a horrible childhood.

Gina gathered the photos together and Regina shifted on the

bench. "I'll have to head off. The youngest kids will be back from school in about thirty minutes."

"Would you have time to talk to me again tomorrow or sometime soon?"

Regina took a big breath. "I'd be happy to write."

"And what about your parents?"

"I have no objection to you going to find them, but I'd like to write first and warn Mum to expect you. We've kept in touch. Not often but every few months or so."

The presence of her unknown father had brooded over the whole conversation. What was the likelihood of her mother ever revealing his name?

Gina took a deep breath and said gently, "Will you ever feel able to tell me about my father?"

Regina gasped. Gina turned in time to see the blood draining out of her mother's face, leaving it the colour of damp paper. Regina's body shook and her pupils dilated.

Gina's heart raced. What was happening? Had her question prompted a heart attack?

"Regina!" Gina gently slapped her mother's cheek. "Regina!" She looked around wildly for help. One hundred metres away, a man started running towards them.

"Put your head down." Gina took off her jacket and draped it around her mother's shoulders.

Percy arrived at a full run. He stopped abruptly and dropped to his knees and flung his arm around Regina's shoulders. "I'm here, sweetheart. Deep breath."

Regina obeyed. The breath rattling in her throat.

Gina sat there numb with shock.

Regina's breaths slowed and with a groan she leaned her head against Percy's chest.

What had just happened, and why hadn't Percy called the ambulance? Did her mother have epilepsy?

"You okay, honey?" Percy's attention was still focused on his wife. He gently stroked her back with a tanned, work-roughened hand.

The colour slowly came back to Regina's skin and eventually she sat up. "Sorry," she said with a weak smile towards Gina.

"That was a panic attack, in case you've never encountered one," Percy said. "That's why I was keeping an eye on you. Sorry if it freaked you out."

"It sure did," Gina said. "I wasn't sure if I should ring the ambulance, but didn't know which direction to run for help."

"That's why I was hanging around. I was fairly sure you'd ask the triggering question."

"Yeah, sorry."

He shook his head. "It's a natural enough question. Look, how much longer are you going to be around?"

"I haven't really decided yet. I've been going day to day."

"Will it be okay for me to give you a call around lunchtime tomorrow? I need to take Regina home."

Gina nodded and watched them go, Percy still with his arm supporting Regina. It warmed her heart to see his care.

Once they disappeared, she sat quietly feeling shaky herself. Then she slowly walked back to her accommodation. It felt like she'd run a marathon. She'd never seen a panic attack before. For a moment, she'd thought her question had killed her mother.

If a simple question about her father triggered such a reaction, it looked very much like she'd never find out who her father was. He obviously wasn't a family member, or Regina wouldn't have been so relaxed about her getting in contact. There'd been no sign of distress when talking about her own family.

Please Lord, help Regina get a good night's sleep and to be able to process all the memories that my coming here have dredged up. Help us all. We need you.

CHAPTER 37

The next morning, the phone rang while Gina was praying for her mother and Percy.

She reached over to pick up the receiver. "Hello?"

"Is that Gina?"

Gina assented. It was Percy. Gina clenched the receiver. "Is Regina okay?"

"Much better, thank you. We've had practise dealing with panic attacks over the years."

Gina laughed weakly. "I've been worried ever since yesterday."

"Your mother wanted me to ring as early as possible. I've just come in from the morning milking."

He'd already put in half a day's work, and she was still in her pyjamas.

"It must've looked like I was stalking you yesterday. Sorry about that, but I was worried about a panic attack from the moment we first saw you last week."

Was it only a week? It felt like she'd been here a month, waiting and praying for news.

"I'm sorry you saw me at all that day. As the mailbox was so far

259

from the house, I'd assumed you'd be eating lunch and it would be fine to deliver my letter."

"Normally you'd have been right, but we'd had an emergency trip to town. Sorry I overreacted. Once we read your letter, we were convinced you weren't the kind of person to intentionally cause trouble."

Thank goodness for people who assumed the best instead of the worst.

"Look, we're very sorry, but Regina isn't feeling up to meeting again. Last night, she asked me to write you a letter about your father. It still won't tell you his name, as even I don't know that."

Maybe one day, when her mother trusted her enough, she'd reveal her secret.

"Regina was worried you might draw the wrong conclusion from her reaction. She wanted to reassure you that your father isn't a member of her family. There is no need to feel uncomfortable visiting them."

The tension in Gina's back and neck eased off. "Thank you for telling me. I had already come to that conclusion."

"I haven't delivered the letter yet because you might decide you don't want to read it. I guess we all wish we had a father to be proud of." He took a deep breath. "We don't know each other, but I must tell you his shame is not yours. You did nothing wrong. This is something I've had to tell Regina over and over."

Gina sat, gripping the phone. Did she want to know?

"Are you still there?" Percy asked.

"Yes, but I'm trying to decide if I want to read the letter or not." She shifted in her seat. "Could I call you in an hour? I'd like to pray about it."

"If you think praying will help, then go right ahead."

So he wasn't a Christian. It looked like she had another family to pray for.

Percy promised to stay near the phone and Gina looked at the clock. Tony liked to get into the office early and he ought to be arriving.

She rang but he didn't answer. She tried again ten minutes later and he picked up.

"Are you okay?" he said. "I didn't expect to hear from you again so soon after last night."

He'd had to deal with her crying yet again last night.

She told him about the letter and her dilemma. Was it better to know the truth or to always be speculating?

"Is your fear of the truth worse than actually knowing the truth?"

Gina hesitated. "I guess I already know it wasn't my mother's fault she was pregnant. I think I'd prefer to know."

"Knowing may help in your future dealings with Regina. You'll know what to avoid talking about and be more understanding of her pain."

"That makes sense. If I don't know, I could unintentionally say things that hurt her."

"Dear Lord—"

Tony moved into prayer without any warning. She'd found it unusual at first but now it made sense. God was part of his life, without any separation into compartments.

"You know Gina's heart. You know she longs to know the truth about her background and to be a blessing to Regina and other members of her birth family. Thank you that Percy and Regina have allowed her to talk with them. It hasn't been easy for any of them, but thank you that you have provided strength and your peace. Be with Gina as she reads this letter. I hate that she is so far away, but I thank you that you are with her. Help her to feel your presence."

And thank you for Tony, who has handled all my emotion with kindness.

*G*ina was watching out her window when Percy's car parked at the front of the bed and breakfast. He got out and walked towards the letterbox.

She rushed for the front door and reached the letterbox just in time to wave to him and mouth "thank you".

Back in her room, she took a deep, slow breath, holding the air for a count of five before releasing it. *Jesus, give me peace.*

There were three pages, with an extra note written in red at the top.

THANK YOU FOR YOUR UNDERSTANDING AND NOT DEMANDING THAT REGINA TALK THESE THINGS THROUGH WITH YOU.

The original letter, written last night, was below.

DEAR GINA,

REGINA APOLOGISES IN ADVANCE FOR NOT WRITING THIS. REVISITING THE EVENTS OF THE NIGHT YOU WERE CONCEIVED IS DEEPLY TRAUMATISING FOR HER. I (PERCY) WILL DO MY BEST TO REMEMBER THE DETAILS SHE SHARED WITH ME AFTER ONE PARTICULARLY BAD PANIC ATTACK.

THE ATTACK HAPPENED IN THE HOME OF A FAMILY FRIEND, A FAMILY SHE'D KNOWN ALL HER LIFE. SHE HAD GROWN UP TRAILING AFTER THE OLDER CHILDREN AND WAS SPENDING THE EVENING BABYSITTING THE MUCH YOUNGER SON WHILE THE PARENTS WERE OUT AT A PARTY.

Gina raised her eyes to look out the window. The sunshine outside was such a contrast to the direction this letter was obviously going. She shut her eyes briefly before looking down at the letter again.

THIS CHILD HAD GONE TO BED AND REGINA HAD FALLEN ASLEEP ON THE COUCH. SHE WOKE TO DISCOVER THE FAMILY FRIEND ON TOP OF HER. HE STANK OF ALCOHOL, AND SHE COULDN'T CALL OUT BECAUSE HIS HAND WAS OVER HER MOUTH. SHE REMEMBERS BITING HIM, BUT IT WAS NO USE.

Where was the wife in all this?

THE MAN SHOVED HER AWAY, AND THEN STUMBLED BACK MUTTERING, "WHAT HAVE I DONE?" TO REGINA'S HORROR HE THEN STARTED TO CRY. GREAT DRUNKEN SOBS. SHE HAD TO RUSH OUTSIDE AND VOMIT.

I CANNOT WRITE ANY MORE OF THE DETAILS. IT MAKES ME SO ANGRY I DON'T KNOW WHAT I'D DO IF THE MAN WAS STILL AROUND.

Was Percy saying the man was dead? Gina had always wanted to meet her father, but maybe this was best. How could she ever talk to someone like this?

YOUR MOTHER HAD NO OTHER WAY TO GET HOME THAN TO WALK. ONCE SHE ARRIVED HOME, SHE CREPT UPSTAIRS BUT OBVIOUSLY COULDN'T SLEEP. HER PARENTS GOT BACK LATER FROM THE SAME

PARTY, AND SHE HEARD HER MOTHER SAY SOMETHING ABOUT MAKING SURE REGINA HAD USED THE EXTRA KEY TO GET IN AND AN ARGUMENT WHICH HAD OCCURRED AT THE PARTY.

REGINA MANAGED TO PRETEND TO BE ASLEEP. IN THE MORNING, SHE DISCOVERED HER FATHER HAD DRIVEN OVER TO HIS FRIEND'S HOME AND BROUGHT THE WIFE AND SON BACK TO STAY THE NIGHT AT THEIR PLACE.

NO EXPLANATION WAS GIVEN FOR THEIR PRESENCE OR THE ARGUMENT, BUT REGINA ASSUMED HER PARENTS HAD BEEN AFRAID FOR THE SAFETY OF THE FAMILY.

The tight ball in Gina's abdomen relaxed. Her grandparents sounded like good people. If they'd known that their friend had gone home drunk and angry, they'd have gone to get Regina. They weren't the kind of people to leave their daughter in danger.

Oh Lord, why did you not let them know earlier about the argument? Once again, Gina looked out the window. If Regina hadn't been attacked, then she wouldn't be here. Would she want that? It was a strange thought. A series of linked events that started as a tragedy but now? Now, she wouldn't ever wish to not be here. *Thank you Lord that I'm here and that you can redeem anything.*

Gina took a shaky breath. There was still more to read. *God, give me strength.*

IT TURNED OUT THAT YOUR GRANDPARENTS MADE A GOOD DECISION IN TAKING THE WIFE AND SON HOME FOR THE NIGHT. THE NEXT MORNING, THE MAN WAS FOUND DEAD IN HIS CAR.

Gina's chest was tight. *Dear God, so sad.* She squeezed her eyes shut. This tragedy was going to take a long time to process. Not only had her father harmed Regina, but he'd then removed himself from the scene. She dropped the letter on the table, wrapped her arms around her waist, and rocked gently. Back and forth. Back and forth, the movement somehow comforting.

Why, Lord? Why couldn't you have given me a better story? A girl longs to have a hero father, and mine is as far as possible from being a hero.

What had Percy said? "His shame is not yours." It was true. Deep down, she knew it was true, but it didn't feel true. At the moment, the shame of her conception was a rock on top of her, crushing her. No wonder her mother still struggled to think about it. *God, help.*

Jesus?

She opened her eyes and lifted her head.

Jesus' beginning might not be the same as hers, but he understood the pain. All his life, he'd have heard whispers about how his mother must have slept around. Jesus endured the shame of a family who'd lost their reputation. Not because Mary or Joseph had anything to be ashamed of, but because no one would have believed their story. After all, virgins don't have babies.

Gina sat up straight. *Dear God, please keep reminding me that my biological father's shame is not mine. Please remind me that I'm your beloved child before I am anyone else's.*

Gina looked down at the still unfinished letter.

YOUR GRANDFATHER APPARENTLY BLAMED HIMSELF FOR NOT GOING TO STAY IN HIS FRIEND'S HOUSE, BUT YOUR GRANDMOTHER THOUGHT THEY'D DONE THE RIGHT THING.

Two households grieving the loss of a father and friend. And what about Regina? Now carrying the consequences of another's sin and unable to say anything without adding to the grief of loss.

Aunt Rosalie had considered Regina stubborn for refusing to name Gina's father. In the days before any awareness of post-traumatic stress disorder, her mother now came across as heroic, doing her best to keep a secret that would only hurt more people. Protecting a family already devastated by the loss of their father.

Dear Lord, help my mother. Heal her. May this terrible story one day be redeemed by you. I don't know how you'll do it, but I know you can.

The final parts of the letter were Percy's personal message to her in which he thanked her for coming.

Her mother had done well in marrying someone like Percy. Someone with his feet firmly rooted in this beautiful part of the world. And someone mature enough to accept and love her as she needed to be loved.

CHAPTER 38

*T*he plane roared for take-off and picked up speed, leaving New Zealand behind. Gina stared out the window at the boats dotted over the harbour.

She'd cut her trip short, but not before phoning Alison to let her know that she'd met her mother and wanted to keep up with what was happening with Alison's search. Gina would call her in a few weeks. Meeting Alison hadn't been an accident. God had his plans for Alison, as he'd had his plans for Gina, and for her mother.

The plane rose through the cloud cover, the wisps of cloud turning into a blanket of white. Then they burst through into the sunshine and Gina saw a familiar snowy peak floating in a sea of billowing clouds. Down below, her mother would be cleaning up from the morning milking.

Yesterday, just before Gina had started the bus trip towards New Plymouth and back to Wellington, her mother had given her a gift. Gina had been closing her backpack when Percy's car glided to a halt outside the bed and breakfast. After a minute, her mother had climbed out and came towards the front door.

Gina opened it.

"I couldn't let you go without hugging you," Regina said.

Gina blinked back tears and stepped back into the hallway to allow her mother in.

"I've dreamed my whole life of meeting you, but I've been afraid," Regina said moving forward. "I'm so thankful I don't need to be afraid any longer."

Gina opened her arms and her mother stepped forward into the waiting circle of arms. Tears burned in her eyes and they clung together. Gina tried to convey in her hug all the words she hadn't yet found a way to express. Life was unfair, but they'd beaten the odds and found each other.

Her mother's mountain dropped away behind the plane. Now Gina had two thousand plus kilometres of sea to home. Home, where she had family and friends. One of her first visits was going to be to her parents, to tell her father everything that had happened —and maybe her mother—and to thank them for the way they'd loved and cared for her.

Yesterday, she and Regina had sat for a little while, arms around each other. Her mother had promised to write.

"Percy and I decided we're going to tell the children about you. They're old enough to know, but we're going to wait until the summer holidays. We all need to get used to the idea first."

It had been a disappointment that Gina couldn't meet them straight away, but not a surprise. Her mother's words were what had convinced her to change her flights. The thought of touring New Zealand alone hadn't been appealing. All she wanted was to get back to Sydney and see Tony.

One question had been burning in her mind and yesterday she'd asked it. "Why did you decide to meet up with me? Especially after I mucked things up at the beginning."

Her mother had swivelled around to look at her. "If you'd just sent the letter, I might not have agreed to meet. I could have ignored a letter or put it off for later, but I couldn't let my daughter, my very own daughter, walk away with the memory of me rejecting her. I couldn't let you feel abandoned again."

Gina had burst out laughing. "I was so upset, thinking I'd mucked up our meeting. I thought I'd never get to see you and it would be all my own fault. Yet it's the very thing that led to you coming."

The God who had overridden her mistake could be trusted to help with the next stages of this journey. Could be trusted to prepare the way for her to meet her grandparents and other relatives.

"*G*ina!"

Tony's voice startled Gina as she came out of customs. She whipped around and his beaming smile was focused on her. Her heart did a little cartwheel of delight. She'd planned to catch the bus home.

He came around the barrier and hugged her. "I've taken three days off work and my in-laws are looking after the children." He took her luggage in one hand and her hand in his other. "The car's outside. We can discuss how you want to use the time as we head back to your place."

They went out through the automated doors and into the blazing sunshine.

New Zealand was beautiful, but it was good to be home, especially with the jacaranda trees in full purple bloom.

"Would you be willing to come and meet my parents?" Gina asked.

Tony glanced at her and grinned. "I hoped you'd suggest that. And what about going up to Aunt Rosalie? She's going to be wanting news."

And Gina had the letter her mother had written to Rosalie to deliver, a letter Regina said would set Rosalie's heart at rest.

Gina touched Tony's arm. "I'd love that."

He reached over and took her hand in his. "I'm looking forward to spending three whole days with you. Hopefully a precursor of a whole lot more."

Tears filled her eyes. She squeezed his hand, unable to say anything. She'd gone looking for who she was, but she should have known all along. She was the much-loved daughter of the King of Kings, and that should always have been more than enough for her. For anyone.

Maybe her birth father hadn't been someone she'd have wanted to know. Maybe her relationship with Regina would take time. Even if Tony's parents weren't exactly enamoured with her, Tony seemed to be. She didn't fully understand why, but she was going to take his love as a good gift from God.

And she was going to remind herself every day whose child she was. Jesus had loved her from before the creation of the earth and died to make her his own.

All these blessings were more than enough. And the future? God would be heaping even more grace into her life. He'd given grace across the miles and he would have more in store for the days to come. Grace for her and for Tony and the girls and for all the members of her family.

How could she be so confident? Well, it was just who God was. Grace all the way and every day. Things might not go as she planned, but God had been running the universe for a long time and he had everything, even her life, completely under his control.

ENJOYED READING GRACE ACROSS THE MILES?

Reviews sell books.

The best way for this book to be discovered by readers is if you get excited about it. Online reviews are one way to share your enthusiasm.

How to write a review – easy as 1-2-3-4

1. A few sentences about why you liked the book.
2. Add a sentence about the sorts of people who might like the book.
3. Upload a review - the same review can be used across different sites.
4. If you loved the book please also share your review on your personal social media, or tell others about it. Word of mouth recommendations are powerful.

FICTION BY CHRISTINE DILLON

This book was the sixth (and final) in the *Grace* series published between 2017-2021.

The digital novels + audio can be bought directly from the author (https://payhip.com/ChristineDillon). You need a PayPal account to make your payment.

NON-FICTION BY CHRISTINE DILLON

1-2-1 Discipleship: Helping One Another Grow Spiritually
(Christian Focus, Ross-shire, Scotland, 2009).

Telling the gospel through story: Evangelism that keeps hearers
wanting more (IVP, USA, 2012).

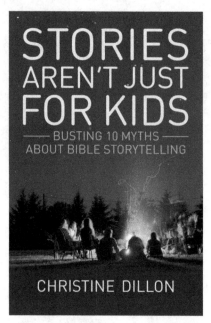

Stories Aren't Just For Kids: Busting 10 Myths About Bible Storytelling (2017).

This book is free for subscribers. It's a taster book and includes many testimonies to get you excited about the potential of Bible storying. All three books above have been translated into Chinese.

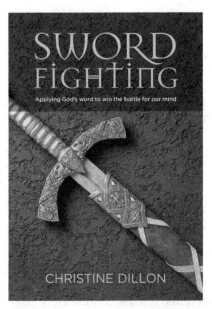

Sword Fighting: Applying God's word to win the battle for our mind
(2020).

This book has just been translated into German, under the title of *Siegreich Sein: mit Gottes Wort.*

STORYTELLER FRIENDS

Becoming a **storyteller friend** will ensure you don't miss out on new books, deals, and behind the scenes book news. (http://subscribe.storytellerchristine.com/) Once you're signed up, check your junk mail or the 'promotions' folder (gmail addresses) for the confirmation email. This two-stage process ensures only true storyteller friends can join.

Facebook: As well as a public author page, I also have a VIP group which you need to ask permission to join.

BookBub - allows you to see my top book recommendations and be alerted to any new releases and special deals. It is free to join.

ACKNOWLEDGMENTS

When the idea for writing a single novel called *Grace in Strange Disguise* was suggested to me in a prayer time in about 2007, my immediate reaction was, "No, Lord, I can't write fiction." But as I prayed about it, my response became, "I can't, but if you want me to write a novel you'll have to give me everything I need."

God took his time preparing my heart and in 2012 I started writing some practice novels. It wasn't until about 2014 that I started on *Grace in Strange Disguise*. There were so many times that I wanted to give up but something always happened to spur me on to the next step. I am grateful that I didn't know at the start of the journey that one book would become two and eventually six. I might have been overwhelmed by the thought of all I had to learn. But now nearly five years later, the sixth and final book in the series is now complete.

I have learned so much along the way and am grateful to those who have helped me. My editors Cecily and Iola, my cover designer, and the teams of people who read an early draft and comment. For this book thanks to Kate B, Lizzie R, Louise Spaulding and to the proofreaders Kate B, Kim W, Sarah L, Lizzie R, Anne M, and Suzanne R. I'm also grateful for the book boosters who read the book just as it launching and put up book reviews. Every review is precious. I especially appreciate reviewers who put up reviews on more than one site.

A special thank you to the librarians at Tamworth and New

Plymouth (New Zealand) libraries and various archivists, all of whom answered my email queries quickly and efficiently.

It has been fun in recent books to use first or surnames to honour various friends. In this book, some of the Dutch names are used to honour friends I see too seldom. Percy's surname honours the couple who led my father to Jesus and they live on same road as other friends and a farm that I loved to spend time on. It has been so fun to travel to Stratford in this book - especially during Covid when I can't visit New Zealand.

Most of all I am thankful to God who led me on this journey. I have learned so much about how he inspires creativity, teamwork, and how he provides everything I need when I cry out to him for help. What a privilege it is to be your child.

ABOUT THE AUTHOR

It's best not to ask Christine, "Where are you from?" She's a missionary kid who isn't sure if she should say her passport country (Australia) or her Dad's country (New Zealand) or where she's spent most of her life (Asia - Taiwan, Malaysia and the Philippines).

Christine used to be a physiotherapist, but now writes 'storyteller' on airport forms. She spends most of her time either telling Bible stories or training others to do so and from 1999-2021 worked with OMF International in Taiwan. Now she will be working with OMF in Australia.

In her spare time, Christine loves all things active – hiking, cycling, swimming, snorkelling. But she also likes reading and genealogical research.

Connect with Christine
www.storytellerchristine.com/

facebook.com/storytellerchristine
bookbub.com/profile/christine-dillon